LIE WITH THE DEVIL

LIE WITH THE DEVIL

A Novel

DAVIN COLTEN

iUniverse, Inc.
New York Lincoln Shanghai

LIE WITH THE DEVIL

Copyright © 2007 by DAVIN COLTEN

iUniverse books may be ordered through booksellers or by contacting:

iUniverse
2021 Pine Lake Road, Suite 100
Lincoln, NE 68512
www.iuniverse.com
1-800-Authors (1-800-288-4677)

Because of the dynamic nature of the Internet, any Web addresses or links contained in this book may have changed since publication and may no longer be valid.

This is a work of fiction. All of the characters, names, incidents, organizations, and dialogue in this novel are either the products of the author's imagination or are used fictitiously.

ISBN: 978-0-595-44336-9 (pbk)
ISBN: 978-0-595-69614-7 (cloth)
ISBN: 978-0-595-88666-1 (ebk)

Printed in the United States of America

To my mom, who always believes in me. To my best friend, I miss you. To hopeful romantics everywhere.

CHAPTER 1

The tranquility of the moment echoed inside my head. I could hear my own heart beating, and for that brief moment, I felt at peace. Everything that I had seen and gone through eluded my thoughts, and home, a place I had longed to reach, I now could not escape.

I closed my eyes feeling this stranger's hand on my body. The warmth of his fingers upon my thigh. The smoothness of his chest upon my breast. My nakedness shook in the cool night air, as I pressed my body closer to him. And I had betrayed myself, my heart, William, as I clasped my hand tighter around his skin.

My chest heaved as I took a deep breath and slid my fingers slowly across my lips. My skin still moist, the vigor coursing through my veins. My body sore from the previous nights journey. I wanted to perpetuate the moment before I would be placed back into society as I had wished for until now. I had changed. The world had changed around me. The war had changed us all.

I closed my eyes reminiscing back to that one precious moment when I was a child. I can see the picture perfectly. The clouds in the early morning spring, blue mixed with yellow, I had never seen a more beautiful sight. My hair messed, my body lying in the grass covered in flowers, feeling the dirt upon my skin, the ground beneath me. The wind moved my skirt higher up my leg, as I smelled the lilac of the flowers scent.

I never told anyone about this place. I would lie there for hours fall asleep and lose time. I felt connected to something; I was part of more than just what was expected of me. And love, what did I know of such a thing? I had never been in love before, it ruined people and brought others closer together, and I never wanted to get hurt. Scared, lost, confused by the game everyone played.

Maybe I was running away from it all, and I went there to get away? Maybe I was running to something, wanting more?

No longer was I innocent to the world, the emerging war had taken a chunk out of the laughter that brought happy families together. Instead tears flowed, death soared, and bloody massacres surrounded me in a world full of peril. When would life go back to the way things once were? Maybe when the war ended, things could never go back to the way they once were? Ruined. Soiled. Broken forever.

I have been shielded from such things, but now I find myself surrounded by it. Smiles are gone, torn by the letters that arrive daily, tearing the hearts out of mothers, killing them inside each day they long for the possible return of their loved ones. A day that might never come. And this is the world that I live in now, all the simple joys are long gone, and the blackened hatred of revenge and sovereignty shine like a banner across the sky. Serenity, I can hardly remember the memory of that word anymore, and I fear all hope is lost.

Today would be the last time I would lie in the field, feeling the freeness of the wind, the world at my feet, envisioning a world without war. The precious moment was fleeting fast, and would soon be gone. When I open my eyes, I will leave this place, the peacefulness, and never return.

I find myself brushing the dirt off my knee. The flowers tangled in my long blonde hair that is now cut short. Running through the grass like an innocent child blinded by the darkened walls that hover in the enclosing distance. I miss my long curls, feeling the material of the dress beneath my fingers, the red lipstick on my lips, distancing myself further from that young woman. Proper. Naïve. Pure. I am no longer that girl.

I see a smile on my face as I am twirling around, till suddenly I hear a gun shot and open my eyes, wide in horror, and the dead silence awakens me into stark vivid reality.

William Cavill, I fear I am lost to you … forever!

Lights flashed and gunshots roared in the distance. Fiery pellets of death swarmed around their bodies, as a stray bullet flew directly passed Dagmara's head, missing her by an inch. Several more bullets followed, as Colin instantly jumped on Dagmara, smashing their bodies to the ground. As they hit the ground, the resistance group fired back, and another bullet tore through Colin's coat, as he shielded Dagmara from the gunfire.

Bullets flooded the air, slicing through the woods, as the resistance group scattered for cover. The Germans moved in closer. A bullet crushed into a woman's skull killing her upon contact, and she fell down to the ground beside Dagmara. The French woman's eyes were wide open as the gun fell out of her hand, and blood splattered on Dagmara. Immediately she wiped off the tiny red droplets of blood, and lowered her face into the dirt.

The resistance group briefly diverted the German soldiers' attention away from Dagmara and Colin, and they took those few seconds, got up, and started to run as fast as they could in the opposite direction.

Suddenly a young enemy soldier barely nineteen spotted them, and started chasing after them on foot. Whistles deafened and more gunshots were fired in their direction, as the enemy approached closer. They were hunted by Germans, like prey to a slaughter, and soon were surrounded by at least a half dozen men. Thrashing shoes smashed down into the ground, as the German soldiers followed in hot pursuit, and the chase turned into a deadly race against time.

Dagmara and Colin ran faster and faster as humanly possible through the woods. Their pulses racing, their hearts pounding feverishly, as the enemies gained in speed. There were too many of them to elude, as the bullets kept coming in heavy force. The fierce predators were relentless; their targets in sight, their aim steady, as they started to close in on their unarmed, helpless victims.

THREE MONTHS EARLIER

The world was at war for a second time. Lives being shattered, years added up into many, more than one wanted to count, while some got to live a privileged life, their head in the clouds.

Dagmara Morrow and her two best friends had been living abroad in Italy for the past several months. Inadvertently caught in the middle, they were on a long waiting list to return home, earlier than planned. They had gotten themselves entangled in the disruption, surrounded by peril. Dagmara loved London, her place of birth, a place where she knew she would have a family and home of her own someday, in the near but distant future.

That day was approaching sooner than she would have liked, and at only twenty, all of Dagmara's close friends were either engaged or married, or on the verge of both. Unlike them she was alone. No husband, no boyfriend, no one to call her his own. That was in part why she had taken this trip to Italy. She had never been to the beautiful country, and wanted to get away from her parents, the pushing. She would find love on her own, when the time was right and not rush into it. No regrets.

Blonde, with a translucent complexion, Dagmara's stunning looks made her the envy of all her friends, classmates, every girl in town. Pulchritudinous someone once called her. Her expressive, blue gray eyes could mystify the most intellectual of men. Her eyes could convey a thousand words without speaking a single one, and many young men had fallen in love with her endearing sweet qualities.

Her slender figure was perfect. Small nose, perky bosom, plump lips, the only thing that one would change about Dagmara, would be to make her less impetuous. She craved the fire, the exciting adventure, seeing the beauty in rare things. Dagmara Morrow never thought about the future, her future, if there would even be one when the war ended.

Light shined in from the window of her hotel room, and the view from the balcony was breathtaking. Slowly she opened her eyes, stretching her legs within the beige colored sheet that covered her naked body. A small crease was indented in the bed from her thin frame. The fresh flowers on the table filled the room with a sweet scent, and Dagmara never had a more peaceful sleep, as she took a deep breath and a smile crossed her entire face.

Being away from home for the first time without her parents, Dagmara reveled in the innovative feeling, and moved out of bed energized and got dressed. Never considering herself vain, she always wanted to make the best first impression. Dressed impeccably, she could wear any outfit, in any color, and still outshine all the other girls.

Kate Bellmore, short for Katherine, and Amelia Ashmore, Dagmara's two best friends in the entire world, were waiting for her in the lobby. They had all grown up together. They had shared and experienced everything together since childhood, able to count on each other when needed.

Kate was taller than Dagmara, with brown hair and eyes. Her olive complexion glistened in the summer months, turning to a radiant tan. Amelia was shorter, her brownish blonde hair and hazel eyes made her the least attractive of the three, but her outgoing personality and forwardness had captured several men's hearts. Not one of them would be left alone in a room for long; they would never be the ones to sit in the corner at a party.

Amelia and Kate loved to dance and swim, while Dagmara preferred photography and painting, the more intimate pleasures one could enjoy by oneself. Kate was the oldest by six months, and was engaged to her high school sweetheart Ian Rutherford. A man she loved since sophomore year. They had already set a date. She would be the first in the group to get married, and then Amelia would follow. Her boyfriend would soon propose, and being the wealthiest of all three girls, it would be a perfect match for any young man wanting a future in business or politics.

Dagmara had dated in school, but not one man had ever captured her heart in full. Temptation, infatuation, mostly on the young men's part, Dagmara longed to find that rare jewel that would captivate her heart the moment she laid eyes on him. The arrogant but sensitive man whose piercing stare would make her heart flutter with silent, savage desire. And she was beginning to wonder, if such a stimulating creature exists?

Tenacious in every aspect of her life, living for the moment rather than the future, *carpe diem* felt more like a suffocating, echoing pull than the predator of time. She even wore a bracelet with the words carpe diem inscribed, reminding her to cherish every moment because it would never come again.

Flames of pulsating passion rose in the falling, awakening hours of the next blackened blood filled day. The long journey had yet to end in the ferocious terrors that lied ahead, hovering in the shadows waiting for their prey. Dagmara Morrow was about to find that her destiny lied in a world full of perilous, rapturous adventures that would ultimately change the course of her life and her future … forever.

Dagmara joined her friends and they ventured off for the day, living in their own little world, trying to distance their thoughts from the sight that surrounded them by the passing of soldiers. Everywhere they looked, young men were in uniform, some barely looked old enough to know how to properly handle a weapon. The city was overrun at times, and no one, not even visitors seemed free from whisper and suspicion.

They had overstayed their welcome, mostly on Dagmara's behalf. Several times they had discussed returning home early. Kate missed being away from her fiancé, while Amelia missed her family, but it was Dagmara who stood alone wanting to stay. She had nothing to go back to, no one waiting for her return other than family members she felt closed off to at times. Unconsciously naive to the hidden dangers that were to come, believing she and her friends would be safe, Dagmara had convinced them to stay.

And that was how the girls had gotten caught up in the political disruption of the country. Everyone was being checked, and double checked, and they had to keep their papers on them at all times. No one it seemed was safe from skepticism, which made entering and leaving the country difficult. In a way, Dagmara and her friends had innocently become victims of the pertinent, dangerous situation that violated them through safe passage.

They had mingled with the locals, accepting invitations to parties and dinners, and had danced and kissed some of the most handsome, illustrious men they had ever met. Kate shied away from all the attention, not offering or giving into any of their affectionate advances. An expert at flirting, Amelia flourished in the fun, but it was Dagmara that surprisingly had the best time.

Unlike most women her age, Dagmara was wiser beyond her years, not closing herself off to mirror images of what people expected. Vivacious, she spoke her mind, she did what she wanted, not conforming to standards, the mundane normality of scrutiny. While most people deceive their desires by not intervening or mentioning them, they become intrigued and watch closely by on those who embrace upon their innovative and perilous secrets. Envying those like Dagmara Morrow.

Fluent in Italian, profiting from her hard work in school, Dagmara impressed many locals, and found the language to be one of the most beautiful to speak, finding their accent along with Irish to be expressively sexy. Dagmara immersed in their culture, but still had not found one man that set her heart on fire. That simply moved her. Moving her in a way that she would feel numb by the penetrating look in his eyes, his hand on hers, a simple kiss on the lips, and she was beginning to wonder if she ever would. Never to feel the love. To know such pain. To have gained nothing, with no insight.

Her friends knew her flaw, she was searching for someone who does not exist, and they had told her many times, but not once did she ever listen. She would never settle for less, and maybe that was more praise than a hindrance, but the latter of the two had kept her alone.

They wandered down the cobblestone streets that were slightly desolate from the usual crowds that hovered in this part of the city. They stopped at a few dress shops, and then proceeded to have a light lunch before they headed back to their hotel. It was there at the last stop that Dagmara Morrow first laid eyes on the man who made her heart skip a couple of beats. The debonair stranger who set her heart on fire. The look in their eyes when they first saw each other, no words could convey what they both were feeling. Their pulses racing, their first impression was expressively unspoken.

The three young women were walking down the street together carrying their packages, enjoying the day. Dagmara had taken several pictures and stopped inside a shop to buy more film. As she emerged from the shop, the wind built in forceful motion, and threw her long blonde curls as she tried to brush the strands away from her face. The gust of wind pushed her off balance. She looked around for her friends who wandered into the next shop, and suddenly, out of nowhere, she bumped right into him.

Wearing his casual civilian clothes, the handsome stranger walked alongside his two friends, when accidentally he knocked right into Dagmara. As they collided, Dagmara dropped her belongings, halting them to a fortuitous stop.

"Oh, I'm sorry," Dagmara said.

"Why don't you watch where you're go … ing," William replied in a harsh tone, saying the last word in almost a whisper as he looked into her eyes.

"I said I was sorry," she protested, hearing the bluntness of his tone.

Catching him off guard, William instantly apologized for his rude behavior.

"No, it is I who should apologize and be more careful," he immediately stated, enchanted with her beauty.

Dagmara smiled at his charming apology. The sparkle in her eyes instantly captured William Cavill in a way that he had never been captivated before by a woman's small, but intimate gesture. The young man could not take his eyes off her, and Dagmara Morrow was momentarily silenced by her own daunting feelings. For the first time ever, she was equally captivated by a man's presence, his physical appearance, as his impressionable, penetrating stare moved deep inside her heart.

He smiled, and a slight dimple protruded in his chin, the only imperfection on his face that she could see, which made him all the more perfect. William's friends watched, as their introduction unfolded. Amelia and Kate walked out of the shop and moved towards them, blocking out the whispers that surrounded them on the narrowing street.

William Cavill came from a wealthy aristocratic family. He was from a long line of Cavills that passed down their estates and impeccable names from one generation to the next. He got his commission in his early twenties just from his family's name, but his incredible eyesight and intrepidness accounted for his ability to fly planes. An RAF fighter pilot like his two friends, he was one of the best.

Well educated, William was extremely distinguished with a charismatic presence. His white skin glowed with a fading bronze tan, and his deep voice mixed with his seductive smile, swept young women into a world where they had never ventured before. Where desire crossed over in infatuation, burning in a liquid fire of lust.

Tall with a sleek body and a perfectly formed ass, his chiseled cheekbones and defined features added to his gorgeous appearance. His eyes were so beautiful, Dagmara found herself lost within his piercing stare that made her whole body tremble with secretive allure. Nobody has the right to be that good looking.

She could not look away. He had not taken his eyes off her for a second. Destiny had intertwined their lives together in a fortuitous encounter, but war, the horrid, blackened act, combined with the sensual act of love, the purity of such a sweet pleasure, had sealed their fate … forever.

CHAPTER 2

He had known a few girls from his past, he had met more wherever they stationed him and his friends, but never had he fallen so fast, so hard. Never had William Cavill been completely entranced by the sight of such a beautiful woman. Her long blonde curls blew freely in the wind. Her eyes sparkled, and she seemed incandescent, her whole body tingled with inciting, unfamiliar temptation.

Dagmara bent down to pick up her bag, and instantly William moved down and helped gather up her belongings that had fallen in their introduction. He handed her the rolls of film.

"Thank you," she said.

Her fingers slightly brushed across his hand. He felt the softness of her skin, and she could barely breathe feeling the tight capacity of their encounter. Their eyes met in an intense gaze, almost touching each other's body in the closeness. She could feel his warm breath on the back of her neck. Her lashes long and curled, as they flickered in his smoldering presence.

A smile slightly crossed her mouth as they stood up together, both in an equally silent, captivating effect. It was in those eyes of his when he looked at her, she could not look away. Everything about the dashing William Cavill seemed perfect. The illusion of perfection that deemed the most dangerous and uncontrollably inviting. He felt the same allure towards Dagmara. Her perfect shaped lips, reddened by color. Her flawless complexion. Her eyes, he was drawn in an unbreakable connection that speeded his heart in deafening, vigorous rhythm.

Amelia and Kate looked at each other noticing the apparent attraction between their friend and this man. Then they looked at William's friends who had grins on their faces, whispering to one another. They had never seen Dagmara so moved by a man before, her eyes had not left his for a second, and with his defined features, his hair messed from the wind, William Cavill looked like a model both girls thought. A handsome human being.

His sex appeal attracted every woman he came in contact with, affecting Dagmara's emotions to a paralyzing haze. Even her friends both felt their pulses race, their breath deepen, as they looked upon the stimulating stranger.

Time had stood still for Dagmara and William, separating them from everyone else. Dagmara looked down for a brief second and then up again, this time with a slight vivaciousness to her smile. The connection deepened in the mesmerizing encounter, and William had not taken his eyes off Dagmara for a second. Locked in a searing attraction. Bound by an unspoken desire. Tortured by the world around.

"I'm William, William Cavill," he spoke in a deep, cultured voice.

His British accent was articulate, and he did not have to say a word, Dagmara could read his thoughts as they looked into each other's eyes. They knew what the other was thinking. He could see her chest move rapidly within the thin material of her dress. A smile crossed his mouth, his pulse elevated with feverish enticement.

Dagmara spoke in the same cultured, British tone. "Dagmara Morrow."

He adored the sweet, innocent quality she possessed. Her pulchritudinous outshined any woman he had ever known. She was not just some girl, this young woman who stood before him, who captured his presence, lie hidden a sensual, bold creature he had to get to know.

"Dagmara," he repeated. "It's a beautiful name, it fits," he added with a seductive charm to his compliment.

Dagmara blushed.

She broke their deep connection and looked away. Then her eyes widened as she looked back up at him.

"You're coming to lunch with me," he told her.

"I am," she said, liking his assertive, spontaneous behavior.

"Yes, and I won't take no for an answer."

Dagmara smiled.

"Come with me, now," he said, his penetrating look overpowering her.

"But I have a prior engagement."

He moved closer towards her. "Break it," he said.

William seduced her with his eyes, and Dagmara could not resist. She could not say no. The invitation was one she could not refuse. She would break her other commitments for the day and go with him.

"All right, I'll come with you," she told him, having the stranger sweep her off her feet and into his world.

Amelia could not wait a second longer and walked over to them as Kate followed, not wanting to interrupt their conversation.

"I'm Amelia, and this is Kate, and you are?" Amelia said, and extended her hand out in front of her waiting for his reply.

William shook her hand, and then Kate's hand, momentarily taking his eyes off Dagmara. "Nice to meet both of you," he said, and then looked over at his friends, and they joined the gathering. "This is Stuart Shelton and Henry Taylor," William noted, introducing his friends to the girls.

Both men were tall and in great physical shape. Stuart was muscular; his light brown hair accentuated his dark eyes. Henry had deep reddish brown hair. His freckled face would turn slightly red in the summer months, and unlike his two friends, his fair skin never tanned. The girls enchanted the young men, as William turned his attention solely upon Dagmara.

William and Dagmara could have stood there all day just looking at one another.

Amelia and Kate went back to the hotel. William took Dagmara's hand in his, and they walked down the street together with his two friends following behind. He took Dagmara to a secluded restaurant, rich in wines, a family owned establishment he had stumbled upon serendipitously. The inside looked more like an authentic Italian home kitchen than an actual eatery. The décor was simple but elegant. The ambiance was beautiful with the laughter of patrons and staff.

They sat together, a table for two.

"How long are you here for?" he asked her.

"My friends wanted to return early, but I persuaded them to stay longer."

"I'm happy you did, or we would have never met," William said with a smile, his dimple protruding inward on his chin.

"So am I," she said, her eyes sparkling with vibrancy, never fully answering his question.

The waiter poured wine into their glasses, and smiled to himself seeing the young lovers. It was like love at first sight, especially for William. He was smitten, immediately. Dagmara was the prettiest girl he had ever seen.

"Someone as beautiful as yourself must have a boyfriend waiting at home?" William inquired in a debonair manner.

A smile crossed her lips. "No, but you must have a girl waiting at home for you?"

"No," he answered, liking her brazenness, enjoying the playful flirtation.

"No?" she replied. "I don't believe you, not a dishy catch like you."

Her flattering comment made him laugh.

They took a few sips of wine, having the delicious taste slide slowly down their throats, when suddenly William heard a noise. Footsteps. A trigger of a gun. Instantly he looked at Henry and Stuart who were already alerted by the same distinct sounds, and then he looked at Dagmara. Without hesitation he grabbed her, pushing her forcefully down to the floor covering her body with his, when simultaneously, massive, deadly gunfire erupted inside the restaurant.

Stray bullets slaughtered through the dining area at a rapid speed, shattering the glass windows, blasting through the front doors, killing people. Shrieking cries were muffled by the loudness of gunfire. Shots aimed directly at the patrons, exploding in the open air, as people shouted and pushed each other out of the way, rushing for cover.

A middle aged woman tripped on some glass, stumbling across the floor, hitting the counter, breaking her neck. Another patron sat frozen in his chair from the gunfire, paralyzed from movement, as a stray bullet sliced through his chest, extinguishing his life the moment the bullet pierced his flesh. His whole body shook, and then he fell face down onto the table, dead.

The windows kept shattering, as the broken glass poured down on people as they scrambled for cover, cutting themselves, slicing with pain. Darkened terror immersed within the restaurant, as William pressed his body down on top of Dagmara as a shield, keeping her safe and out of contact with the bullets. Blood thickened in red pools surrounding the dead bodies, as the fiery pellets scorched through people's flesh in excruciating pain. And screams, terrifying, haunting screams deafened from the injured bodies that lie sprawled upon the dirty floor.

Then the gunfire started to subside, and the savages holding the pistols started to retreat back through the front doors, when William, Stuart, Henry, and a few other soldiers grabbed their guns and started to exchange fire. Rapidly William reached inside his coat pocket, his fingers clasped tight around his gun, as the weapon moved in front of Dagmara's face. Her eyes opened wide seeing the barrel brush over her body, as William moved off her, and started firing at the assailants.

The deadly bullets swarmed in the heated moment of peril, surrounding Dagmara and the other innocent victims that lied helpless to defend themselves.

Fearless within each shot, William stood up and started firing at the intruders, as Stuart and Henry were right alongside him, courageously firing at the enemy. Instantly the rebels started to run out of the establishment, and took off sprinting down the street. The uproar started to simmer, but not before several people were badly wounded, some stumbling to their bloody, untimely deaths. And all the while Dagmara lie motionless, unable to move let alone breathe. Her heart pounding so fast as the smoke choked her lungs from the fumes.

An uncommon chivalry coursed through the veins of William Cavill and his friends. They possessed strength and leadership at a time of emergency and confusion. A quality that not only impressed Dagmara, but drew her closer to William, as she looked up at her savior.

"Quick, after them," a man in uniform yelled, and several men followed out the door after the gunmen.

William did not run, instead he turned back around and looked down at Dagmara. He lowered his gun and bent down, and helped her stand up. He brushed the glass and debris off her body, making sure she was not hurt. No bullet wounds, not even a scratch. The blood on her clothes was not hers. Her face was dirty; the smoke blackened her porcelain skin, as William's finger smudged her cheek wiping away a tear.

She wanted to say something, but she could not. Speechless by the traumatic experience, Dagmara had never been in the middle of gunfire before, always able to walk through the streets without that fear. But now that naive innocence was lost, and she could no longer move freely within the city without grave peril.

William brushed the glass off his coat as Stuart and Henry moved over to them. Sirens in the distance surrounded, but the predators were already long gone, as Dagmara moved across the floor, carefully, hearing the crushing of glass beneath her shoes.

Unlike William who was already used to this type of attack upon civilians, Dagmara was not, nor would she ever get used to such ghastly, disastrous sights. In the midst of all the rush, plagued by the very being of her heart, she thought first of her new friend before any other. The tightness of his clasp around her hand hardened, as William rushed her out of the restaurant through the commotion to safety.

As Dagmara passed through the shattered door, she closed her eyes to the blood-drenched sight that surrounded her in a dreary image of awakening haunt.

That night Dagmara did not tell Amelia and Kate of the horrid attack she was involved in. They would immediately want to expedite leaving, and she would then have to leave William. War was breaking out in other parts of the world, and would reach them shortly. Soon it would be too late for them to leave, to get out of the country, and Dagmara could not allow her friends to be placed in danger, along its wrath, but she was compelled to stay having just met William Cavill.

Dagmara had to stay just a little while longer, so she remained silent about the attack, the murders, everything she had witnessed, keeping the dark secret hidden. And all the while she hoped she had made the right decision. That staying longer had not jeopardized their lives, and allow her friends to get caught in the crossfire or worse. She could not fathom such a notion, or have their deaths on her hands.

CHAPTER 3

Dagmara did not need to explain; her friends understood perfectly, and were delighted by William's invitation for dinner the next night. They were happy for their friend, and would make some excuse for her absence at the dinner party that evening.

Dagmara slipped into a form fitting dress made out of silk. The thin material was soft against her skin, and the black color against her fair complexion and light blonde hair made her look absolutely stunning. Her deep red lipstick and long black lashes accentuated her beauty. Her eyes seemed lilac in color, and she was radiant, full of excitement towards the forthcoming night.

William approached the hotel lobby, and saw Dagmara walking down the stairs. Her long, almost painted on dress, her curls bouncing in the air, she looked lovely, and he could not take his eyes off her, not for a second in the entrancing sight.

He greeted Dagmara with a seductive look in his eyes, and kissed her hand. Dressed impeccably in a black tuxedo with his hair slicked back, William Cavill was definitely the most handsome man Dagmara had ever seen.

And just like that, Dagmara found herself having a candlelight dinner with William Cavill that evening at one of the most expensive restaurants in Venice. He ordered a bottle of wine, one of the best, and she was equally impressed with his fluency in Italian. William was fluent in several languages, including German and French, both highly regarded as useful skills during the war. And neither one thought about their friends, the war, or how long this moment would last. They were alone together for the first time, just the two of them, with no interruptions.

The band started to play, and a torch singer in a sequined dress entered the middle of the stage positioning herself in front of the mike. Couples started to dance to the slow, engaging music. William extended his hand to Dagmara, and swooped her onto the dance floor. The curvaceous singer had a deep, sultry voice as she began to sing an enchanting song.

Light on his feet, William was an excellent dancer as he glided across the dance floor, another innate trait he inherited from his father. He had done this before, quite often, with many women. Dagmara felt weightless, her feet barely touching the floor beneath her high heels. The intimate dance speeded up her heart in rapid movement. He held her close, enfolding her in his arms, as their bodies pressed tight against each other. Synchronized in rhythm, their bodies became one.

William could feel her perky breasts against his chest through the thin material of her dress. She rested her head on him, her arm around his back, the other clasped tight within his hold, as they danced to the slow song, moving in sensual motion.

He twirled her around; she looked up at him, her eyes sparkling in the dim light. The seductive glance stimulated his loins with fiery temptation, as he pushed her closer to his body, and then slowly leaned in and kissed her. One, long, enamoring kiss that illuminated the entire evening.

His mouth devoured her lips, caught up in the pleasurable embrace. Her whole body trembled feeling his manhood press against her. That was how tight he held her; Dagmara had never danced so close with a man before. Her heart fluttered in the heavenly feeling.

Swept away in a world all on their own, that song would become theirs, as the music became faint and the shadows of people and their heavy voices seemed to fade in the distance. The dance floor became their own, just the two of them, as if no one else was around, blocking out everyone else. Mesmerized in the ardent seduction, wanting to perpetuate the moment for as long as they could, Dagmara and William kissed, and kissed again, till her lips became numb.

It was like she was living in a fantasy, a beautiful dream she never wanted to leave. From that moment forth, they became inseparable. Their romance took over in passion and long awaited love. Dagmara hardly saw her friends over the next few weeks. They spent almost every moment together. Whether lying on the beach, cuddling under the stars, or dancing the night away in a posh club,

Dagmara had unleashed her fervor and her shielded heart, allowing William Cavill to infiltrate both.

She encouraged his amorous advances. Their lips became one, ravenous in their passionate love affair. Desire felt within her entire body. Her loins set upon a blaze of fire. Her heart deepening in uncharted, newfound love. He was completely enchanted with Dagmara, from her entrancing beauty, he loved everything about her. She made him laugh; she made him smile, even at a time of war. They were happy, they were very happy together, and the initial attraction soon blossomed into a meaningful relationship that solidified in devotion.

William would give her the world if she let him, and in return, Dagmara would always look at him in the same charming way. Nothing it seemed could penetrate through their perfect little world, except the dream dark city that surrounded, could puncture a hole, and rip them apart, forever. The ferocious war became increasingly more dangerous, every second, especially to the innocent victims that got caught up in the movement. Nowhere it seemed was safe, and before it was known, Dagmara had gotten herself trapped in a deadly, bloody realm.

"It's like I've known him my whole life, even though we've just met. I can't explain it, the way I feel when I'm with him. It's like, I can't breathe," Dagmara told her friends, her face flushed with excitement. "Don't you see what I'm trying to tell you both, I think I'm in love with him. I think I've fallen in love with William Cavill!" Her eyes sparkled in the new revelation. Her lips widened in a blushing childlike innocence, as her breath deepened with heightened anticipation.

Both Amelia and Kate stared at Dagmara and then looked at each other in surprise, knowing that it was too sudden to have fallen so hard, so fast in love, but that was their friend Dagmara. She was never like them in the romance department, always viewing love as such a dangerous game. A game that poisoned the heart and weakened the brain.

"That's wonderful Dagmara," Kate replied.

"I'm happy for you," Amelia said.

Amelia and Kate knew they could not tell their friend what they both were really thinking, what they were dying inside to say. Dagmara would never believe them. Strong willed, impulsive at times, no one could talk Dagmara out of anything once she had made up her mind. She knew what they both were thinking, as she was thinking the exact same thing. But she decided to throw caution to the wind and embrace the moment of carpe diem fully, embracing the feeling with every bone in her vigorous body.

Love was grand and it felt wonderful and expressively new. The innovative feeling felt for the very first time was something Dagmara Morrow could not explain, let alone justify in words. The feeling was heavenly when she was with William Cavill. His arms wrapped tightly around her, and when he kissed her, his lips devouring her mouth, maybe this is what everyone has been talking about. Blissful, tempting fervor, and she wanted more.

She craved the feeling that elevated her thirst. The desire consumed her thoughts. Her mind clouded by her passionate actions, especially by his amorous advances. Warmth coursed through her body as his lips touched her mouth. His hand upon her skin, she trembled with excite. She could not fight the temptation. She could not resist, and gave into the riveting feeling. The invigorating feeling that overpowered her heart.

It was romantic floating in the arms of William Cavill as they took an intimate gondola ride in the moonlight hour. The stars twinkling in the dim lit sky, the serenity of the moment blossomed into a love affair that deemed unbreakable. He kissed Dagmara, several times. Slow, long, savoring kisses, like a man should kiss a woman. His kisses made her toes feel numb. Enfolding her in his arms, she felt safe, she felt untouchable, unlike any feeling she had ever felt before. And for the first time ever, Dagmara Morrow saw a future with someone. A man she wanted for a husband, a lover, and a companion in life.

Her vibrant eyes melted him inside, inciting him with escalating vigor. She had captured his heart, and as their lips touched, he softly caressed her cheek. She opened her eyes giving him an inviting smile to kiss her again, as the gondolier maneuvering them in the water briefly looked at the young lovers. He smiled seeing the beautiful picture, that within all the darkness that hovered in the shadows, there could still be light. Not wanting to disturb their kiss, or interrupt their deep, engaging smiles, the gondolier looked upon the waves of the darkened waters.

Then suddenly before they knew what had happened, the tranquility was shattered by gunshots, several of them, coming from a close distance. Instantly William and Dagmara opened their eyes looking all around, as they heard screams from different people, getting louder as they turned the corner. The gondola shook in the water as they moved to stand up, and then they saw flashing lights up ahead, and the commotion that was unraveling in the streets.

As they moved closer, they saw the massive confusion. People running, shouting, the sirens deafening in all the madness. A small outburst had erupted between a resistance group and the government, and as they stepped back onto land, William and Dagmara looked straight at each other. They knew what they had could not last forever, wanting it to go on, not wanting it to end. They were only fooling themselves. They could not perpetuate their romance, any longer. No matter how much they tried, it had to end, soon, but Dagmara never thought it would be so sudden, wanting to spend more time with the man she had fallen in love with, the man who had captured her heart.

"Hurry we must go!" William shouted to Dagmara in a tone that frightened her. He clasped his hand tightly around hers, almost hurting her with his grip, and they took off running towards safety.

They ran swiftly in the opposite direction of the chaos, and Dagmara looked back, only once. She saw several police officers rushing to the scene. They were firing random shots into the crowd. She watched as an innocent boy fell to the ground, falling to his death. The sight was ghastly. Blood surrounded his body, as people trampled over him, stomping on him to get away.

William and Dagmara tried to make their way through the crowded streets, pushing, shoving, as William guided her towards his hotel. She saw lights all around. Gunshots deafened her ears. Her heart feverish in fright, as if she was trapped in a stampede. Trembling with fear, her heart beating so fast, she could barely catch her breath, as William moved them farther and farther away from the peril to a safe place.

William had left Dagmara in his hotel room and joined up with his friends, and they spoke to their commanding officer. She sat alone in his room, as the quietness echoed loudly inside her head, her mind thrashing with thoughts and unwanted images of the evening's terrifying events.

She knew she had overstayed her visit. She should have gone back months ago with her friends. It was not safe being there anymore, anywhere for that matter. Countries being overrun, people slaughtered in bloody battles, but Dagmara had stayed through it all, disregarding Amelia and Kate's pressure to leave. She had convinced them to stay, and in turn, she had somehow sealed their fates, but she had also met William. William Cavill, the man she could see a future with, the man she felt she could spend the rest of her life with in harmony. She had primarily stayed for him. To be with him.

Dagmara waited impatiently for William in his room; barely able to control her body from shaking, feeling the cold chills of the night crawl upon her skin.

She felt as if she was silently dying inside, her heart suffocating in the agonizing wait. Dagmara was scared of William's return, knowing the news would be something she would not want to hear.

And she wished at that very moment, for a world not at war. Dreaming of a world that would let them be together. Not sending him back into the depths of darkness, *to lie with the devil once more!*

CHAPTER 4

It seemed like hours had gone by as Dagmara waited, pacing around the room, till finally she lied down on the bed and closed her eyes. Her body felt weak, she had not eaten in awhile, and her blood pressure had plummeted. She needed a glass of orange juice, but she could not go down to the cafe, nor did she want to leave the room and miss William's return. She would wait for him to come back, when suddenly she dozed off, falling into a slight dreamlike state, and heard footsteps approach the door.

Her eyes rapidly opened, the knob started to turn, she looked up, and saw William standing in the doorway holding a bottle of juice. He had remembered her delicate condition. With everything else happening around them, within all the violence, he had put her first, placing her as his top priority.

Dagmara smiled happy to see him, and slowly drank the orange juice, afraid to ask him what happened. What this meant for him, and especially what it meant for them? Would there even be a them after tomorrow, or even tonight? Would this night be the only night they would ever have to spend together?

Her mind scrambled with questions as William sat beside Dagmara, looking at one another in complete silence. She could see in his eyes the answer was not one she wanted to hear. The news was not good. That night she was going to tell William Cavill she loved him, but she never got the chance. His eyes conveyed sadness, a tortured feeling from within, and then suddenly the smile on his face disappeared, shattering her dreams, her hope of a beautiful future. All was lost when the smile on her face smoothed into sadness, knowing something was wrong, something between them had changed.

"I have to tell you something Dagmara," he said, and then she knew. Her heart felt like it was going to break seeing the look in his eyes. She had known all along, wanting the romance to last forever. The moment was fleeting fast, as their love affair came to a thundering halt just as rapidly as it began.

"I don't want to know," she said.

"I just got my new assignment. I leave tomorrow."

"Tomorrow!" Dagmara replied, raising her voice.

"I have no choice, I have my orders. We both knew this was coming."

"But I didn't think it would be so soon, so terribly soon."

"I know. Do you think I want to leave now, to leave you, just when I've found you," William said with passion.

"When?" she asked.

"I fly out tomorrow morning."

"Where will you be going?"

"For now, I can't tell you, it's a secret mission. My commanding officer reassigned Henry, Stuart, and I after tonight's outburst. I wish I could stay here longer with you, but I have my orders."

Dagmara knew from the moment William stepped foot inside the room, she could see the look on his face. Their time together would be cut short, and tonight within the remaining hours was all they had left. And when daybreak came, they would be separated, moving farther and farther apart, not knowing if they would ever see each other again?

"Then we only have tonight … together," she said, barely able to get the words out.

William did not answer her, unable to face Dagmara and the dreaded question. Instead he got up from the bed and walked away. She moved towards him, started to say something, and then stopped, not wanting to say what both of them were thinking. That it could be the last time they ever see each other. He might go off to war and die, and never come back. She might never see him again after this night, and the prospect was unbearable, as Dagmara shook from the horrid notion. The world was unfair, tearing apart young lovers.

"It's not safe for you here anymore, for anyone," he turned around and said to her. "You have to leave tomorrow, I've already made arrangements for both you and your friends to leave in the morning. You must promise me Dagmara, that you will be on that flight, no matter what. You must get out of here!"

"I don't want to leave you, not now … not when I've just found you," she told him with the same passion.

"You must, I must know you are safe."

"When do you leave?" she asked.

"Ten."

"Then I will stay with you till then."

"No, you must ..."

Dagmara did not let William finish his sentence as she put her finger on his mouth silencing him, shaking her head no; she would stay with him till he left. He would not change her mind. She would take the next flight out, her friends would go without her, and she would stay with him, for as long as they had.

"I love you, you must know that by now," William told her.

His words moved her, as if she was hearing them for the very first time from a man.

"As I love you," she finally said to him, never saying those three words to another man before, she said them to William.

They kissed.

Long and deep was the passionate embrace, sealing their hearts with a powerful kiss. And as the connection between them tightened, a tear of sadness slowly ran down her cheek, as they looked into each other's eyes not knowing what the future let alone tomorrow and the day after would bring.

And just like that, the spell had been broken. War took over, and William and his friends were given their assignments. He did not have a lot of experience as a fighter pilot, but his youthful endurance, aligned with his intrepidness, along with his father's impeccable name, had gotten William and his friends a great commission. Not one of the Cavill men lacked the courage of their convictions, nor did Stuart or Henry. Fearless in battle, men of honor, the peril that surrounded them in every direction, they did not fear death.

William moved closer to Dagmara, his body just pressing against her. His fingers gently caressed her face, feeling the softness of her skin, and then he leaned in closer and kissed her rosy red lips. Perfect in form. Long, slow, mesmerizing was the hypnotic effect.

That night, they engaged upon a passion they both enjoyed. They knew they would only have this one night to spend together, whether making love, or just cuddling in each other's arms, they would only have this one night. William pressed her into his body more, feeling her breasts within her dress, arousing his loins. The darkened, bleak mood had rapidly turned sensual, as he started undoing the front of her dress, button by button.

His hand moved smoothly through the thin material. He had done this before, several times, this was not new to him. William had made love to a woman before, and Dagmara's inexperience showed through her hesitant actions towards his sexual, amorous advance.

"I've been with a woman before," he told her.

"Then you are more experienced than I."

"If you're not ready, I don't want to push you …"

"No … I want to," she told him, letting go of her propriety. There was nothing to fear, but the fear of losing him, of never seeing him again after this night.

He kissed her on the side of her neck, and Dagmara became less hesitant, as her whole body trembled by his touch. The innovative feeling coursed through her body with excitement, as William Cavill took his time, slowly unbuttoning her dress.

He kissed her lips again, and then moved her dress down her body, as the material fell to the floor. She stood in a sheer white slip and matching silk stockings. Her long blonde curls fell around her shoulders, as her eyes sparkled in the dim light.

William could see the outline of her naked body beneath the slip, instantly stimulating his loins. Her slender, ripe figure enticed him, as he started to unbutton his shirt. She watched as he took off his shirt and undershirt, and then his pants. Her loins warmed. His tall, sleek figure equally enticed her, as his smooth chest flexed in the coolness of the night.

William Cavill was the first man Dagmara Morrow had ever seen undressed, and as the layers of clothing were being removed, William was the perfect embodiment of a man. She could not take her eyes off him, not for a second.

Dagmara unhooked her stockings from her garter belt, rolled them down, one at a time, and took them off. Then she took off her slip, removing all her undergarments, as William moved closer. Goose bumps formed on her delicate skin as he moved near her naked body. He kissed her mouth, her cheek, moving his lips down her neck. William led Dagmara over to the bed, and they slipped in under the sheets, her naked body lying next to his. As they lied in bed together, naked, kissing passionately, she could feel his hand moving down her body to her inner thigh.

This was all new to Dagmara; she was not experienced in the art of seduction, or in making love. William had romanced many women, and for the first time ever, Dagmara felt somewhat at a disadvantage. But she was eager to learn, and soon her body took over within the sensuous feeling, inciting her with newfound warmth.

He moved her hand on his body. Her heart started pounding fast, as he moved her hand down lower. William took his time with Dagmara, slow was his approach. His seduction smoldered in intensity, as he kissed her lips hard, harder, his vigor scorching to be unleashed. William had wanted Dagmara from the first moment he saw her, but unlike other women he had made love to in his past, he wanted his time with Dagmara to be special, especially for her. Deep, long kisses were his style. His fiery seduction rapidly heated the bed, as their bodies started to glisten.

His lips devoured her mouth, their pulses raced, and Dagmara felt like she was floating on a cloud. William moved his lips down her neck, and started to move his body on top of hers. She could feel his manhood press against her, his thigh moving over her leg. Suddenly she stopped, pulling back, and broke apart their intimate connection. He opened his eyes feeling her lips move off his mouth, and his body tightened.

"Can we just lie here together like this," she said, not wanting to go further. Not wanting to make love to him now, to give him her most intimate embrace.

He looked at her for a long, mesmerizing moment, looking down into her beautiful blue eyes, then shifted his body off hers, and lied down next to her in bed. William looked at Dagmara somewhat puzzled, not understanding her proposed refusal?

Softly his fingers caressed her face, her eyes conveying a virtuous innocence in expression. "If that's what you really want," he said.

Dagmara nodded yes, but that was the exact opposite of what William Cavill truly wanted. He wanted her, here, now, wanting to make love to her. Tantalized by the way her body already made him feel, he wanted her ripe, untouched beauty, and soil it in a night of unbridled passion to satisfy his own sexual craving.

Not wanting to leave things this way, William would wait until they were reunited, and look forward to a proper night of passion, not wanting Dagmara to compromise her virtue for him, and for the war. He respected her too much. He loved her too much to take that away from her, to have her do that just for him.

He moved closer to her, enfolding her in his arms, cuddling in the late night hour, feeling each other's warmth. Their lips kissed in a long, amorous embrace, feeling each other's nakedness.

They did not make love that night. Slightly disappointed, William would wait until he came back from the war, to have that to look forward to, rather than have the memory to take with him. Dagmara felt safe within his arms, in his bed, and in a way, it meant more to her to just lie next to him naked, than to have made love. A closer more intimate connection, as he held her around tight.

The moment was powerfully significant. The silence shimmered, as his manhood yearned to be free. Her tongue slid softly over the ripples of his abdomen, as she kissed his smooth chest. Her bosom silently cried out in ecstasy, as William cherished the feeling, memorizing every curve. How soft her skin felt, her breasts against his chest, kissing her neck, her moistened lips. His fingers outlined her entire body, as if he was an artist, and she his model.

CHAPTER 5

A slamming of a door in the next room, heavy talking in the halls, luggage being carried away awoke the young lovers, bringing their night to a close. Their naked bodies cuddled, his arm wrapped around her waist, his head rested on the pillow.

William Cavill was the first man to ever see Dagmara Morrow naked, and she never felt closer to a man. A moment she would always remember. Her friends would have disapproved of her staying in his hotel room, and especially staying overnight in his bed, so she conjured up a lie, telling them she had stayed in the room next to his. Somewhat disbelieving, they accepted her story, not questioning her further. But they had not acquiesced so easily to her staying behind and not leaving with them on the early morning flight. They wanted Dagmara to come with them, but she refused, wanting to spend every last second with the man she loved.

Amelia and Kate did not fully understand her connection with William Cavill. The passion. The love. Not comprehending how quick such a thing could happen, they knew Dagmara and William had a lot in common. Never seeing their friend in love before, real love, not just high school crushes, they begrudgingly accepted, and allowed Dagmara to take the later flight home. They would pack her belongings, and let her family know of her late arrival, and she would explain the rest.

It was not safe for anyone anymore; the flights leaving were heavily delayed for security purposes. And against their better judgment, wanting Dagmara to come with them, Amelia and Kate told their friend to be careful. Unknown to them at the time, this would be the last time they would speak to Dagmara under these heightened circumstances, expecting her safe return. She had thrown caution to the wind and stayed behind to be with William. Dagmara would have rather taken the same flight with her friends than traveled alone, but she stayed behind for him.

Dagmara opened her eyes that morning to a new fervid day. She squeezed William's hand and kissed his fingers, feeling his nakedness next to her own. It was a blissful feeling she definitely could get used to. She never had a more peaceful sleep. She smiled, if only her parents could see her now, what would they think? What would they have to say? Dagmara always had a wild, adventurous spirit, never conforming to anyone's rules.

And just like that, over the course of one passion filled night, Dagmara had become the more experienced of her two friends.

"What are you smiling about?" William asked, as he playfully kissed Dagmara's neck, turning her around.

"Nothing," she said with a mischievous look in her eyes, twirling his identity discs with her finger.

He did not press her further, allowing Dagmara to have her secrets, as he had his own. William brushed a strand of hair from her face, and kissed her rosy lips, tasting her strawberry sweetness inside his mouth.

"I could lie here in your arms forever," she told him.

"Then I accept the invitation."

"Could you imagine it, just the two of us, leaving everything else behind," she said, and snuggled closer. "We could run off together where no one could find us."

"You would do that for me?" he asked.

She looked at him with eyes of love, and then passionately kissed him on the lips with her impetuous response.

Then suddenly her smile turned to sadness. "I don't want to leave your side, not for a moment … because I fear if I do … I will never see you again. I will lose you forever!"

"No, you must never say that," he said to her powerfully, looking her directly in the eyes.

William moved over to the side of the bed, grabbed his coat, and reached into the pocket, slowly withdrawing a small box. As he turned back around towards Dagmara, she saw the small object and turned away, not wanting to look inside.

"No," she protested.

"I thought about it last night after I got my assignment, so I went to a nearby store. And I know it's not much, if we were back home, I would get you a really big diamond to show you how much you mean to me. How much I love spending this time with you. How much it has meant to me."

She turned back around hearing the agony and sincerity in his words. William opened the box; a small diamond ring was inside. She looked up at him.

"I know how I feel about you, and I think I know how you feel about me. What I'm trying to say so inarticulately is … I want you to marry me Dagmara. I want you to be my wife."

"You want to marry me?" she said, her heart pounding fast.

"Yes, I love you. Will you marry me Dagmara?"

Instead of being overwhelmed with happiness by his romantic proposal, Dagmara could barely breathe.

"How can you ask me that, now? I can't accept this," she said, not wanting to hurt him.

Not understanding her refusal, William pressed further explaining his reasons, his intentions for her, as Dagmara moved out of bed and stepped into her slip. Hurriedly William pulled on his pants, moved over to her, and stopped Dagmara from putting on her dress and leaving.

He grabbed her around; she looked up at him.

"If I knew you were mine, and mine alone," he started to say, as she shook her head no, trying to get away from his tight hold.

"No, I can't. I won't!" she protested.

"Why not?" he asked, raising his voice.

She did not want to tell him why, how could she? How could Dagmara tell the man that she loved, that it was not fear holding her back from accepting his offer. She could not accept his ring and had to turn down his proposal of marriage, because she did not want to be made a widow before she became a bride.

A tear slowly slid down her cheek, her eyes sad in thought of such a horrid premonition of events. "You'll go off to war and die!"

"NO," he said to her, grabbing her face tightly in his hands, looking her straight in the eyes. "No, not if I have you to come home to," he told her, and passionately kissed her on the lips. "I want you Dagmara. I want to keep you safe, protect you, take care of you, isn't that the whole purpose of my life."

Her lips softened into a smile as she kissed him back, accepting his offer of marriage. As William began to bend down on one knee and slide the ring on Dagmara's finger, she moved down to him on the floor and took the ring out of his hand. She took off her necklace, slid the diamond ring through the small chain, and placed it back around her neck.

Dagmara held the ring in her fingers and told William, "I'll keep it here, close to my heart until you return."

It was not exactly what William had intended, wanting to see the ring on her finger, but he understood, and would wait until he returned home to properly place the ring on her fourth finger. Another enjoyment he would have to look forward to when he returned home from the war.

William kissed Dagmara with his entire body as they stood up together. The kiss had sealed their fate, locking them in an unbreakable connection of a future. A future they would both look forward to with open hearts.

As they finished getting dressed, there was a knock on the door; Stuart and Henry were standing in the doorway. Dagmara was buttoning up her dress, her slip slightly showing, as William zipped up his pants, and looked over at them.

"I'll meet you guys downstairs," he told them and closed the door, as they smirked at each other and left.

Dagmara brushed her hair, smoothing out her long curls, and colored her lips with red lipstick. As she looked into the mirror, William was standing behind her. She turned around to him. For the first time since she met William Cavill that day on the street, he was dressed in his uniform, and he looked more handsome than before. To him, Dagmara was the one who looked lovely; her blonde curls accentuating her light colored eyes.

"I think you missed a button," he told her, and placed his fingers on her dress readjusting the alignment.

"Thank you," she said with a blushing smile.

Then he brushed his finger over her lips, smudging her lipstick, and kissed her on the mouth. A perfect kiss.

Guests were bustling about, busy closing their accounts and finishing their stay at the hotel, as Dagmara and William joined Stuart and Henry at the small café in the lobby. Dagmara looked at all three men sitting at the table in their uniforms, she could not help but feel happy and sad at the same time. Three friends go off to war together, but how many of them return? She did not want to know the answer.

William was a gentleman, he did not share his passion filled evening with his friends, nor did his friends ask or make sexual innuendos about last night's apparent tryst. They did not know all the facts; neither did her friends, and if they were to come to their own conclusions, let them. Perhaps when William was alone with Stuart and Henry, he would divulge some private details of their intimate relationship, as Dagmara might do the same with Amelia and Kate.

They did notice one thing different about their friend, and as soon as they saw the diamond ring around Dagmara's necklace, they knew what it was.

"You two are engaged?" Stuart asked.

Dagmara smiled at William, as if his friends had uncovered their secret.

"Yes, I've asked Dagmara to marry me," he said elated.

"And I accepted."

"We haven't told anyone yet, not even our families, it just happened this morning. I'll officially propose to Dagmara when I get back to London, and properly place a larger ring on her finger," William explained to his friends, feeling slightly embarrassed by the small size of the stone.

"So sudden," Henry remarked.

"It just kind of happened," William told them.

Henry and Stuart were surprised by the news of their friend's engagement. Not that they had anything against Dagmara. She was beautiful, charming, and came from a good family, so they could not ask for a better match for their friend. They knew William's father would accept her into the Cavill family, but they had never seen their friend act in such an impulsive manner before. Debonair was his style when he seduced the ladies, but commitment after only a few weeks, they were speechless.

"Well congratulations," Stuart said.

"Yes, congratulations to both of you," Henry added.

"Thank you," Dagmara replied, as they shook hands with William, and took turns hugging Dagmara and giving her a kiss on the cheek.

Both men were enchanted with her. Smelling her perfume as they congratulated her with warm wishes in a tight embrace. Admiring her beauty, slightly envious of their friend's impeccable choice.

"Both of you will have to come to our wedding," Dagmara told them, and as easily as those words flowed from her mouth, she felt an acute pulling deep inside her heart.

Not knowing what the war wound bring, hoping it would keep both William and his friends safe, she could not help but feel sad at such a joyful occasion, having that blackened thought plague her mind every breathing second. In the midst of tragedy lied romance, a love that ignited the flames between two passionate people.

William kissed Dagmara on the lips, in front of his friends, for the whole world to see. Her pulse racing, as she kissed her soon to be husband on the lips lavishly hard, not wanting to ever let go. Knowing in a few hours they would be saying their goodbyes, hoping it would not be the long kiss goodbye, and tomorrow would bring serenity to a new dawn.

CHAPTER 6

Stuart and Henry waited on the side, enabling William and Dagmara to say their goodbyes in private. Her flight home would be taking off shortly, and they only had a few precious minutes left to be with one another, savoring the moment until the next.

Dagmara was on the verge of tears. For the first time ever, she knew what it was like to be in love, for someone to love her. Her heart felt like it was being gutted out of her flesh, breaking in two. It was hard for her to say goodbye, to anyone, so Dagmara was happy she had stayed behind. Those few extra hours meant the world to her, cherishing each second she had left with William Cavill.

Dagmara had disobeyed Kate, Amelia, and William's urging for her to leave with them on the earlier flight, as her own stubbornness would not accept any of their reasoning but her own. Guided by her heart, following the feeling for the first time, she placed a smile on her face for William, not wanting him to see right through her. Not wanting him to know she was scared, for him, for her, for them both.

He took her hand in his.

"I will miss you deeply Dagmara."

The way he said her name, each time, melted her heart with the penetrating look in his eyes. His thick eyebrows were uneven as his hair tossed in the wind, shifting from side to side on his forehead. His lips, perfect in form, and the dimple in his chin, the only imperfection on his face that Dagmara or anyone else could see, would be the one thing she would remember most about his face, which made him all the more handsome in her eyes.

A cold chill whipped around Dagmara's body, as the wind picked up in force. His hands warmed her skin, as her curls swayed around her face. Her lips full and red, her cheeks rosy from the coolness, as her eyes entranced him with an everlasting look of beauty. To William, he could see no flaws; Dagmara was absolutely perfect in every way.

"Will I ever see you again?" she asked him.

"There is no certainty in life, but by the farthest star in the evening sky, they can never take away our tomorrow, when yesterday is ours forever …" William replied.

"I love you, you know that don't you," she told him, as a tear fell from her eye.

"As I love you," he told her, catching the tear on his finger.

"I always will!" she stated passionately.

"I will come back to you, I promise you Dagmara. We will see each other again."

No words could express the tormenting feeling that blackened their hearts in such a promising bright future. They knew that this could be the very last time they ever saw one another again. The last time they ever kissed and held each other, feeling the warmth of the heated memory of their naked bodies lying next to one another. That tomorrow and the day after would be in forever ruin, helpless in knowing the outcome of their own destined futures.

Would he come back to her? Would William return from the war alive? Would Dagmara still be waiting patiently for his unexpected return someday in the near but distant future? Would the day come when she received a letter like so many others, the horror would overshadow in grieving pain, and she would never see him again? Would she be waiting with no means to an end, not knowing if she was remembered or forgotten? Nothing could be worse than that.

Nothing she thought could ever repair the emptiness that lied within that darkened, shattered hole. That fleeting, futile layer of hope. All was but lost. Everything she had turned away from was now right in front of her.

Their passion could never be erased. Their love could never be matched. They would remain lovers for the rest of their lives, even if it was only in spirit. Nothing could ever come between them, or could it? Was anything ever forever? Neither of them knew the answer to that profound question that plagued people for centuries, but for them, they would soon find out.

William Cavill kissed Dagmara Morrow once more, one, long, impassioned kiss, as she wrapped her arms around him tight, and kissed him back with the same amorous vigor he bestowed upon her mouth. Her lips were fiery hot as they kissed for several minutes, wanting to perpetuate the moment, as observers watched in whispering smiles as they passed by the young departing lovers.

Their lips were inseparable in the steamy embrace, till Stuart tapped William on the shoulder and broke their kiss apart. He told them their time was up, and Dagmara had to leave. Her flight was about to take off, and neither of them wanted to leave the other, but they knew they had prolonged the inevitable.

Dagmara reached inside her coat pocket, pulled out a small photograph, placed it in Williams's hand, and closed his fingers around the image.

"Something to remember me by," she said tearfully.

"I could never forget you, you know that Dagmara."

"Then walk away, now, and don't look back. Remember me as I am now," she told him.

"She has to go William," Stuart urged, as the stewardess started to close the doors.

"I'll write to you, every day," he said. Seeing her hesitation to leave, William had to get Dagmara on the plane; he had to make sure she was safe. "You must go, now," he said strenuously. "You must leave me. Go!"

The powerfulness of his tone brought forth his assertive behavior, dying inside each second by having to push her away, pushing her to leave his side. But William had to, he had no other choice. He had to let Dagmara go. He had to let her leave.

Overwhelmed with emotion, Dagmara kissed William on the lips, hard, and then walked away. Running towards the half closed door of the airplane, walking away from William Cavill and a future together.

William watched Dagmara walk away from him, and his body immediately felt the pain cutting into his chest, like a dagger had sliced through his heart, and he wished for the first time since the war had begun, since he became an RAF fighter pilot, that he would cowardly run away, just so he could be with her. To wake up next to Dagmara in the morning, and every morning after that. To fall asleep in each other's arms every night. To feel her naked body lying next to his, her soft, smooth skin, her lips upon his mouth.

Dagmara did not look back at William, not once, because if she did, she would not be able to get on the plane and leave. It would be too unbearable. Tears streamed down her face as she handed the stewardess her ticket and boarded the aircraft. She did not look back, even though everything inside of her was screaming to do so. To look upon his handsome face once more, and capture that everlasting image in her mind.

She could still feel his lips on hers. Her heart aching as she sat down in her seat, wanting to feel the warmth of his arms around her, his naked body lying next to her in bed, once more. Dagmara held the necklace in her hand and kissed the ring; kissing the only thing she had left to remember William Cavill by, other than the sensual, loving memory.

Stuart and Henry saw the love in William's eyes as he watched Dagmara board the plane, and then he opened his clenched fist, and looked down at the photograph that Dagmara had given him. The small picture was slightly crumbled. The black and white ink on the paper was good quality, and her image was captured perfectly in the beautiful picture. A slight smile crossed her mouth; her eyes conveyed a look of intrigue, her curls fastened by several clips.

He did not follow her request by walking away and not looking back. Instead William stayed behind and watched. Watching as the door to the aircraft closed, sealing her in, separating them, as he held the tiny picture in his hand. The only remembrance that was real, besides the forever lasting memory of the night they shared together in his hotel room.

William watched as the plane took off down the runway, and then rose higher and higher in the air, separating them farther and farther apart, till the figure of the plane became small to the eye. He looked at the photograph of Dagmara Morrow, and then placed it inside his pocket knowing she would be safe.

"We have to go," Henry told him, as both he and Stuart were unable to ease their friend's pain.

After several, long, agonizing minutes, no longer able to see the airplane in the sky, William Cavill turned away from a life that could have been, from a life that maybe now will never be. And as he walked away, farther and farther within each step he took, he walked away from Dagmara Morrow, the woman he loved, walking away from that future, to an unwritten one.

"We have our orders, and we will carry them out," William stated to his friends assertively, pushing back the tears that plagued his heart. Not succumbing to that weakness.

The courageous fighter pilot was back in control of his emotions, as he walked forward now with determination for success, and not failure. His attitude had dramatically changed from the lovesick young man, to the intrepid, mature soldier. William Cavill could no longer think of Dagmara Morrow anymore, or of their future together, as the tenacious fire that fueled his strength, the very life that he breathed, proclaimed his soul once again.

Dagmara settled into her seat and wiped away the tears as she looked out the window. The people and airport below became smaller and smaller in image, till finally she could not see them anymore. They were now tiny pebbles on the ground, placing farther distance between Italy and herself, between she and the ferocious war, especially placing farther distance between she and William.

She looked out among the clouds and closed her eyes. "I pray to the stars to watch over you," she said softly. "Be safe my love!"

Soon Dagmara would be home in England, surrounded by friends and family. Half of her heart was looking forward to seeing her parents, Amelia and Kate. The other half was aching inside never to return. To leave the place where she was born, where she had lived in her youth, and never come back. For fear of losing the feeling she felt inside her heart this very moment. That it would be lost, forever, and never come again.

William put on his flying gear, and got ready to go up in the air to begin his dangerous and very deadly mission. Each assignment he took with risk, especially this particular one. He knew this might be his last, he might not return home, as he placed the picture of Dagmara on the control panel, and rubbed the image with his fingers. No, he could not think of her, his future wife, he had to keep his mind on the pertinent peril that lied ahead, but the more he looked at her face, the more he became choked inside with suffocation, unable to think clearly.

Then he kissed the photograph and placed it inside his jacket pocket. It was better not to look upon her face, or he would not be able to fly as he always had, without fear. If he thought of her, he might not take the dangerous chances and make safe choices, and he could not start doing that now. His unit, his friends, his captain all depended on him, and his valor.

"My heart is forever yours Dagmara."

And with that last thought being of his fiancée, William Cavill aligned his aircraft with the other planes and waited for command to take off. Waiting with intrepid intensity that coursed through his veins, hardening his heart.

And as William took off in the air, followed by Stuart, Henry, and several other planes, the fighter pilots went forth into the unknown territory that lied ahead in their path. Undaunted they gained speed, whispering like hummingbirds in the open sky, and William Cavill moved closer and closer to peril, soon to be placed directly in the middle of battle.

Both moving in opposite directions, what lied ahead for William and especially Dagmara could not have been known by either. Thinking she was safe on her way home, hoping he would stay safe, they thought only of each other.

CHAPTER 7

Amelia and Kate arrived safely home. They met with Dagmara's parents who were displeased to hear that their daughter had not returned home with them. The girls told the Morrows she would be on the next flight, and that she had stayed behind to be with William. Her parents had heard of the Cavills, and although they were unhappy she had not returned home with her friends, they were surprised and very delighted to hear that their daughter had made the acquaintance of William Cavill.

They knew how selective Dagmara was, knowing she must really fancy this young man to have stayed behind. They were also pleased to hear that William's affections were placed solely upon their daughter. He came from a very wealthy and influential family; a union between the two would be most profitable. But they did not know that Dagmara and William were engaged, and were to be married as soon as he returned home from the war. Dagmara had never gotten the chance to tell her friends before they left. She had not spoken to them after William proposed.

Her friends and family expected Dagmara home within a few hours, as they waited patiently for her arrival.

"Dagmara Morrow Cavill. Dagmara Cavill," she mused to herself. "Mrs. Dagmara Cavill." The words sounded exquisite to her ears. "Dagmara Cavill, doesn't it sound wonderful," Dagmara said to the person sitting next to her on the plane, and then she relaxed back in her seat as a smile crossed her face.

A spray of bullets came flying at his aircraft from all different angles, as William Cavill and his friends were completely surrounded. As the enemy moved in close, William fired back at the German aircrafts, shooting down several planes that crossed his path. His eyes shifted right and left rapidly moving, as his hands crossed the control panel, his plane gaining in momentum and speed, changing in direction.

He climbed high above the clouds, and then maneuvered down lower trying to evade a plane that was right on his tail. Then he pulled back, slowing in speed, and allowed the enemy to move in front of him, as he placed his plane directly behind, and fired.

Outsmarting the enemy with his quick and very dangerous move, William destroyed the plane and took out another German. Henry and Stuart kept firing at the enemy, taking out several more, and then they began to move closer together in unison with the other planes, heading straight into deadly, enemy territory.

William maneuvered his aircraft with incredible depth perception and speed, never faltering for a moment, his eyesight, impeccable. He persevered forward intrepidly with his friends alongside him, and then they began a massive attack, as the enemy airplanes flew straight towards them ready to kill.

Direct in contact, William fired and fired at the planes. He shot down the enemy aircrafts one by one, trying to elude the predators and avoid getting killed. He did not think of the planes he was shooting down, or of the men he was killing, their faces haunting him in the black of night. Nor did he think upon the numerous enemy aircrafts moving straight towards him in terrifying peril. He thought only of her … Dagmara.

Unable to sit patiently, refusing a drink, Dagmara floated off into a dreamlike state contemplating the two words that repeated over and over in her head like a broken record.

> *Dagmara Cavill.*
> *Dagmara Cavill.*

Then Dagmara looked out the window at the clouded sky, when suddenly her eyes opened wide, and the entire plane shook in ferocious force. Then there was another rapid tilting and a loud explosion.

They were under attack!

The airplane had been hit, twice; the second shot took out one of the wings, as the plane began to lose altitude and rapidly decreased in speed, descending at a quickened pace. Dropping below the clouds.

Screams, deafening screams of terror echoed inside the aircraft, as passengers and crew were thrown to the floor, as the explosions erupted further inside the plane, demolishing more of the aircraft. Windows started to break. Pieces of the plane started to come loose, as the airplane took a spiral nosedive downward at an enormous speed.

Faster and faster the plane twirled in the sky, as the captain and his crew tried desperately to signal for help, trying to gain control of the aircraft long enough to maneuver it level. As if the airplane was a twisting funnel, the plane twirled and twirled in a sickening, forceful motion, moving faster towards the ground.

"Help me," an older man yelled, as his wife tried to fasten his seat belt.

Passengers went flying in the air, crashing into the aircraft at all different angles, smashing them to their terrifying deaths. Fright, crying babies, and blood consumed the compartment, as the passengers thrashed into one another, unable to control their own bodies at the rapid, horrifying speed.

"We're going to die. We're all going to die!" a woman screamed.

"Shut up," a man shouted.

The people needed to remain calm, but everyone on the airplane knew what the woman was saying was the truth, and even though the man and the other passengers did not want to hear the words out loud, they themselves believed them to be true. They were all doomed. And as the airplane came crashing towards the ground, they were all, each one of them … already dead!

The lights went out and darkness thickened, as screams swarmed in staggering formation, the smoke clouding the air, and before anyone could feel the massive, forceful hit, the airplane smashed into the ground, shattering the plane into several pieces. Families were separated; tearing apart loved ones from each other's arms. The passengers, desecrated, as bodies were thrown to the ground being trampled in motion, as the aircraft fell on top of the people, killing them instantly upon contact.

Black air formed around the debris, as the redness of blood splashed within the large area of the separated body parts that were scattered throughout the wreckage. Clothes covered in fresh blood. Dead bodies dangling from the aircraft, still fastened to their seats, as the airplane finally came to a thundering halt, and quietness surrounded.

No more tears, screams had long ceased, and for the moment, nothing on the ground moved. Everything was still!

The wind blew a cold breeze across the massive destruction, and without warning, no one could have foreseen such a horrid tragedy among innocents, trapped helpless in the sky, intertwined in a deadly war. An enemy fighter plane had shot down the aircraft carrying civilians, and as the smoke filtered through the air in thickening suffocation, there were only three survivors remaining, everyone else on board was dead.

A middle aged woman who had her two year old son ripped from her arms, an old man who was badly wounded, and one young woman. Dagmara Morrow was among the three survivors. Miraculously she had survived, but not unscathed, hurting her left arm, she had scrapes and bruises all over her body. Her face was dirty, her forehead was bleeding, as she could barely breathe, let alone comprehend what had just taken place.

For several minutes Dagmara had been knocked unconscious from the plane crash. Her head had hit part of the window on the way down as she held on for life, closing her eyes, lifting her feet to her chest, her head down to her knees. Her whole life flashed before her eyes, as the spiraling motion of the plane made her nauseous, and she leaned over after regaining consciousness and threw up. She wiped her face several times with her right hand, unable to smell anything but the smoke, her lungs consuming the tainted air.

Dagmara tried to focus her eyes on the disastrous sight, as there was so much blood, everywhere. Everywhere she looked she saw dead bodies lying on top of each other, under pieces of the airplane. Body parts thrown all over mixed with people's belongings. Bludgeoned bodies surrounded her on the ground, and the stench of fresh blood filled the blackened air that hovered above her head in darkness.

Her last thought before she hit the ground was of William Cavill, the handsome young man she had just gotten engaged to. And somehow she had survived. She had lived through one of the most terrifying, deadly catastrophes of her entire life. And thinking that the worst was over, she was unsuspecting to the petrifying horror that lied ahead, as the worst had yet to come!

∾

Dear Dagmara,

I wrote to you before I left, knowing you would receive this letter when you returned safely home.

By the time you read this; I will already be on my way.

For now, I cannot tell you where I'm headed, nor can I tell you when I will be returning. I can only tell you how much I enjoyed our time together, and how much I will miss you … and love you!

Forever Yours,

William C.

William mailed the letter to London after he watched Dagmara leave, and as the letter arrived at the home of Dagmara Morrow waiting to be opened, William was flying high above the clouds in enemy territory, fighting his way through German aircrafts. But the letter without a return address on the envelope would wait for a long reply, as Dagmara was now fighting for her own survival somewhere in the midst of unknown, enemy territory. She was now in the middle of the war, along its deadly wrath, intertwined accidentally by fate.

Dagmara tried to sit up, her body felt incredibly sore from the forceful impact of the crash, and as she moved her upper body off the ground, she instantly saw a group of men moving through the wreckage. They were all carrying weapons as they walked around looking for survivors. Not knowing if the three men were enemies, Dagmara saw up close the spoils of war that went to the vicious, unmerciful victors who took great delight in other peoples tragic misfortunes.

They grabbed wallets, tore scattered jewelry from the clutches of dead people's hands, and immediately Dagmara knew they were not friends, they were enemies, German soldiers. The old man who was badly wounded from the crash saw the men, and started making noises, trying to alert his presence.

One of the men spotted the injured survivor, and all three men rushed over to him. And right before Dagmara's eyes, they shot the man in the chest, several times with laughter. The wounded man reached out with his hand, trying to move his body, crawling to escape, as the assailants shot him again, this time in the head, ending his suffering. They maliciously executed their prisoner without trial, being both his judge and jury.

The horrid sight was too graphic for Dagmara's eyes, as she turned away, not wanting to look upon the fiendish creatures that became the man's executioners. They shot the innocent survivor in cold blood, feeling no remorse. No qualms of conscience for their actions. Each of the men fired several rounds into the corpse, like target practice, and then in the air, as the bullets smashed into the dead bodies that lied on the ground.

Dagmara was paralyzed from movement, suffocating inside, unable to breathe, frightened to make a sound and alert her presence. Her heart pounded feverishly witnessing the brutal murder. Gasping for air, her chest felt tight, her whole body stiffening in acute numbness. She had to think fast. She had to do something before it was too late, before they spotted her, and she became their next victim.

What could she do? She had no weapon, no gun to defend herself with from the vile predators that fed upon the dead and undead. Her mind scrambled and she lied still among the corpses, and then suddenly she saw a piece of metal torn from the plane.

Slowly, quietly, her life depended upon her quick action; Dagmara reached forward with her fingers, grabbed the sharp metal in her hand, and dragged it towards her body. The metal was so acute, that it instantly cut into her skin, digging into her flesh, inflicting enormous pain. Blood started to form in the palm of her hand as she moved the object closer to her chest, withstanding the pain, remaining silent.

She could not scream and cry out for help, they would immediately silence her before she had a chance to escape. They would kill her like they had killed the old man. They would kill her without hesitation, as Dagmara clenched the piece of metal tight within her hand. She was a survivor, and would use her last breath, her last ounce of blood within her bones to defend herself, for her life!

CHAPTER 8

The men rustled through the dead passengers' belongings looking for treasures and searching for more survivors to torture, when suddenly Dagmara saw the middle aged woman begin to move in the wreckage. After the woman witnessed what had happened to the old man, she freed herself from the large object that had fallen on her leg, and got up and started to run. She tried to run fast with her injured leg, trying desperately to get away, when the three men easily caught up with her, and threw her down on the ground forcefully with their strength.

One of the men hit her in the face hard, as the other two men held her down on the ground with their bodies. The men tore at her clothing, tearing off her dress, as she screamed no, screaming for help, pleading, begging with the men to stop, to let her go. She tried to get away from them, but her efforts were futile. Her words were not heard, her struggling was useless, wrestling with the savages, overpowered by their strength, and the more she screamed no, the more pain she received, as the dark haired man hit her in the face again, drawing blood from her mouth.

The vile assailant sat on top of her, pressing her into the ground, and then unzipped his pants, and raped her.

Suddenly the woman was silent, whether she had passed out from hitting her head against the ground, the strong punch in the face, or the shock to her system from her body being violated, she lied still. The echoing silence pierced into Dagmara's head like a scalding blaze of terror, not knowing if the quietness or listening to the woman's screams was worse.

She could not do anything for the woman, as Dagmara closed her eyes, not wanting to watch further, unable to witness the vehement attack upon the woman. Then the man on top of the woman moved off, and traded places with the second man, and then the third. Each of the men took their turn raping the woman, holding her down against her will on the dirty, bloody ground.

And after they were done with the woman, and they had violated her all they wanted, they shot two bullets into her scull, savagely killing her, silencing their actions upon reprehension. They did not even cover up her half naked body when they were done.

Disgusting filth Dagmara thought as she opened her eyes, witnessing the horrible attack by the vicious enemies. Then suddenly the men heard a noise that rattled them, and they looked over in Dagmara's direction. Instantly she lied still, as if she was one among the dead, barely moving her chest in breath, as the men lifted up their guns and looked at one another.

Then they heard another noise coming from the opposite direction that momentarily diverted their attention away from Dagmara, and she took those brief seconds of opportunity, and moved herself closer to the body that was lying next to her on the ground. She moved the dead man's hand over her chest, her leg under his, displaying the image that she was one among the many that lie in the crash. Smelling the fresh blood made Dagmara feel ill again, as she moved the man's arm higher on her body, covering herself, making it appear that she was part of the disaster.

She looked dead. Her clothes were covered in blood. Her face dirtied from the smoke. Her body ailing in pain, as she smelled the stench of the decaying corpse, unable to breathe. But Dagmara stayed courageous, and would not let herself be violated by the fiendish creatures. She would rather sacrifice herself, taking her own life to the hollows of death, than allow those men to place a finger on her while she still breathed.

Dagmara clutched the metal tighter in her hand and closed her eyes, not knowing what was to come.

The men had gotten spooked by their own licentious actions, and not knowing if they were being watched, they rapidly rushed off, taking whatever money and possessions they had found, and ran away in a panic not wanting to get caught. And as the enemies were fleeing, Dagmara waited several minutes to see if they would return, but they did not, nor did anyone else.

Swiftly she pushed the man's heavy arm off her chest, and moved his body away. Her clothes were full of warm and dried blood, dirt all over her skin. Her head was bleeding, her dress torn, her knee scraped. Slowly Dagmara stood up, sore, her thin frame ached in excruciating pain, but she could not think of that now. Her left arm felt sprained, but she had to get away from this place of death, especially if those savage men returned with an unsatisfied thirst, wanting more.

Dagmara looked around for her belongings, her purse, but she could not find anything. No money, no clothes, no means to get her help. She was completely alone for the first time since she left London, since she left her friends, since she left William in Venice. She was the lone survivor of the devastating plane crash, and now she was alone in a foreign country. France. She knew no one in France, nor did her family. A stranger in the midst of war. No papers, no identification, she could easily be thought of as a traitor, a spy, and taken and tortured as a prisoner of war.

Instinct for survival, no time for tears they would have to wait, locked away in fear, Dagmara moved around inbetween the desecrated bodies, when her eyes suddenly opened wide in horror, and she saw the woman who was sitting next to her on the plane. Her head decapitated from her body. The sight was ghastly, as Dagmara shunned away from the gruesome picture. The sight of the woman's hand still clutched to her purse made Dagmara feel ill.

Then Dagmara moved around in the wreckage, and came across a bag full of young men's clothing. Swiftly she took off her dress, slipped into a pair of pants, and buttoned up a shirt over her slip. The clothes were a size too large, as she stepped into a pair of shoes, found a handkerchief, and tried to clean her face looking into a piece of glass. She wiped away the blood from her forehead, and wrapped the cloth around her hand to stop the bleeding. Then she smoothed her long blonde hair into a tight knot, found a hat from another man's body, and placed it on her head.

The image of Dagmara Morrow now looked like a young boy and not a woman, especially an upper class woman. No lipstick, no dress, no long hair. Dagmara believed that if she was found and taken, it would be best for her captors to think she was a young man rather than a woman. Better to be shot, than raped and murdered she thought. Also, Dagmara figured she would be able to move about more freely in the nearby town without people staring at a woman alone.

She tried to wipe the blood off her hands. Her fingernails were black underneath, as she looked at the piece of glass, her new reflection, and a tear slowly slid down her cheek. Only hours ago she was lying in the arms of William Cavill, the man she was going to marry, feeling completely safe, the world at her feet, and now, she was so far from that moment. Dagmara wiped away the tears from her eyes, as she had to be strong if she was going to survive, and took off on her own, not knowing where she was headed, or what she would find. Or rather, who would find her?

The Morrows waited for their daughter, but the plane never arrived, and Dagmara did not return home. Soon hours turned into many, and then they received the unexpected, devastating news that the flight Dagmara had taken, crashed somewhere over France. The worst of the shocking news was hearing about the destruction of the aircraft, and the disaster that lied below on the ground. At present, there were no remaining survivors. All who were on board were presumed dead.

Bereaved, Mrs. Morrow dropped to her knees as her husband caught her from falling to the ground, holding her around in his arms, tying to console his grief stricken wife. They comforted each other, as their only child was presumed dead. They were full of sorrow for the way they had last treated Dagmara, especially for the way they had parted. The words that were spoken, not knowing that they would never again see their daughter alive.

They waited at the airport for several more hours, wanting answers, demanding to know exactly how this calamity could have occurred. Tears streamed down Mrs. Morrow's face, as she sat with her husband, waiting to hear the confirmation of their daughter's death. A team of men had been sent to the crash site to identify the bodies, and at the moment, their daughter was considered dead by the officials. All the passengers were.

A few hours later, Mr. Morrow telephoned Dagmara's friends telling them what had happened. Both Kate and Amelia broke down in tears, paralyzed by the inconceivable news.

"No, that can't be," Kate shouted.

"Please tell us if you hear anything," Amelia said to Mr. Morrow calmly, and then hung up the phone.

The girls stared at each other in shock.

"Dagmara can't be dead, she just can't be!" Kate shouted hysterically, not wanting to believe the horrid news.

Amelia kept shaking her head, not wanting to hear those words, not wanting to imagine such a terrible fate for their friend.

"It will be okay Kate," Amelia told her, holding her around, trying to calm her nerves, to stop her from shaking. "I don't believe it either. It just can't be true. Dagmara can't be dead ..." Amelia said, as the word *dead* echoed loudly inside her head, as she tried to be strong.

Both girls were beside themselves unable to breathe let alone think of anything but Dagmara and what she must have gone through. Only a few hours ago they had left Italy, leaving without their friend, leaving Dagmara behind to travel home alone. They could think of nothing but the notion that if Dagmara had left on the same flight as them, they would have all arrived safely home together. And as both girls thought upon that disturbing fact, they were dying inside wishing they had convinced their friend to leave with them.

They sat by the phone in Kate's room and waited, waiting impatiently with hope and sadness in their hearts, tears streaming down their faces, waiting for another phone call from Dagmara's father.

Several hours passed, and then the phone finally rang in the late night hour, waking up both girls. Immediately their eyes opened hearing the second ring, and answered the phone. As they picked up the receiver, they looked at each other, neither of them wanting to hear what Mr. Morrow had to say. Not wanting him to confirm the unofficial news they had received earlier.

Mr. Morrow told the girls to be strong, and that Dagmara's body was not found among the crash, but they were unable to find everyones' body, and at the present, only parts of people were left among the ruin, and so far, she was not among any of them. Her belongings had not been found either, as there was hardly anything left of the disaster area to be recovered. They still were investigating, and would be doing so all through the night to the next morning and after, however long it would take to identify all the bodies.

Dagmara was on the passenger list, confirming she had taken the flight, and at the moment, she was presumed missing. Her body had not been identified, so she was momentarily taken off the list of dead and placed on the list of missing people, as were so many others.

Not knowing if their friend was alive or dead, all they knew was that the count was still zero for survivors, which brought little hope if any for Kate, Amelia, and Dagmara's parents, bringing them no solace in the unforeseen, inexcusable tragedy.

CHAPTER 9

With no means for shelter, and no one searching for her, there would be no rescue for Dagmara Morrow. Cold, hungry, and tired, Dagmara aimlessly walked the road looking over her shoulder as if she was being followed. The Vichy government now controlled France, and enemy soldiers in German uniforms patrolled the streets bringing terror to all who inhabited the neighboring cities. There was no peace, unrest on every corner, as locals band together to fight against the men who terrorized them with gunfire, taking away their liberty.

Dagmara had never seen such a horrible way of life. People afraid to walk the streets or even go into town for food, for fear of being shot or mistaken as a traitor. Hardly anyone gave her notice as she made her way to the nearest town, walking for several hours, as miles added up into many. Her feet hurt from wearing the shoes she found, as she tried to keep them on her small feet. Her dainty frame was completely covered by the oversized clothes; her slim figure and young face made her appearance look like a boy in his teens.

Able to pass without much speculation from the enemy soldiers who marched up and down the streets, instilling fear in the hearts of all who crossed their paths, Dagmara kept her eyes down, not looking into their faces. Looked upon as a young French boy as she walked past a group of German soldiers, she held her breath the entire time as she brushed passed them into an alley. Dirty, alone, she felt like crying, as she pressed her back against the stone wall. Never had Dagmara been more frightened in her whole life.

Nightfall was almost upon her, as Dagmara roamed the desolate streets looking for shelter, water, anything she could find of valuable use. She contemplated going to the police, but she did not know if they could be trusted. They were under Vichy rule, and could think of her actions as treason, and throw her in jail or worse. She had no friends here, only enemies among strangers. She could not trust anyone; they might turn her over to the police just to save their own life or someone they loved.

Unknown to Dagmara, no one would be looking for her, no one would have expected she had survived and wandered away from the crash. She was alone on her journey, lost, scared, not knowing what to do.

The room was cold as William sat in the corner with a pen and paper writing another letter to Dagmara. He had written a second letter, and received no response. Hoping his letters were reaching their destination in England, he decided to write another, the only thing that brought him some peace at night. His only link with her.

William had gone against his father's wishes and placed himself directly in the enemy's path. Instead of being assigned a safe place, he remembered the argument he last shared with his father on the subject. Now, William wished he had not been so coarse with him; perhaps he should have listened to him for Dagmara's sake.

Dear Dagmara,

I have not heard any word from you. I hope you are safe my love. I have written to my father telling him about you ... us. He looks forward to meeting you.

He and I did not part on the best of terms, but all is forgiven now, and I so look forward to my return and being with you.

We lost another man yesterday, his plane was shot down ... he was right next to me.

Stuart teases me about my letters, but I will write a thousand if this war takes that long. ... I hope it will not!

Forever Yours,

William C.

"I hope it will not," William whispered, as he finished the letter, unable to write anymore as the light from the candle burnt out.

He looked over and saw the other soldiers fast asleep in their beds, but he could not sleep, there would be no rest for him till he was with his future wife. William sealed the envelope, then kissed his fingers, and slid them down the front side of the envelope over Dagmara's address.

Stuart opened his eyes and smiled, knowing his friend had written another love letter to his sweetheart. Somewhat envious that his friend had a woman waiting at home and he did not, having no one to write letters to, Stuart closed his eyes and envisioned that Dagmara was his fiancée and not Williams.

Running as fast as she could, barely able to see in the dark, Dagmara tried to quicken her pace as she stumbled over her large shoes. Two German soldiers were chasing after her on the desolate street, as she looked around for a place to hide. She turned the corner as they pursued her in the terrifying chase, increasing their stride, gaining in distance, when suddenly, out of nowhere, a hand reached out and grabbed her, pulling her in towards the dark.

Hidden in the shadows of the blackened alley, she was dragged off the street, concealing her from sight. The soldiers ran straight passed the alley, running down the street to the next.

A hand was placed over her mouth to keep her quiet, muffling a scream, as another hand was placed firmly around her body, keeping her still. Unable to move, Dagmara could feel the stranger's chest pressed up against her back. The brush of his hand over her breast as he held her around, his fingers on her lips. Her heart pounded feverishly in fright, trying to calm her nerves, as she watched the German soldiers pass by.

Her savior held her close to his body, and after the men disappeared down the street, he released his grip and turned her around. Slowly he took his fingers off her mouth as Dagmara looked up at him. Colin Murphy's face was slightly hidden in darkness, but his piercing stare made her heart flutter, as if he was looking straight through her. She noticed his physical appearance. The Irishman was sexy with a taut physique and an arrogant demeanor.

Looking into her beautiful face, he knew instantly she was not who she pretended to be. Her long black lashes, rosy lips, to pretty to be a boy.

"Hurry Colin, we have to get out of here," Brady said to him.

Colin looked at her. "If you want to live, come with me now!" he told her in a strong Irish accent.

Without saying a word, she clasped her hand tightly around his fingers, and followed him down the alley. As they ran down the narrow passage in darkness, following closely behind his friends, only once did Colin Murphy look back at her. The moonlight moved upon her face with a shimmer of light, he saw her hold her hat down over her head, and he knew his intuition was right. His eyes did not deceive him.

Not knowing where she was going, or where these men were taking her, Dagmara went with the stranger, allowing him to take her to safety. Rescuing her from the armed men, eluding the predators from the clutches of death, Colin had already made a big impression on Dagmara Morrow.

A small run down house was where they were hiding out in France till they could make their way home to Ireland. Dirty and vacant, a family had left in a hurry, leaving their belongings to ruins. Colin, his brother Brady, and his two Irish friends had been staying in the house, evading the German soldiers, and especially the police. Dagmara looked around the place, not used to living in such conditions.

Mark Quinn, a heavyset man with large hands immediately saw the disdain on her face, her apprehension and disgust at their surroundings.

"What, you think you're better than us? This is not good enough for you?" Mark Quinn snapped at her insolently.

"No … I," Dagmara started to say, trying to make her voice sound deep.

"Why did you bring him here?" Mark Quinn asked, looking straight at Colin.

"I couldn't just leave him on the street," Colin told his friend.

"Well, I don't trust him," Mark Quinn commented, and took another puff off his cigarette.

"He's just a kid," Brady intervened, coming to her defense.

Without even knowing her, Mark Quinn, Colin's best friend, had taken an instant dislike to Dagmara, and Brady had done the exact opposite. And the closer Dagmara looked at Brady's face, the more she saw the familiarity between he and Colin, knowing they must be related.

"Are you hungry?" Colin asked her.

"We hardly have enough food for ourselves, I'm not going to share my food with the likes of him," Mark Quinn stated with a poisoned look in his eyes, puffing away on his cigarette, as he stared at his uninvited guest.

"Why don't you give the kid a break," Brady said, coming to her defense again.

Impudent on purpose, Mark Quinn brushed past Dagmara hitting her in the shoulder as he grabbed an apple. "I'll be keeping an eye on you. You better watch your step. Wouldn't want anything to happen to you," he said, took a bite of his apple, and stormed off.

Insulted by his deliberate rudeness, Dagmara knew Mark Quinn was not a man she could trust, not wanting to be left alone in a room with him. His large frame, his thick Irish accent muffled his words, and the vicious intent in his eyes when he looked at her, scared Dagmara.

"Don't let him get to you kid, he's always like that with strangers," Brady commented.

Dagmara smiled at Brady, his kindness was unexpected.

"Come on," Colin motioned to her, making no apologies for his friend's behavior.

Colin's room was small and damp. The place looked as if it had been ransacked and not cleaned in a long time.

"Where did you find him?" Dagmara asked.

"You mean Quinn?" Colin said, intrigued by her articulate British accent, knowing there was more to her than he first presumed.

"How could you be friends with someone like that?" she stated with superiority.

"He's been my best friend since I can remember. He grew up with Brady and me, and he didn't always have the best childhood or parents, in and out of orphanages. Quinn can be rough at times, but you don't know him like I do."

Dagmara started to say something when Colin overlapped her words, defending his friend's behavior.

"We're all not as privileged as you it seems," he said to her, his arrogance flowing strongly through his words.

"What do you mean by that?" Dagmara asked, taking offense at his remark, the underlying of his words.

Instantly Colin grabbed Dagmara's hand and turned it over, and rubbed his finger over her soft skin. Her delicate hand felt nice within his touch, and the more he felt her softness against his fingers, the harder he was towards her.

"I bet these hands have never seen a days work."

Immediately Dagmara pulled her hand away, insulted by his impertinent manner, backing away from the stranger who for a brief but fleeting moment was her savior.

"I don't have to stand here and defend myself or my friends to you. You don't have the right. You don't know Quinn, you don't know anything about him or me, so why don't you just keep your opinions to yourself, and we'll get along just fine," Colin stated in a harsh tone, angered that she was looking down upon him and his friends.

He made her feel bad about her wealthy upbringing. Colin Murphy was the only man who ever made Dagmara Morrow feel this way. Provoked by her snobbery, looking down upon his humble upbringing, she had not intended to argue with the stranger and bring conflict between them. Impetuous in manner, Dagmara sometimes spoke brazenly without thinking of the consequences. It was not her intention with him.

"I know what you think about us. That we're the scum beneath your aristocratic shoe. Not worthy to sit beside you. I saw the look on your face when you stepped inside the house. Who are you to judge us," Colin stated with resentment, bringing a certain prejudice to her pride.

Colin had already made up his mind about Dagmara even before she opened her mouth. She had not meant to cause friction between them, that was the last thing she wanted, and the more he disapproved of the way she behaved, the more she wanted his approval.

"You can clean up in there," Colin motioned towards the bathroom.

He looked her up and down, noticing the clothes she was wearing were too big for her small frame.

"I'll see if I can get you something that fits better," he said, and walked out of the bedroom.

The harsher he was towards her, the more of his rogue like manner shined, and the more Dagmara Morrow was unsure if she could trust this man, but she was stuck with them for the night. Colin was a complete stranger, and although he had rescued her from those men on the street, she now found herself in a precarious predicament in a country at war.

CHAPTER 10

Dagmara walked into the bathroom and looked at herself in the mirror. She splashed some water on her face and wiped off the dirt with a towel. She felt dirty and wanted a hot shower, but she would settle for just having her face and hands clean. As she finished, Colin entered the room holding a shirt and a pair of pants for her to wear, and as she moved towards him, he saw her freshly cleaned face for the very first time. Underneath the dirt lied her beautiful, porcelain complexion. Her beauty equally enticed him in allure and frustration.

He threw the clothes at her.

"Try these on."

She caught the clothes as they hit her in the face. His domineering stare was powerful, not yielding to her beauty.

"I'm sure they'll fit."

"Try them on now," he said to her in an imperious tone.

Dagmara hesitated for a moment seeing he was not going to leave; she started to unbutton her coat. Colin watched as she took off her coat and looked up at him, then turned her back towards him, and started to unbutton her shirt.

"I forgot something," he said, and abruptly left the room closing the door.

Hurriedly Dagmara took off her shirt and buttoned up the new one. Then she took off her pants and slipped into the new pair. The clothes were a much better fit, as if they were made for her size. She started to button up the pants, struggling with the top button. As her fingers tugged on the last button, the door suddenly opened, and Colin walked in carrying a glass of water and an apple. Instantly she looked up at him, he saw her struggling with the buttons.

He placed the glass and apple down on the dresser and walked over to her.

"Here, let me do that."

"No, I can do it," she said to him and backed away.

"Let me help you," he said, pushing her hands away.

Colin moved closer to her, and placed one hand on her hip and buttoned up her pants. Her heart raced as he placed his strong hands on her body. Her slender figure fitted the clothing perfectly, as Colin could feel her pelvic bone beneath the material. His hands slightly moved onto her stomach, she trembled by his touch, and he could feel her body shake.

He noticed the buttons on her shirt were uneven and started to readjust them. His fingers made their way to the top button, and she could feel his hand slightly brush across her chest. He could feel her heart pounding fast. She lowered her face feeling incited and scared by the stranger's touch upon her body. He looked down at his hand upon her shirt, moved his hand to her chin, and moved her face up to his. As she looked into his eyes, feeling the closeness between their bodies, the sensual chemistry awakened, suffocating them both in a pulsating silence.

Dagmara saw the look in Colin's eyes as he looked upon her face. She knew then she had not fooled him, even though he had not mentioned it before, he could see right through the mirage. He knew she was not a boy.

He moved his hand to her head and took off her hat; she let him do so without saying a word. Her long golden curls fell down around her shoulders, forming around her face, and Dagmara Morrow was the most beautiful woman Colin Murphy had ever seen.

"If you knew, why didn't you say anything?" she asked him.

"You must have had a good reason."

"Why are you helping me?" she wanted to know.

"Why are you trying to hide?"

"I thought it would be best if people took me as a boy," she began to say. Colin could see her hesitation, as Dagmara thought back to the plane crash, the woman who was savagely raped and killed by those fiendish predators. "Traveling alone, there are a lot of lonely men out there. I thought it would be safer for me this way."

Surprised by her answer, there was an entire mystery surrounding her.

"How did you wind up here with those men chasing you?"

"I was in Italy, I was headed for home, London, when my plane was shot down and …" Dagmara hesitated again. She was unable to tell Colin of the horrid, bludgeoned sight, seeing the massive dead bodies sprawled all over the ground. Blood and death surrounding her everywhere.

"We heard about the crash. You were on the flight?"

"Yes."

"But I heard there were no survivors," Colin said in astonishment, as she stood before him alive.

"There were two others, that's all I saw. I don't know if anyone else survived."

"What do you mean *were* two others?" Colin inquired further.

"German soldiers came, I think they were German, and they started to loot among the remains. I first saw an old man and they killed him. And then I saw a woman and …" Dagmara was unable to finish her story. Her mouth became dry, choking in a haunting memory.

Colin could see the pain in her eyes, she had witnessed something so horrific, she could not describe it in words, and for a brief moment, he actually felt compassion towards her and not disdain. He even wanted to comfort her, place his arms around her, but he did not.

"She's dead … they killed her," Dagmara finally told him, not able to tell him the rest. The abhorrent remembrance she had a front row seat for, never wanting to revisit that place of darkness, ever again.

"I'm sorry," he said to her in a nicer tone, trying to imagine what it must have been like to survive such a terrible disaster, only to face another. What she must have gone through and seen. He could see it in her eyes, she was a survivor, and whatever she witnessed after the crash, had not killed her spirit, it had only made her stronger.

"Why didn't you tell your friends?" she asked him.

"As you said, there are a lot of lonely men out there who might take advantage of a young woman like yourself."

"And you're not one of them?"

"You think me interested in you?" he replied, slightly offended by her insinuation upon his character.

"I do not presume as much," she told him, not meaning to slander his intentions.

"I'm not like that," he answered, raising his voice, defending himself. "You think I would be interested in a rich, spoiled girl as yourself," he said to her insolently.

She took a step back from him.

"Don't worry, your kind never interested me. I wouldn't sully my hands with the likes of someone like you," he told her in a harsh, impertinent manner.

His impudent words angered her, but she did not correct him in his assumption, even though he was wrong, he was definitely wrong about her.

"I hate people like you. I loath the rich upper class who think they are so much better than the rest of us, just because we don't have money or a name."

"Then why are you helping me?" she asked him again, puzzled by his blatant dislike for her, not understanding him.

Colin did not answer her, unable to tell Dagmara the real reason behind his motives, but they were anything but cruel. Instead he touched her hair, feeling the silk like texture in his hands.

"You'll have to cut it off."

"And what makes you think I will accept your help," she said with arrogance, still distrusting him.

The toughness of her character vibrantly illuminated Dagmara's face, accentuating her blue eyes in striking color, and Colin Murphy found her uncommon audacious quality to be most refreshing.

"What makes you think I will help you?" he said to her in the same tone, looking her straight in the eyes.

"I need to get home," she stated in a nicer tone, longing to be with her friends and family.

"We were headed in that direction back to Ireland before we got stuck here. You can come along if you don't slow us down," Colin told her, never actually answering her question why he would help her.

"And what do you want in return?" she asked him, slightly scared of his answer.

Suddenly Colin moved closer to her, frightening Dagmara with the dark look in his eyes. Her heart beating fast, the space between them tightened.

"I bet you're worth a lot of money," he said.

"Is that all you want?" she asked.

He moved even closer, almost touching his body to hers.

"I'm only in this for the money, that's all."

"I can't cut my hair," she protested.

"Then I'll cut it for you," he said to her arrogantly, not softening to the vanity she placed upon her long curls.

Dagmara knew she had no choice, Colin was right; she had to cut her hair, giving realism to the boyish image. He took out a pair of scissors from the drawer and moved towards her with the sharp object. The innocence in her eyes penetrated his hardened exterior, and for a brief second, Colin felt bad about making her cut her hair, especially since he was the one doing it. Then she closed her eyes, relinquishing the vanity she felt made her beautiful.

He moved closer and looked at her face. Unwanted temptation arose.

Dagmara felt the closeness of their bodies again, but Colin did not take advantage of the situation, nor did he kiss her, although the thought had crossed his mind more than once. Instead he grabbed her hair in his hand, and started to cut off her long, blonde curls.

The strands fell to the ground as Dagmara opened her eyes seeing the dirt underneath his fingernails. Up close Colin looked in his mid twenties, but his eyes conveyed a wiser, older soul. He was not upper class like William Cavill, nor was he well educated. He did not attain any of those debonair, illustrious attributes that William vibrantly possessed. He was the exact opposite. Inexplicably, Dagmara found herself becoming attracted to this man. His eyes, alluring. His arrogance, seductive. This stranger who did not fit her station and status in life, they now became allies, her only chance for survival.

As he cut off her long blonde curls, Colin suddenly felt betrayed by his own hardened anger, repressing his feelings for this young woman, not succumbing to her beauty. The girls back home did not strive for anyone better, they were more than happy to have someone like Colin Murphy as their boyfriend. He could have any girl he wanted back in Ireland, but he wanted Dagmara, like he wanted all women he met, except he knew he could never have her. They came from vastly different worlds, and their own backgrounds at birth had sealed their fates in life.

When he was finished, Colin put down the scissors and Dagmara looked into the mirror. Her hair, short, her long curls, gone, and her reflection scorched in a silent scream as she looked at her new image in the glass. Vain, she felt her beauty had been lost, cut away with the strands of her hair.

A tear slid down Dagmara's cheek, and as she looked back into the mirror, she saw Colin standing behind her. He saw her tear, her hair, her clothes, yet to him, she still was the most beautiful woman he had ever laid eyes on. Her prettiness had not diminished, it was just the opposite. Pulchritudinous her image was to him, as she turned around and looked him straight in the eyes.

He loathed the rich, spoiled aristocrats, lathering his contempt, but with her, it was different. She was different. He was different. She made him feel different. With her, he found compassion, attraction, and unwanted desire.

"Then we have a deal," she said, and wiped away the tear, feeling slightly embarrassed by letting him see her cry.

Colin put out his hand, but instead of extending her hand to him, Dagmara leaned in slowly and gave him a kiss on the side of his face. Not expecting such a show of gratitude, especially from her, the gentle kiss was felt inside his entire body. The smoothness of her lips as they pressed against his cheek, tantalized him. Colin felt unhinged by her bold action, by the softness of her kiss, by his own weakness.

Then suddenly his face turned to anger, and he wiped away her kiss, brushing his hand over his cheek, several times, as if he was repulsed by her display of friendship. She saw the disdain again in his eyes as he looked at her, as if he could not stand to look at her face without gritting his teeth.

Perplexed by his reaction to her gesture, Dagmara became equally angered by his contemptuous demeanor, and immediately her eyes hardened in stare. If she had felt anything at all for this stranger, it was now gone, replaced by the sudden outburst of his impetuous response. She could never be friends with a man like him, let alone anything more, and she longed to return home, to be in the arms of her future husband, William Cavill.

Colin looked at her without saying a word, and then stormed out of the bedroom. He walked in a hurried pace through the front room and out the door, ignoring Brady and his friend Cillian as they tried to speak to him. He did not want to talk, to anyone, as he sat down on the step and lit up a cigarette.

He took a long puff off his cigarette, contemplating their conversation, everything that had transpired. The anger he felt inside slowly diminished, as he rubbed the back of his hand across his face, still feeling her warm lips upon his skin. And he wondered why she had kissed him, wondering why the kiss had affected him in this way? Perplexed by her action, by his reaction.

The harsher he was towards her, the more he wanted her, and the more he knew he could never be with her. And from that moment forth, Colin Murphy was bound to Dagmara Morrow for the duration of their journey home.

CHAPTER 11

Exhausted from the long day that seemed as if it would never end, Dagmara curled up on the small bed, and placed the blanket over herself for warmth. She fell asleep within minutes, and shortly thereafter, Colin came back inside to apologize for his rude behavior, when he found her sleeping in his bed. She looked so peaceful, not wanting to wake her; he took another pillow, lied down on the floor and covered himself with his coat, allowing her to have his bed. Quiet in movement he did not want to disturb her, as he turned out the light, and closed his eyes to sleep.

By the early morning hours, the fires had burned out, and most of the bodies were accounted for. There were still several people they could not find or identify that were on the passenger list, and Dagmara Morrow was one of them.

Dagmara's parents wanted to send a search party for their daughter, but the French government would not allow anyone to come into their country for that purpose. They would conduct the search themselves, not wanting the English to be involved. Not wanting them to uncover the truth about what had actually happened. Not wanting the English to know that the airplane carrying civilians was shot down, the Vichy government falsified the documents stating that it was a malfunction in the engine system that made the plane crash. Not wanting to cause enormous uproar among the neighboring countries, the quick cover up was immediately executed.

Contrary to what spectators thought, or word formed in gossip, it was not the French who were at fault for this particular disaster, but that did not console the distraught, grieving families in England that waited to get word if their loved ones were alive or dead. Many family members gathered around in a small room waiting to hear the official news about the crash. Mr. and Mrs. Morrow stood together impatiently at the front demanding answers, answers that never seemed to come.

Unable to send anyone to look for their daughter, there would be no rescue party sent to find Dagmara Morrow. No one would be searching. If their daughter was still alive, she would be on her own, without help, without anyone but herself for survival.

The next morning, the handle to the bedroom door turned quietly, and Mark Quinn stood in the doorway. He saw Colin sleeping on the floor, and then looked over in the bed and saw the stranger. His eyes inflamed with anger as he watched her sleep, and then closed the door.

Instantly Colin opened his eyes and looked over at Dagmara. He knew Mark Quinn was clever, he would figure it out soon if he had not already, and as he looked at the young woman sleeping in his bed, he realized for the first time since he met her last night, he did not even know her name.

Dagmara opened her eyes feeling someone watching her, and looked straight at Colin. After the impudent way he had treated her last night, she did not know what to expect from this man. He was a stranger, but she knew no one else she could trust. The way he looked at her, what was he thinking she wanted to know? Why was he so secretive, wondering what he was thinking about, as he looked at her mysteriously without saying a word.

She looked down on the floor next to the bed and saw a pair of boots. Colin had placed them there last night, in a gesture to say he was sorry for the way he had acted. He could not tell her in words that he was not repulsed by her kiss. She would not believe him. Not believing that it was the exact opposite. The softness of her lips still imprinted on his cheek.

"Thank you," she said to him, and slipped on the boots and tied the laces. They were a much better fit than the shoes she had found. She could walk in them without tripping, or run fast if she needed to escape.

"I'm Collin," he said in a nicer tone.

"What's your last name Colin?"

"Murphy."

"Colin Murphy," she repeated, he liked hearing her say his name.

He did not need her approval, nor did he want it. He did not need her friendship, but he found himself silently wanting it.

"I'm Dagmara Morrow."

"Dagmara Morrow," he mused. "Let me introduce you to the others."

Dagmara widened her eyes in surprise.

"I thought you weren't going to tell them?" she said, not understanding him.

"I have a feeling they already know."

He threw her hat in the trash, no longer needing it to cover her hair and conceal her false appearance. They walked into the front room and found Brady and Cillian sitting at the table, Mark Quinn was standing off to the side with a devious look in his eyes.

"Is it true?" Brady asked his brother.

"Yes," Colin told him looking over at Mark Quinn.

Dagmara stepped to the side of Colin. They saw her short blonde hair, her radiant eyes, her beautiful face. Mark Quinn had told them what he suspected, that the young boy was not a boy at all, but a girl.

"Why didn't you tell us?" Cillian asked.

"I was going to, but I see Quinn beat me to it."

Mark Quinn just looked at Colin, thinking he had done him a favor.

"Then I guess it's lucky for us to be in the company of such a pretty young woman," Brady commented, already smitten with Dagmara.

Brady's kindness did not sit well with Mark Quinn, and the more everyone accepted her, the more the animosity rose, as he regarded her as his new enemy. Mark Quinn would not allow her to come between his friendships, especially with Colin.

"What's your name?" Cillian asked her.

"Dagmara."

"What a beautiful name," Brady commented.

While Brady and Cillian were making a new friend, introducing themselves to Dagmara, delighted to make her acquaintance, Colin had not taken his eyes off Mark Quinn.

"She will be the ruin of all of us!" Mark Quinn shouted, looking straight at Colin, and then stormed out of the house.

Colin noticed the fierce look in his friend's eyes, the way he looked at Dagmara with fiery contempt. He had seen that look before.

The more Brady and Cillian got to know Dagmara, the more they thought of her as a sister, their little sister who they would look out for and protect. Brady especially was sweet on her, neither of them commenting about the shortness of her hair. She was amongst friends she believed, she would be safe, but little did Dagmara know that among the group of strangers that befriended her, lurked an enemy. One that would be watching her every move. One that was clever, and very, very dangerous!

They could no longer stay in the house, they had to keep moving and try to get out of France. None of them had any papers on them for identification. A few Francs was all the money they had between them. They could not trust anyone, and would have to keep to themselves while they moved about, but the longer they stayed in one place, the farther they were from home, and the closer their liberty was in peril.

Rebels swarmed in every corner. German soldiers marched the streets in a brigade. The resistance opposed Vichy rule and fought for their freedom risking their lives while trying to defend their country. Colin and his friends did not want to get mixed up with the resistance, and kept to themselves as they moved about on foot by day, barely sleeping at night, watching over their shoulders, constantly. Nowhere was safe.

Starving families, dead bodies, blood everywhere was all Dagmara saw as she kept close to Colin and his friends, keeping her distance from Mark Quinn. They tried shielding her from the gruesome images they came across, but Dagmara did not look away, and those memories would forever haunt her in thought.

She barely slept anymore; scared the enemy would find them, frightened that they would be murdered in their sleep. Her eyes closed purely from physical exhaustion, putting her to sleep every night, and the dirty places they stayed in, were the worst of conditions. But Dagmara never complained, nor did she look upon her new surroundings as she once did when she first stepped inside that house those long nights ago. She felt no better than them now, and in a way, she felt they were the ones to be proud, not her. They were used to these situations, adapting easily to their new surroundings, and maybe their tough upbringing had helped them survive making them stronger, as Dagmara's upbringing had only weakened her.

They were all equals she now believed, knowing how wrong she had once been. Dagmara did not think about hunger, it had been days since she last had eaten anything more than a piece of fruit. Her feet were tired, her body was sore, she longed to feel warmth, to be clean and find a safe shelter. Colin noticed how brave Dagmara was, never once complaining about anything. She was strong, he knew she was a survivor, and she needed to be if she was to make it out of France, alive.

The flame flickered in the wind as William sat at a table writing another letter to Dagmara. The small candle was all the light he had, and still he wrote, never giving up, never wanting the war to beat him. He kept writing letters wherever he was stationed, no matter the circumstances, he would always find a way. Time is all he had at the moment, and that in itself was his enemy; it gave him too much time to think. To think about what was to come, and not knowing what was next. His future was unwritten; it was not up to him anymore if he survived, and he felt his fate now lied solely within her hands.

She would bring him back. She would keep him safe. She was now and would be forever in his heart. William would give Dagmara anything she desired, as there was nothing he could not give her with his wealth and love. He would deny her nothing, and in the end, he would ultimately give her the world, if she let him.

The pen moved on the paper, and William hesitated for a moment, contemplating what to write, his mind temporarily clouded, wondering why he had not received any letters in return. His last few letters contained a return address. Why had his love not written to him? Why was Dagmara torturing him in this way? Not knowing the answers made the feeling worse every day a letter did not arrive with his name on it. William tried to concentrate and finish the letter, when Stuart walked over to him and placed a piece of paper down in front of him on the table.

William looked up at his friend. "What's this?" he asked.

The look on Stuart's face expressed how deeply sorry he was for his friend. He could not tell him what was written on the piece of paper; William had to read the contents himself.

"I'm sorry," Stuart said, not knowing what else to say.

"Sorry, for what?" William asked. "You look as if something terrible has happened. What is it?"

"Just read it," Stuart replied.

William grabbed the piece of paper and started reading the contents, when suddenly his eyes opened wide in horror, and the paper fell out of his hands. The pain was unbearable, not wanting to comprehend the news. His chest tightened, suffocating him.

Henry noticed his friend's distraught composure and rushed over to them.

"What's wrong?" Henry asked, wanting to know what was going on, as he picked up the piece of paper from the floor, and started reading the contents.

"I didn't want to be the one to have to tell you," Stuart said, as he placed his hand on William's shoulder with empathy.

"I'm so sorry William," Henry added, after he finished reading the contents. "Do they know for sure?" he asked Stuart.

Stuart shrugged, as they looked at one another in the unsettling silence, knowing the agony their friend must be going through, feeling his loss.

The contents of the piece of paper that was not intended for their eyes, had informed William Cavill and his friends of the names of the victims who were killed in the plane crash. The flight from Italy to England had crashed somewhere over France, and at the present, there were no survivors. Dagmara Morrow's name was on that list. She was reported missing and presumed dead. And the word *dead* deafened inside William's thoughts seeing her name next to those letters. A numbing feeling engulfed him inside, as if a bullet had sliced through his heart in that instant in excruciating torture, unable to breathe.

"NO, I won't believe, this can't be true. It just can't be ... Dagmara can't be dead! They're lying. They're all lying!" William shouted in a moment of anger, fear, crumbling the letter in his hand, and then he stormed out.

Both Henry and Stuart were stunned by the devastating news. They did not want to believe what was stated on the piece of paper either.

"He didn't even get a chance to marry her," Stuart said.

"I know, he didn't even get a chance to say goodbye," Henry said sadly.

Henry and Stuart knew they would not be able to ease William's pain. No matter what they said to their friend, it would not make any difference; William Cavill had to grieve on his own.

CHAPTER 12

"No this is not real, it just can't be happening, this just can't be true!" William kept repeating, because if it was true, that would mean everything he was doing was for nothing. There would be no purpose to his assignment; there would be no purpose to his life anymore. Everything would be meaningless. Futile. Everything he did was for her. His intrepidness was fueled by her love, the notion that he would soon be coming home to Dagmara. That he would return to England and marry her, and make her his wife. But all that would be lost now, stolen, taken from him, gone.

He took out her picture from his pocket; he had not looked at the photograph since the day they parted, since the day he saw her leave and get on the airplane. All this time he was laboring under a misapprehension, thinking she was home, safe, with her friends and family waiting for his return. William never thought Dagmara did not make it home, that her life would be in peril. That it would be the last time they would ever see one another again. He never imagined anything would ever happen to her, that it would be him instead who would be shot down and possibly killed, but not her.

Never again to kiss her sultry lips, to hold her in his arms, to feel her naked body against his own, would be a fate much worse than death. He loved her that much, more than life itself, and at that very moment, William Cavill wished they had married, or at least slept together, or both. But they did neither, wanting to wait till they were reunited, and he had said yes. He had said yes to everything she wanted, placing her wants above his desires and needs. With her, she would always come first.

"NO," he shouted into the desolate night sky. "You can't be dead, I won't allow you to be … because you're going to be my wife," he said, breaking down in tears. "I love you. I love you so much Dagmara, more than you know."

His words trickled off in silence as tears streamed down his face in anguish and regret. And for the first time ever, William Cavill hated life, the very air he breathed, not wanting to go on without her.

"I love you. I love you!" he shouted over and over again, not caring who was listening.

William fell to his knees bereaved, as the pain scorched through his body with deep seeded torment, torching his heart into flames, destroying every dream he had about them, and a life that could have been.

The photo of Dagmara crumbled in his fist; tears fell down his cheeks as he looked up into the stars and yelled in anger, "I defy you, I defy all of you who have done this to me. To take her away from me!"

Stuart and Henry rushed to William's side hearing him scream, not wanting to draw attention to their friend's behavior. They moved to pick him up, and he pushed them away, not wanting their help, wanting to be left alone.

"Come back inside, killing yourself won't do her any good," Stuart implied. "It said presumed dead, she might still be alive," he suggested, giving his friend a glimmer of hope.

"She could be hiding out somewhere. Maybe she got to safety and that's why they can't find her," Henry added.

William suddenly looked up at his friends, hearing their words, his vision blurred by the tears. He knew his friends were only trying to make him feel better. He would catch his death if he stayed any longer in the cold night air. His body was glistening with moisture, and the coolness of evening made him cough several times. But at the moment, William Cavill did not care. William Cavill did not want to live, but he also did not want to die. What his friends were saying to him could be true, but it was a slim chance of hope that Dagmara was still alive. That she had survived the plane crash and wandered off somewhere, and that is why they had not found her body.

As William stood up, Henry and Stuart's words resonated in his mind, dominating in thought, but still he felt all hope of happiness gone. Like a butterfly beginning to fly, the life had been swept out of his body and crushed by the wing of a predator. His chest tightened as he steadied his breath, unable to control his emotions.

He loved Dagmara Morrow more than he had ever loved any other woman. More than he had ever thought. More than he had known. And he wished he could go back to that moment of bliss, to feel the warmth of her naked body lying next to his, her lips on his mouth, as that beautiful vision of them together in his hotel room flourished inside his aching heart.

Suddenly his heart started to radiate with hope, as he smoothed the crinkled photograph that had distorted Dagmara's image, and placed it back inside his jacket pocket. William wiped away the tears, and then the image of Dagmara was abruptly shattered into a terrifying, bleak existence.

Gunfire exploded in heavy force. Darkness swarmed around the entire camp. Explosions in the near distance went off simultaneously, one after the other. Bullets ricocheted off the ground hitting several soldiers, catching them off guard as the enemy closed in, in deadly force, and they were under attack!

The smell of sulfur awoke Dagmara, Mark Quinn had lit a cigarette, and the smoke filtered through the air around her nose. She opened her eyes and saw Colin and the others asleep, and decided to try to make peace with Mark Quinn, especially for Colin's sake.

She got up and walked over to him. He noticed her approaching, and did not even acknowledge her presence, nor did he offer her a cigarette. Instead he rudely turned around and blew smoke straight into her face. The smoke trickled away in the wind; Dagmara did not turn her face away, as her eyes had not shifted from his. They stood staring at one another, not saying a word. Usually Dagmara would never make friends with a man like him, not wanting to associate with someone who regarded her with such animosity, but she wanted no friction between them on their journey, and figured it was better to have him as a friend than an enemy.

"Why do you dislike me so much?" she asked him.

He did not answer her as the animosity elevated. Mark Quinn had taken an instant dislike to Dagmara the moment Colin brought her into their lives, even before he knew she was a British upper class young woman.

"What wrong have I done you?" she asked him again.

"You really want to know?" he replied in his thick Irish accent.

"Yes."

"I see the way he looks at you. I know he likes you even if he doesn't say so, even if he won't admit it, even to himself."

Surprised by his answer, Dagmara realized why Mark Quinn disliked her so much, because he was jealous, but not of his friend, of her. Bringing her along with them, envious of the time she and Colin spend together.

"If you're afraid I'm going to take him away from you …" Dagmara started to say.

Angered with her assumption, Mark Quinn threw his cigarette to the ground, frightening Dagmara, and then moved closer to her. "You don't know what you're talking about," he said with contempt, looking her straight in the eyes.

"I think I do," she said, standing up to him and not backing down.

"You come in here with your pretty little smile, dazzle him with your charms, and think you can have him. That you can take him away from me. Colin would never want someone like you. He loathes your kind just like I do," Mark Quinn stated with a detesting tone.

"Why do you feel threatened by me?" she asked, almost afraid to hear his answer.

"Threatened," he said, raising his voice, getting more upset. "I've known him longer than you, and believe me, he'll never want you, he'll always choose me. You can never come between us!" he warned in a chilling tone that made Dagmara's skin crawl, as his eyes increased in blackened peril.

And then Dagmara realized why Mark Quinn disliked her so much, hated her with a passion. It was simply because he felt threatened. Threatened by her friendship with Colin. Threatened that she would take Colin away from him. That she would come between them. And as Dagmara figured out the answer to her own question, her eyes opened wide, like an innocent child overhearing a dangerous secret.

"Does he know how you feel about him?"

Angered by her blatant question, Mark Quinn suddenly became furious, not wanting to hear the words out loud, especially from her. He had concealed his feelings from his friend, never telling Colin the truth. Never telling Colin that he loved him, not just as a friend, but more. Not like a brother, but as a lover. And now his dislike for Dagmara turned to a scalding hatred that thickened by the second, because she figured him out. She knew his truth. She uncovered his secret. Revealing the deep dark secret he has concealed since childhood.

Forcefully Mark Quinn placed his hands on Dagmara's shoulders, and pushed her up against the wall, taking her by surprise. Her head hit the wall hard, as her heart started pounding fast, scared of what he might do to her for discovering his secret.

"You think you're so smart, that you've figured out everything," Mark Quinn shouted, frightening Dagmara, holding her against her will with his strength.

His eyes fumed with violent intentions as he moved himself closer to Dagmara, pressing his body into hers, pushing her harder into the cold wall. The look in Mark Quinn's eyes was more of desperation and fear. Fear that she would tell Colin. Fear that he would lose his best friend. And that look of panic, of jealousy, scared Dagmara more than the force of his hands against her body, as Mark Quinn would do anything to keep his secret from being revealed. And before Mark Quinn had a chance to go further in carrying out his threat, Colin swiftly appeared from the side having been awakened by the loud confrontation.

"What's going on Quinn?" Colin asked, having overheard the end of the conversation, suspicious of their private meeting.

"Nothing," Mark Quinn stated, releasing his grip around Dagmara, and then backed away. "We were just having a friendly chat, that's all," he replied, and flashed Dagmara a hardened smile, warning her not to say anything to Colin, and then walked back inside.

Trying to catch her breath, Dagmara watched Mark Quinn walk away from her, and then looked at Colin. He knew something had transpired between them, more than his friend had admitted, but Dagmara did not tell Colin what she knew, or what she suspected. Easily she could have told Colin that his best friend was secretly in love with him, and had been for a long time, but she did not. She did not want to come between their friendship; it was not her place to tell him, as Colin would never believe her, so for the moment she remained silent.

"Are you all right?" Colin asked.

She placed her hand on her head, feeling the hard hit.

"I'll be okay," she told him.

Colin waited for her to say more, wanting to know what had happened, but Dagmara remained quiet about their conversation, and Mark Quinn knew she would not say a word. He read her well. She knew his secret, and that made her a liability, an inconvenience to him. A danger. A threat.

The next morning the animosity towards Dagmara increased, and Mark Quinn did nothing to hide his contemptuous feelings towards her. Colin immediately became aware of the fact after last night's confrontation. Whatever transpired between his friend and Dagmara had only pushed them farther apart, and he found himself smack in the middle. Colin did not want to be placed there, to have to choose between his best friend and a girl he just met. He would without question choose Mark Quinn over her, not wanting to lose his friendship. Mark Quinn had saved his life when they were little, and he felt indebted to him ever since.

Quietness overshadowed their journey by day, and towards nightfall, Dagmara felt more like a stranger among the close knit group than a member over the next few days. They settled into a deserted barn that evening, and the conditions were as cold and dirty as the other places they had stayed in on previous nights. But luxury was not a priority, nor manageable under their circumstances, and lucky for them, they had not been caught trespassing on the owner's property.

Brady and Colin had left together to find some food, while Dagmara was left behind with Cillian and Mark Quinn, and for the first time since the plane crash, since the horrible disaster, she felt alone. An uneasy feeling plagued her inside being placed in the awkward situation. Dagmara excused herself from Cillian and wandered outside. She loved the openness of the night. The tranquility it brought, bringing back images of happy childhood memories. The flowers, her long hair blowing in the wind, she touched the shortness of her strands, lost in sadness.

Roaming through the field alone, Dagmara did not know she was being followed, and it was that night that Mark Quinn decided to make his move. He followed Dagmara into the quiet fields. The damp grass beneath his feet made a squashing sound, and suddenly Dagmara looked behind her hearing the noise. The moon was covered in the night sky, and she could barely see anything let alone who was following her. The more she walked, the closer he stepped, and the distance between them tightened in vicious intent.

As the squashing sound moved terrifyingly close, Dagmara abruptly stopped and turned around, but it was too late, as the violent predator was already upon her, and she could not escape.

The hit came from behind pushing her down onto the ground, knocking her half unconscious. The forcefulness of his anger hit Dagmara with a robust amount of pain to her body, as she struggled to free herself from her assailant. She kicked and screamed, as he tried to place his hand over her mouth to muffle the sounds, but her screams were not heard by anyone. The strong hold around her body was tightening, as she tried to fight back using all her strength.

For a brief moment, Dagmara broke free, got up, and started to run towards the barn. The wetness of the grass made her trip, and she stumbled onto the ground. She tried to pick herself back up, when forcibly she was overpowered again by the man's body, and he jumped on her taking them both down to the ground.

He hit her in the face this time, and placed his body on top of hers to hold her down. She kicked and fought as he tried to hold her hands steady and take control.

The second hit crossed her cheek, she began to lose strength, and her struggle decreased, as the vicious predator had her firmly within his grip. He lit a match in the darkness, illuminating a small light, and as the wind rapidly blew out the flame, those few, petrifying seconds were long enough for Dagmara to see her assailant's face. The look in his eyes was frightening, as she looked into the fierce, cold-blooded eyes of Mark Quinn. Paralyzed momentarily by seeing his face, she could not believe that it was him. That he had attacked her.

"I warned you, you wouldn't take Colin away from me," he shouted, enraged with hatred and embarrassment.

He scared Dagmara with the dark gleam in his eyes, now knowing what he was capable of doing.

"I didn't tell him. I won't tell him. I swear!" Dagmara protested, trying to reason with him, but Mark Quinn did not listen to her words, not wanting to hear her lies, even though she was telling him the truth.

"I won't let you come between us!" he yelled.

His ferocious demeanor derived from Dagmara knowing his secret, knowing the truth about him and his real feelings for Colin Murphy. He could not under any circumstances have her tell him. He could never allow Colin to know. It would ruin everything. She would ruin everything he believed, as there was only one way to silence her, to make sure she would never tell … he would have to get rid of her.

And before Dagmara's eyes, Mark Quinn immersed into a man full of desperation, spiraling out of control, and suddenly, forcefully, he clasped his hands tightly around her throat!

CHAPTER 13

Dagmara squirmed and pushed, but she could not get him off her. His strength on top of her body was overpowering, and as she struggled for life, for the very air she breathed, he increased the pressure in his strong hands applying more force. Mark Quinn wanted to kill her, and then Colin would never know the truth. He would blame her death on the enemy soldiers, as he looked down into her eyes, crushing her throat.

Her vocal cords became weak, her body losing strength, as Dagmara was barely able to struggle anymore, giving way to his devious plan. Clever in his vicious intentions, Mark Quinn had purposely sent Colin and Brady out, staying behind with she and Cillian. He watched in the corner as Dagmara wandered off, and then knocked Cillian unconscious with a hit to the head from a tree branch. His diabolical plan was perfect, and he was determined to follow through seeing no other way out.

Dagmara Morrow's hands fell weightless down around the side of her body, and she could feel the life being sucked right out of her soul. She had survived a plane crash, she had survived and witnessed a brutal rape and murder, and now, she became a victim again, but this time she was unable to help herself and get away. And as her body lie beneath his, hardly moving, becoming limp, Mark Quinn's hands tightened in strength. His eyes full of malice, hatred coursing through his entire body.

Then suddenly Mark Quinn heard footsteps thrashing towards him in the dark, and as he looked up, before he could see him coming, Colin jumped on top of him, pushing him off Dagmara, saving her life.

They rolled over each other several times, as neither of them wanted to hurt the other, but they were at a crossroad in friendship that now had to end. They could no longer be friends, and neither Colin nor Mark Quinn wanted the other as their enemy, as they stood up facing each other ready to fight.

"What are you doing?" Colin shouted, disbelieving his eyes, not wanting to see his friend act in such a violent manner.

"Don't you see, I had to, she was going to ruin everything. It would be the end for us!" Mark Quinn yelled.

"What are you talking about?" Colin asked.

"You're going to fuck her just like you did all the others," Mark Quinn shouted, his rage taking control of his emotions.

Brady and Cillian rushed over and moved towards Dagmara, when Colin put his hand up telling them to stay back, he would handle the situation alone. Mark Quinn started to move towards Colin, and he backed away, not understanding his friend's actions, why he would do something like this.

"Don't you see, I saw you, I saw the way you looked at her. I knew she would poison you against me. That you would take her side over mine."

"You're talking crazy Quinn, you don't know what you're saying. Why don't you just calm down and we …" Colin began to say, as Mark Quinn resorted to desperation, took out his knife, and pointed it at his best friend.

His breathing quickened, his anger increased, his stare hardened, as Mark Quinn immersed into a monster right before Colin's eyes.

"You want to hurt me now?" Colin asked, as he began to see his friend for what he was, for whom he has probably been all these years.

"No, I don't want to hurt you Colin, I would never hurt you. Don't you see that, don't you realize how much you mean to me. How much our friendship means to me!" Mark Quinn shouted again, as tears streamed down his face. "I did it for you!"

Angered by his friend's words, Colin moved closer to him, and Mark Quinn lifted the knife in his hand.

"You're nothing but a coward!" Colin yelled, infuriating his friend. "All these years, I always felt I owed you for saving my life when we were kids, and I guess I never wanted to see what you have really become. I defended your honor, countless times, even when I knew I shouldn't have. When I knew you were wrong, I took your side over everyone who said a cross word about you."

"Then you see why I had to get rid of her, why I did this. She was ruining everything," Mark Quinn stated, trying to convey his reasoning for his actions.

Colin stepped closer and reached for the knife, when instinctively Mark Quinn reacted by defending himself, and slashed his arm, tearing Colin's shirt, drawing blood. The flesh wound did not make an impression upon Colin, as he reached forward aggressively to take the knife away from his friend before he really hurt someone, and they both fell to the ground struggling for control of the weapon.

Brady and Cillian rushed over to help, but the fight was over with before it began. The knife fell out of Mark Quinn's hand, and he rolled over on the sharp blade. The knife went straight into his chest, piercing his heart, and as Colin moved off his body, he lied sprawled out on the ground.

Mark Quinn looked up at his friend, grabbing the knife that was lodged in his flesh, his hands full of blood. Breathing his last words, blood seeped out of his lips as he opened his mouth to speak. "You fucking blaggard!" Mark Quinn said to his best friend in a barely audible tone, then his hand let go of the knife, his eyes widened in a frightening, painful stare, and he was dead.

Colin stepped back from Mark Quinn's body. His friend's words sliced through his heart in agonizing betrayal, as he looked down at his hands that were full of blood. His friend was dead. He had killed his best friend; even if it was unintentional, accidental, Colin felt he was to blame. He could have easily fallen on the knife and been the one to die, but he did not, and now he had to live with the consequences of his actions.

And as that sentiment resonated in Colin Murphy's mind, oppressing his thoughts heavily, he looked over at Dagmara, and his eyes hardened in stare. How easily her beauty had blinded him, allowing himself to fall prey to that alluring weakness. And he wondered how something so beautiful, so enviable, could be the cause of so much pain?

Brady rushed over to see if his brother was injured, but the blood on Colin's hands was not his. Cillian had a small bump on his head from the hit. He bent down and checked Mark Quinn's pulse making sure he was dead.

"What do we do now?" Brady asked his brother.

Colin walked over to Dagmara and bent down beside her in the grass. Noticing the tears in her clothes, he lifted her chin up, and saw a bruise on her cheek. Then he moved her face higher up to his, and saw the imprint of Mark Quinn's large fingers on her neck. The bruises from his hands formed on her skin, already turning black and blue in color. Then he extended his hand to her, and helped Dagmara stand up, as she was momentarily disoriented.

"We can't stay here tonight, someone might have heard us. We have to keep moving," Colin told his brother and Cillian, and then looked at Dagmara. "I'm sorry that he hurt you, for what he did to you," he told her, as he placed his fingers on her throat, gently rubbing her skin.

She felt the pain in her neck, her skin bruised heavily by the force of Mark Quinn's strength. Dagmara did not say a word to Colin as she looked at him with her eyes, and then placed her hand in his. They hurried back to the barn and started gathering up their belongings, as Colin placed a wet cloth on Dagmara's throat trying to ease the discomfort. And each time he looked at her, he was unable to look at her, thinking of her suffering. The accident. His friend's death.

Suddenly lights flashed and gunshots were heard in the distance, and they knew they had been spotted. Rapidly Colin grabbed Dagmara's hand and they all took off running into the field at a quickened pace.

Whistles deafened and more gunshots were fired in their direction as the enemy approached closer. They were hunted by German soldiers, and soon were surrounded by a dozen men. The owners of the property had placed a call to the police, notifying them of thieves on their property. Thinking they were spies, they immediately sent a unit to capture them, and take them in for questioning.

The soldiers kept firing, and several bullets swarmed around each of their bodies in the dark fields, as they lowered themselves down to the ground. The soldiers could not see them clearly, as they randomly fired shots into the field hoping to hit them. Then a German soldier stumbled upon Mark Quinn's body, and they found themselves under attack, as the commanding officer ordered his men not to bring the prisoners in for questioning any longer. Shoot to kill.

Rapidly Colin pushed Dagmara down to the ground beneath him, shielding her body chivalrously, as Brady and Cillian were right in front of them. They had no weapons, they were completely unarmed and could not defend themselves against the fast, deadly speed at which the guns were being fired.

Brady looked back at his brother, as Colin motioned for him and Cillian to stay down low to the ground.

"Stay right here," Colin whispered in Dagmara's ear, and then moved along the ground, slithering like a snake towards his brother and Cillian.

"What should we do?" Cillian asked him.

If they got up and started to run, they would easily be spotted and shot, killing them all without demanding surrender. Colin could not allow his brother and Cillian to get hurt, and now he had another to consider, as he looked back in the grass at the young woman who was covering her head in her hands. He had to protect her. He had to think of her safety along with their own. Colin owed her that much, especially for what his friend had done, feeling partly responsible for Mark Quinn's violent actions.

"What are we going to do with her?" Brady asked his brother.

They now had Dagmara to consider, and as the gunfire increased in magnitude, Colin made the only possible decision. They had to split up. They could no longer travel together. There were too many of them to evade, as the soldiers moved in closer. By separating, it gave them all a greater chance to get to safety, to make it to the train station, to make it out of the country, if they went different ways and met up later.

"Brady listen to me," Colin started to say to his brother, hoping that he had made the right decision, and not placed a death sentence on all their heads. "You and Cillian go the way we originally planned, and I'll take Dagmara and go another way."

"NO," Brady refused, elevating his voice among the gunfire. "We're not splitting up!"

"I can't lose you, you understand that Brady. I couldn't face mum if anything happened to you. I'm responsible for you."

"I can take care of myself," Brady told his brother.

"Yes, I know you can, but this is the only way. I won't argue with you. I can't drag her all over as we had planned, she'll never make it. I'll have to go a different way with Dagmara, and meet up with you both."

"Where?"

"The station."

"But how do we know we can even trust that man," Cillian interjected.

"We'll have to, we have no other choice. I want both of you to watch your backs and stay far away from the towns. Keep on the back roads, and I promise I'll meet you there," Colin told his brother, trying to convince him this was the best course of action.

"You promise?" Brady said, scared for his brother, not wanting to leave him.

"Yes," Colin said shaking his head, and then grabbed his brother's hand and told him, "I promise you Brady, I'll find you, both of you!"

Brady smiled at his brother, wanting to believe him, wanting to believe in him, but the gut wrenching feeling in his heart and the bullets that flew passed their heads told him not to let go of his brother's hand.

"Now get going, they're getting closer," Colin ordered his brother.

Not wanting to leave, Brady begrudgingly agreed, and clasped his hands tightly around Colin in a big hug. Colin hugged his brother, hoping that he would make it, that they all would. That this would only be a slight parting and not a goodbye. That he would live to see his brother's face again, knowing the possibilities of failure was high.

"Now go!" he urged his brother, and rapidly Brady moved his body lower to the ground and started moving away from his brother.

"I know what you're doing. I didn't want to say anything in front of your brother, but it's suicide Colin," Cillian stated, knowing Colin had divided them up not because of Dagmara, but for his brother.

"You can't tell him."

"I think you're making a mistake. We shouldn't deviate from the plan. It's too dangerous, we should all stay together," Cillian stressed.

"You must promise me Cillian, that if we don't make it, I mean, if I'm not there to meet you and Brady, you'll go without me. That you won't stay behind and wait for us, or come looking for us. I don't care what Brady says to you … you have to get him on that train!" Colin insisted, stressing the urgency and importance of his wishes.

"I understand," Cillian told him, reassuring Colin that he could be relied on and trusted.

"It will be your last chance to get out of France … both of you must take it!" Colin stated strenuously.

"I promise you Colin, we'll both be on the train. You just get yourself there, safely, and with the girl," Cillian replied, hugged Colin, and then started moving along the ground following after Brady.

Colin watched as Cillian and his brother moved farther and farther away from him, moving farther away from the peril. Then he turned around and started moving back along the ground towards Dagmara. He saw the German soldiers moving in closer, and knew he had to get them out of there fast. He would divert their attention away from Brady and Cillian, placing a target on he and Dagmara. Not wanting to place her in danger, he was forced to do so. He had no other choice. It was the only way.

Dagmara looked up at Colin as he moved next to her on the ground. "We're alone now, Brady and Cillian are going on ahead as planned. We'll meet up with them later."

Her eyes opened wide not understanding why Colin had separated them, until another bullet flew straight passed her body, almost hitting her, scraping her coat. Instantly Colin moved them lower to the ground, and then Dagmara realized that they were going to lead the enemy in the opposite direction, placing all the gunfire on them, diverting their attention, while the others got away to safety.

CHAPTER 14

"When I count to three, we're going to start running in that direction," Colin told Dagmara, and then he took a long look at her face, seeing her innocence, and gently caressed her cheek with his hand, knowing what he was asking her to do.

And as Colin said three, they both got up and started to run as fast as humanly possible in the opposite direction of Brady and Cillian, as the enemy soldiers caught a glimpse of two people moving in the field, and started chasing after them on foot.

The trick had worked and the soldiers rushed after them, as Brady and Cillian got farther and farther away, hoping that Colin and Dagmara would do the same. Thrashing shoes smashed down into the grass, as the German soldiers followed in hot pursuit, and the chase soon turned into a lavish, deadly race.

Dagmara and Colin ran faster and faster through the fields, as the enemies gained in speed. There were too many of them to elude, as the bullets kept coming, continuously. The predators, relentless.

Running several miles without stopping, both Dagmara and Colin were physically exhausted, and still they kept moving at a quickened pace, never slowing down, as they looked back and saw the enemies closing in on them.

They reached the top of the hill, and a bullet suddenly flew directly towards their bodies, and struck Colin in the shoulder. The forceful impact from the hit pushed Colin off his feet, he lost his balance, and fell. As he fell down to the ground, he rolled over the hill and took Dagmara with him. His hand still entangled with her fingers, they started rolling down the hill together picking up speed.

Their hands broke apart as they rolled in a tumbling motion towards the bottom of the bumpy hill. They smashed into several rocks, hitting the ground hard, unable to slow themselves down in the forceful motion. Then they crashed into a few larger rocks at the bottom of the hill, and both Dagmara and Colin lied still, their bodies not moving.

The German soldiers stood at the top of the hill and looked over the side. They fired several shots at the fugitives, their bullets missing them by the long distance. As one of the soldiers was about to climb down the hill, another put out his hand and stopped him from moving downward.

"Shouldn't we go after them?" the young soldier asked.

"Look at them, no one could survive that, and even if they did, they'll be dead soon enough. We have orders to get back into town."

The young soldier shook his head in compliance, and the soldiers left their victims and ran back to join the others and regroup.

William stood and watched the fire grow brighter within the numerous explosions that surrounded him. Henry and Stuart ran back inside, grabbed their guns, and brought William his gun, as they stood three together against the enemy. The sneak attack had occurred in the late night hour, taking them by surprise, as William Cavill's entire unit was intentionally taken off guard giving the enemy the advantage.

Ambushed in the middle of nowhere, with no help on the way, more soldiers gathered around William and his friends, ready to defend themselves in fearless valor.

They had no time to get to their planes, they would not be able to get them up in the air let alone off the ground in time, as the explosions erupted with fierce loudness, approaching closer. William and his friends were not fully prepared for hand to hand combat, they were fighter pilots, and did their best fighting in the skies, and they were great at it. William Cavill was at the top of his class, but his skills would have to be used in a different way this time.

Massive gunfire burst in thundering commotion surrounding them from every angle, as William, Henry, and Stuart stood intrepid, and then started rushing forward without an once of fear in their bodies. Henry and Stuart fired several rounds into the enemy lines, as William suddenly turned into a different person, savage in nature. He lost all control, and stormed directly ahead of his friends towards the front line into the blackened hole of fiery death.

Nothing to live for anymore, feeling he had lost everything by losing Dagmara, William Cavill transformed into a fierce, armed creature that stormed the gates in a nightly attack. He ran straight into the darkness unable to see anything, as his friends yelled to him to stop and come back. But he did not hear them, let alone listen to their words, as he raced forward with speed and determination, laced with an overt courageousness, heading straight into the enemies trap.

The heroic William Cavill fired his gun, taking down many enemy soldiers, one after the other, as he kept firing and firing. His pain consumed him in torment. His heart felt hollow, as he defied the stars in every direction, killing as many men as he could. The blood coursed through his veins like fire, burning, unable to stop, and as he looked back at his friends who were rushing after him, shouting for him to come back, they were too late to catch up with him. An explosion hit directly in front of William, and blackness swallowed him in his despair.

His body was thrown several feet in the air, and then he fell weightless towards the ground, as he crashed hard, covered by smoke and debris. More explosions simultaneously erupted around him, as his friends were caught in their own misfortunes, and were taken down by the enormous blasts.

Stuart took a bullet to the head, and was killed instantly upon contact, his body slamming into the ground. Henry fell to his knees as a bullet pierced through his chest, slicing through his flesh, and then another bullet sliced through his body, drawing more blood, as he lie on the ground in excruciating pain, unable to move, unable to run for cover.

The soldiers moved to Henry's aid, and dragged Stuart's body away, as William Cavill; the third of the three musketeer friends lied in darkness. His body lied still on the ground, not moving, his hand still clasped to his gun. His forehead was bleeding, his eyes were closed, his face covered in dirt. The bloody battle roared in devourment, and men yelled in command, as courage swarmed among the brave fighting soldiers who tried to defend themselves and their country.

William's unit was completely outnumbered, until suddenly they saw lights in the sky. Several neighboring fighter pilots came to their rescue, and fired upon the enemy. The German soldiers began to retreat and run for cover, as they were overpowered by the gunfire of the planes, but help did not get there in time to save Stuart Shelton, he was already dead. He died a painless death, never feeling the torture that his friends endured. Henry Taylor screamed in enormous pain, his body having multiple convulsions, unable to control his own movements, as two men carried Henry on a stretcher taking him to the nearest doctor.

Amid all the chaos and gunfire that was disbursing, and violent, ear-piercing screams deafened in the withering wind, William Cavill's body had not yet been found. He lie motionless in the same position on the ground, covered in dirt. His face blackened, his eyes closed, his chest not moving, and the fate of his life now lingered somewhere inbetween the shadows of twilight, on the brink of death.

Slowly Dagmara opened her eyes, feeling pain in every part of her body. She moved to sit up, as every bone in her body was sore. Her lip was bleeding, her clothes torn, and her eyes momentarily glossy from the hard hit against her head as she crashed into the rocks. Luckily, she had no broken bones. Then she looked over and saw Colin. He was not moving. His body lie still. Panic consumed her, as she slowly moved over to his side.

She turned Colin Murphy over onto his back. His forehead was cut, his clothes ripped and dirty like hers, and his shoulder was bleeding from the bullet wound. Colin had hit his head against a rock as they tumbled, and was momentarily knocked unconscious. Immediately Dagmara wiped the mud from his face, and tore a piece of material from her shirt. She wrapped it tightly around his upper arm to cover the opened wound, to try to stop the blood from flowing. Then she checked his pulse. He was still breathing. Colin Murphy was still alive.

Feverishly Dagmara scrambled to help him, not knowing what to do, she looked all around, but there was no one in sight. They were completely alone. The German soldiers had left awhile ago, and not knowing where she was, they were lost. If only Brady and Cillian were here, they would know what to do, they would be able to help Colin, but Dagmara hoped they had gotten far away from this place of death, and wherever they were, they were safe.

"Please don't die on me," Dagmara said, overwhelmed with fear of being left alone, of losing him, as tears fell from her eyes. "I can't make it without you. Don't leave me here alone. I need you Colin Murphy," she shouted, hoping he would hear her.

More tears ran down her cheek, sliding off her chin and onto his face. Scared, not knowing how to get them help, to get them to safety, with no weapon to defend them with if the soldiers returned, Dagmara leaned towards Colin's mouth, and gently outlined his lips with the soft stroke of her finger.

Colin Murphy meant more to her than she realized. He had saved her from those soldiers, he had saved her from Mark Quinn, and he had saved her that long night ago when they first met on the street. Not even knowing who she was, he had helped her and taken her with him, and given her shelter.

In her eyes, Colin Murphy had in someway replaced William as her savior. William had saved her from loneliness, from her overbearing parents, and she loved him. She loved whom she was when she was with William Cavill, but with Colin, he had saved her from the clutches of death more than once. And in someway, he had even saved her from herself.

His arrogant, sometimes rude, impetuous manner attracted her to the dangerous side he possessed, but he was also kind, a side not many people got to see. Behind the strong exterior, behind his rough demeanor, lied hidden a handsome, vigorous gentleman.

Upon instinct, Dagmara leaned in closer towards Colin's mouth, and kissed him on the lips. Not knowing why she had done so, inexplicable to ever tell him why, she kissed him, hoping in someway to breathe life back into his body.

Gently she pushed her lips onto his, when suddenly Dagmara's eyes opened wide, as she felt Colin's lips kissing her back. Immediately she broke their lips apart and moved back from him. He licked his bottom lip and then opened his eyes, tasting her sweetness inside his mouth.

"Colin, you're awake. You're alive!" she said with a huge smile. "Are you all right, how do you feel?"

He looked up at her, trying to focus his eyes on her face, still feeling dazed from the hard hit against his head.

"Are you okay," he asked, thinking of her first.

"I think so."

"What happened?"

"You were hit, and then we both went over."

Colin moved his finger to her mouth and wiped away the blood. He noticed a bruise on her forehead, and her knee was scraped and bleeding. Miraculously they both had survived the long, downward fall. They had survived without any major injuries. Bruises would heal.

He noticed the piece of material tied around his arm, and then saw her shirt was torn. She had grass in her hair, and her face had smudges of dirt covering her beautiful, porcelain complexion.

"Can you walk?" Dagmara asked him.

Slowly she helped Colin stand up, and instantly he felt his whole body spasm with acute pain racing up his spine. Feeling no broken bones, Colin steadied himself on his own two feet, and they both looked up towards the top of the hill seeing the high distance they had fallen. Then they looked at one another, and Colin placed his finger on Dagmara's cheek, wiping off some of the dirt. A smile creased in her lips, as his piercing stare shimmered in the darkness. Her heart started pounding fast.

He extended his hand and she placed her hand in his. Slowly they started walking together in the dark, walking towards the unknown, in search of a warm place to stay for the night, and stay out of the enemies reach.

CHAPTER 15

They walked for miles, tired, cold, dirty, and stumbled upon a small run down bed and breakfast. Inside they found an old lady who wore thick glasses and ran the establishment. Her husband had died a few years back, and she was left alone after her only child was killed in the war. The French woman felt sorry for the two young men, as Colin told her Dagmara was his younger brother. She saw their clothes, they had no money to give her, and they desperately needed a place to stay for the night.

The old woman had helped several people hide from the Vichy government, and did not ask if they were on the run or just lost. Needing no explanation, she gave them a room for the night, expecting nothing in return. The kind hearted woman was happy to help people, especially youngsters, reminding her of the grandchildren she never had.

Mrs. Beart walked with a slight limp as she moved up the stairs and showed them to their room. There was one bed inside with a chair, and a small dresser and a washroom. Both of them needed to rest and clean up before they were on their way tomorrow. The tight quarters they were to share for the evening would only be for one night Dagmara thought, no one had to know, especially William.

Dagmara was so happy to clean her face and hands from the dirt, and Mrs. Beart had given them some medicine and bandages. Colin started to unbutton his coat, and there was a knock on the door. He placed his finger to his lips telling Dagmara to be quiet, and then he motioned for her to stay in the bathroom as he opened the door. Mrs. Beart had brought them a tray with one sandwich and two small glasses of milk, and underneath, she was carrying a clean shirt.

"I thought you and your brother might be hungry," she said, and gave Colin the tray. "I thought you could use this," and handed him the clean shirt. "I would offer you more, but this is all I could find," she told him; unable to see clearly through her thick glasses that his younger brother was actually a girl.

"Thank you, but you need not give us your food, you've already given us enough just with a place to stay for the night," Colin replied.

"Nonsense, you and your brother are young and strong and need your strength, I'm just an old woman with my days numbered," she said with a smile, and then closed the door.

Colin had never come across such benevolence. This woman whether she knew it or not, had taught him a valuable lesson, that even amongst enemies, there will always be friends. This old woman had aided many in a desperate time of need, helping them elude German soldiers, helping them escape. If it were ever found out that she was helping these people, they would take her into the middle of the street, in front of everyone to witness, and execute her for harboring fugitives. But she took the risk, not hesitating from fear.

Slowly Colin took off his coat and shirt. His shoulder was covered in dried blood. Lucky for him, the bullet had only grazed his skin, slightly cutting his flesh, and had not gotten lodged in his body. As he removed his undershirt, his rippling abdomen flexed in the coolness of the night. Dagmara tried not to stare, but was unable to look away, incited with unwanted feelings.

Dagmara cleaned the wound, then used the medicine Mrs. Beart had given them, and bandaged Colin's shoulder as best she could. The blood had stopped; her quick thinking under the urgency of the situation had allowed her to add pressure to the wound. Colin watched in amazement as she tended to his injury. Her efficiency. Her undaunted behavior not looking away from the blood. She was tough, and the more time they spent together, the more Colin found himself becoming increasingly attracted to Dagmara.

Her soft hands touched his skin, and he flinched slightly from the coldness as she applied the medicine to his forehead. At the same time the attraction grew, Colin could not forget what had happened in the fields. The image of Mark Quinn's body staring up at him would forever haunt him. His best friend was dead, and he felt responsible for his death. If only he had listened to Mark Quinn, and not brought her into their group. If only he had given her shelter for one night and sent her on her way, maybe his friend would still be alive?

But that was just a conceived notion of mere reality, and he could not undo the past. He had made his choice. He had helped this young woman, and in a way, he felt he had betrayed his best friend, a friend who had once saved his life. Never to have regrets, Colin Murphy now had one.

Her shirt was almost torn to shreds as Dagmara opened her coat. Her pants had holes in them at the knee. She started applying some medicine on her knee, when Colin took the cloth out of her hand, bent down, and applied the medicine to her wound. He placed a bandage over the scrape, then stood up, and gently wiped his finger across her lips with the medicine. Then he tilted her chin up to the light, and saw the large handprints outlined on her throat. Her skin had already turned dark in color from the bruises, and Colin could not take back what his friend had done, he could only try to make it better.

"I am sorry for what he did to you," Colin said again, looking Dagmara straight in the eyes.

"You don't have to apologize for him."

"I'm not apologizing for him, but for myself," Colin told her, and walked over to the tray of food. "The nice woman thought you might be hungry. You should eat something."

Keeping his feelings hidden, Colin hardly ever apologized for his behavior, but with Dagmara it was different, he was different, as he found himself expressing emotions he thought he could never have towards someone like her.

She would be the ruin of them, she would come between them, Mark Quinn had told him once, but he never listened, and now, he knew his friend was right. Dagmara Morrow had already taken a special place in his heart.

Suddenly Dagmara fell off balance and Colin caught her in his arms. Weak from lack of sleep and food, she fainted for a few seconds as he carried her over to the bed. Colin picked her up in his arms like a feather. She had lost weight since he first met her, so had he. The rosy color in her cheeks turned to a pale, whiter color, as he brought her the glass of milk. Dagmara took a sip as she regained consciousness, and saw Colin looking down at her. Then he tore off a piece of the sandwich and moved the bread between her lips. Forgetting about the hunger, Dagmara felt woozy as she tried to sit up, and then rapidly lied back down feeling dizzy.

"You haven't eaten in awhile, take another bite," he told her, and handed Dagmara half of the sandwich.

Slowly Dagmara took another bite and then Colin handed her the glass of milk to drink.

"You need to eat too," she said to him.

"No, you must keep your strength up, I'll be fine. I've gone before without food for days, you're not used to it."

Dagmara picked up the other half of the sandwich and shoved it into his hand, Colin started to give it back to her, she refused. He gulped down the glass of milk, and ravished the food as if they were starving, and they were.

Neither one of them spoke about what happened after the fall, as they sat on the bed together reminiscing silently about the kiss. That was all Dagmara could think about as she finished the glass of milk, wondering if Colin was thinking the same. As if they were reading each other's mind, Colin kept thinking about how soft her lips felt against his mouth. How he enjoyed the ardent gesture even more this time when she had placed her lips on his instead of his cheek. Unlike the time before, he did not wipe away her kiss, not wanting to wash away the beautiful sensation.

Dagmara started to cough; she had swallowed the food too fast, and then lied back down on the pillow still feeling weak. Her blood pressure had plummeted.

"You need to rest," Colin told her, gently brushing a golden strand of hair away from her face.

Dagmara was still pale as she tried to steady her breathing taking in a few large breaths.

"You should get some sleep," he added.

Dagmara tried to stand up but felt dizzy, as Colin steadied her from falling. Then he started to unbutton the rest of her coat, took it off, and did the same with her shirt. The closeness between their bodies heated up the room, as she felt his hand brush gently across her chest. She sat down on the bed as he untied her laces and took off her shoes, then unbuttoned her pants and slipped them down her legs taking them off, undressing her.

She brushed the dirt off her slip; her silk stockings had holes in them, as Colin placed her clothes on the chair, then turned back around, and saw Dagmara standing by the small lamp. The sheer material of her slip form fitted her body perfectly. Her slender figure curved in all the right places. Even with her short hair and the darkness of the room, Colin Murphy found Dagmara Morrow to be simply irresistible. He could not look away.

Dagmara slipped in under the sheet and pulled the blanket to her chest, as Colin washed up in the bathroom. Her eyes were closed as Colin turned out the light and then took off his pants. The moonlight shined in from the window, as Dagmara opened her eyes and saw Colin standing in his underwear. The trickle of light smoothed across his bare chest, his firm bottom, having the body of a Greek god, as he turned around and faced her. Suddenly Dagmara felt incitement in her loins as she stared at Colin Murphy's half naked body.

The illusion of perfection, he was incredibly sexy, and at that moment, she could see no flaws, he was perfect in every way.

"I thought you were asleep."

"I couldn't sleep," Dagmara said, shivering from the cold.

Colin sat down beside her on the bed, and everything inside of him was screaming to kiss her, to feel her sultry lips again on his mouth. He wanted her. He silently yearned for her. He wanted simply to tell her how he felt.

"Tell me about yourself?" she asked him.

"What do you want to know?"

"Do you have a girl back home?"

Surprised by her question, the hesitation in his eyes told her no.

"Why are you so interested?"

"Just making conversation," she said with a slight smile.

"My dad ran off when I was little, leaving me mum and Brady, leaving me in charge to make sure they were taken care of. Brady hardly remembers him, but I do," Colin told Dagmara, as he reminisced back upon his childhood memories with anguish and unresolved feelings as he looked out the window into the moonlight sky. "And I swore to myself that I would never become like him, to marry and drink all day and night, leaving my children to the cold hands of strangers."

The hardened strength of his voice, the anger still fumed within the remembrance of his darkened past, as Colin lost himself deep in thought.

"I'm sorry," she said with compassion looking up at him, and then gently touched his hand.

He looked down at her hand on his, not knowing why he had told Dagmara about his father, about his childhood. Why he had opened up the wound that had never properly healed? No matter how much Colin Murphy tried to forget, to lock away the disturbing memory, it would always be with him, till death.

"Before he left that night, he had come home and stumbled through the door drunk. You could smell the liquor fuming from his bones, and mum confronted him about some young bird he was seeing. They started yelling at each other, and then in a heated rage, he hit her, and she fell down, and then he started kicking and kicking her … and I remember running down the stairs, and then he started hitting and kicking me. And I hit him back this time; I wasn't going to let him do this to us anymore. And we fought, and I remember Brady crying and mum screaming, pleading with him to let me go. And then I grabbed the gun that he kept in his drawer … and I aimed it straight at his face

… and I told him if he ever laid another hand on me or mum … I would kill him, and he knew I would … and that was the last time we ever saw him."

Colin turned his face away from Dagmara, not wanting her to look into his eyes, to see through his damaged soul. He had never told anyone that story before, not even in the throws of passion with the many girls that had shared his bed. Dagmara was the first and only person he had ever told. If only she knew how special that made her.

The moonlight shined in through the window illuminating the room with light, as the silence thickened within the small surrounding of the bed. The agony of his tortured past, even now when Colin spoke about his father and that night, the painful memory tore him up inside with resentment. The anger he felt brought forward his thick Irish accent that protruded through his words, as Colin was momentarily lost in his own little world, distancing himself from Dagmara, placing himself back in that moment.

Then he looked back down at Dagmara. He could see in her eyes how his story affected her, touching her heart. They were so different, yet so alike, and he did not want to hurt her with his impertinence, that was the last thing Colin wanted to do, and the more he looked at her face, the more frustration coursed through his bones aching to be with her, to be someone else, to be someone who she could love.

"I bet I know everything about you," he said, his arrogance returning.

"Go on then, tell me," she told him, and moved her body up on the pillow.

"You had a wonderful childhood and peaceful dreams. Life has treated you very well. You can have anything you want because your parents are wealthy, and you use your charms to the fullest. You're strong, and you're not afraid in this world because … because you're beautiful," Colin said, as Dagmara's eyes widened hearing the last three words.

"I want to try that," she told him, and sat straight up in the bed looking into his eyes, holding the sheet to her chest. "You're very courageous, and you live dangerously on the edge. You live more in the moment, but you're plagued by the past. You're passionate, and you want people to think you're tough and nothing hurts you, but that is not who you really are."

Her words surprised him with insightful intuitiveness, as Dagmara moved closer to Colin, getting to close to the flame.

"You don't know what you're talking about?" he said, and backed away.

"I think I do … you're running away from the pain of your past, but you keep it so close to you, to your heart, so you don't get hurt again. But you don't have to be afraid of who you are, to let people in, to see the real you, because …

there's so much more to you Colin Murphy," she said, understanding him, and slowly caressed his cheek with her hand, softly letting her fingers glide down his face.

Abruptly Colin moved away from her off the bed, not wanting to hear the truth, as Dagmara was the first person to ever really understand him, which somewhat scared him. She saw through his hardened exterior, as Colin never wanted to let himself get too close to a person, never wanting to get burned. Dagmara could see in his eyes the agony, got up out of bed, draped the blanket around her, and went to him.

She touched his arm, and rapidly he turned around.

"You think you know me, why, because we've shared some days together, a few close moments. That means nothing. You don't know anything about me!" he said in a harsh tone, raising his voice, intentionally taking out his anger on her.

She could see the pain in his eyes, and knew he did not mean to lash out, especially at her.

Dagmara started to say something and Colin interrupted. "You don't know how much I've hated you, but for all the wrong reasons. Because you're beautiful. Because you're rich and well educated and I'm not. Mostly I've hated you … because of the way you make me feel when I'm with you."

Dagmara stared at him for a moment, surprised by his words. "How could you possibly say that to me now, when the first night I met you, you couldn't stand to look at me without gritting your teeth. I saw the disdain in your eyes, how you wiped away my kiss. I don't believe you!" she shouted, getting upset.

Impulsively Colin grabbed Dagmara around and kissed her hard on the lips. Then he leaned in towards her more, succumbing to the lustful vigor that was fulfilled by the pleasure of their embrace. A perilous pleasure that would ultimately spiral into a climatic betrayal of his own heart. Fighting off the desire, the loath he had for the upper class, Colin Murphy gave into the sensuous feeling, and kissed her again.

As Colin's lips touched her mouth, allowing another man to kiss her, to be that close, Dagmara Morrow had betrayed her own heart. She had betrayed the small round object that lied hidden next to her chest. She had betrayed William!

CHAPTER 16

The agonizing, forbidden pleasure, the sensual, stimulating seduction coursed through Colin's veins, as he immersed himself deeper into the infatuating kiss, pressing his body into hers.

Colin Murphy's kiss was intoxicating. A fire so tantalizingly dangerous, Dagmara wanted to be burned in it night after night absorbing the flame. She ignited his passion that fueled his vigor. A sensuous, alluring feeling, their searing embrace erupted upon their bodies like a hurricane of lust.

Allowing Colin to kiss her, Dagmara did not push him away. His lips lusciously warmed her skin, arousing every bone in her body, rapidly speeding up her heartbeat, and for a brief moment, Dagmara and Colin found themselves lost in their own little world within the kiss. The war that surrounded them, the enemies that lied ahead in their path, all was placed aside, as Colin devoured Dagmara's lips.

Abruptly Dagmara broke their lips apart, opened her eyes, and pushed Colin away. As he moved forward to kiss her again, she gently placed her hand on his mouth, and slid her finger slowly around his lips, excited by the provocative gesture. He placed his hand on hers, and kissed her finger, slightly moving it inside his mouth. Seducing her with his piercing stare, she could barely breathe being so close to his body in such an intimate manner.

Dagmara moved closer to him, and the blanket fell out of her hands down to the floor. He pressed himself against her, placing his hands around her back, and then kissed her passionately on the lips. She could feel his manhood press against her. The space between them was nonexistent, as he could feel her perky breasts through her slip, pressing into his chest, taunting his loins. And he wanted her, to throw her down on the bed and make love to her.

It was then in that moment, that Colin realized he was wrong about her, he was wrong about Dagmara Morrow from the very beginning. He had hated her for all the wrong reasons. He had hated her because she was beautiful. He hated her because she was rich and he was not, because a woman like her could never be his. Mostly he hated her … because he was beginning to fall in love with her.

Suddenly Dagmara pushed Colin away, not succumbing to his sexual, ardent advance. His mouth lunged at her lips, and she pushed him back, not wanting to allow the moment of weakened lust to go on further. She might have wanted him, she maybe even desired him, but she definitely did not need Colin Murphy; he would only bring her trouble. She would not be unfaithful to her heart, to William; to the man she loved and would soon marry. The only question was, how faithful would her heart be to her?

Upset, tormented by the desire he expressively possessed for Dagmara Morrow, Colin thrashed around the room and kicked the chair across the floor. His actions frightened her. His burst of anger, impetuous. Then suddenly he turned around, and started coming towards her. The look in his eyes ran a cold chill up Dagmara's spine, as his arrogant manner and dislike for her, and everything she stood for, had fully returned.

"Why can't we be together!" he shouted.

Not wanting to answer him, Dagmara stood silent, which angered him further.

"It's because you think I'm not good enough for you, isn't it. That since I haven't had a proper upbringing and education, that I'm not worthy of your affections? Is money the only thing rich people really care about!" he said in a livid tone.

His impertinent behavior angered Dagmara with his painted accusations.

"You want to know the real reason why," she said, raising her voice, looking him straight in the eyes.

"Yes," he shouted, standing inches apart, as the heated argument elevated.

"Because … when I'm near you I can't breathe … because I don't trust myself when I'm with you!"

Colin was speechless, never expecting an answer like that, but that was not the only reason, it was only partially true, as the small round object heated next to her heart. Dagmara Morrow was already engaged to a wonderful, handsome, highly distinguished man. A man she loved. A man who greatly loved her.

Frustrated by his explosive actions, her words, by being deprived of having her, Colin Murphy forcefully grabbed Dagmara, pushed her up against the wall, and kissed her on the mouth, unleashing his fervor. Taking her by surprise, Colin vigorously kissed her, as he held her in his hands, swallowing her whole.

He overwhelmed her.

Dagmara resisted at first, but he would not let her go, persuading her to give in … and she did.

Aggressively Colin kissed her lips and then her neck, and tore down the thin strap of her slip from her shoulder. He pressed their bodies tight, as his other hand moved higher up her leg. He felt her silk stockings beneath his fingers, as his hand moved underneath her slip, touching her thigh. The sensual feeling intoxicated his senses, feeling her sultry smooth skin against his hand, he abruptly stopped, and broke their heated red lips apart.

"You must stop me!" he said breathing heavily, as he looked straight into her eyes, wanting Dagmara not to allow him to go further, unable to stop himself.

Instantly she slapped him across the face breaking their connection, and pushed him away, as they stared at one another breathing hard. Furious by his impulsive nature, by the forceful manner in which he treated her, indulging in his lustful yearn, Colin hated himself for hurting her. Not intentionally wanting to hurt Dagmara, and taint her propriety.

Upset by what transpired between them, the way he treated her, Dagmara opened the door, dashed out of the room, and started running down the stairs. Immediately Colin pulled on his pants, half buttoning them, and rushed down the steps after her to bring her back inside the room.

"Dagmara," he said, softly calling out her name, not wanting to wake up the old woman. "Come back here."

The wind gust through the opened door in the late night hour, as Dagmara ran outside in only her slip, her bare feet feeling the coldness beneath her toes. The freezing temperature whipped through her bones as if she was wearing nothing at all.

"Dagmara stop!" Colin yelled, as he grabbed hold of her, and she struggled to get away. "It's freezing out here, you'll catch your death."

"I don't care," she said upset, not thinking of their situation.

"You're acting childish, someone might see us," he told her, as he looked around the desolate street, and then brought Dagmara back inside and closed the door before anyone had a chance to spot them. Then he picked Dagmara up in his arms and carried her back up the stairs to their room.

Peering out from the corner of her bedroom door was Mrs. Beart. The old woman watched in silence, witnessing the outburst, hearing everything, watching as the young man took her back upstairs.

Colin placed Dagmara down in the bed and covered her with the sheet. Then he picked up the blanket from the floor and covered her shivering body for warmth. He started to move off the bed, she grabbed his hand not wanting him to leave.

"Could you sit with me, just for a little while?" Dagmara asked him, wanting to feel safe.

Seeing she needed the security of his closeness, he moved next to her on the bed, enfolding her in his arms.

"Can we be friends?" she asked him nicely, no longer upset.

"Friends?"

"Yes, why can't we just be friends."

He tried to warm her body with his hands as she snuggled closer, and then Dagmara closed her eyes feeling the heat from his body, knowing he would protect her. Letting go of his anger, Colin thought about what she had asked of him. He never did give her an answer. The temptation turned to yearn, taunting him, as he lied next to her in bed. He wanted more than her friendship, wanting more than just being friends. They were not brother and sister, they were anything but that.

A few minutes later, Dagmara fell asleep. Colin saw her eyes close, her leg bent in the sheet. He let her sleep in his arms, not wanting to disturb her. The feeling felt nice feeling her body next to his, as he held her around and closed his eyes, and then drifted off to sleep.

The next morning, Dagmara opened her eyes and saw Colin sitting in the chair across the room staring at her. Not knowing how long he had been awake, how long he was watching her; she slowly sat up in the bed. The look in his eyes, there was something different about his demeanor towards her; they had grown apart and not closer since last night.

By accident, the necklace had fallen out of her slip, and Colin saw the round object, the stunning, sparkling diamond ring. The mystery as to why she was wearing it, why she had not told him, angered Colin Murphy with his own pending frustration about his feelings for her. The dubious predicament they were placed in became even more entangled by the deceit, by their impassioned expression of lust.

He had been watching her for a few hours unable to sleep, watching as she wrestled in the bed, her body becoming one with the sheet. How peaceful she looked. Her kissable lips, her short blonde hair; he still yearned to bury his face in her long curls. Curls that were no longer there. He hated the way he had treated her last night, upset at her for not telling him about the ring. He mostly despised the man who had given Dagmara the diamond, asking her to be his wife.

Why had she not told him? Why was she keeping it a secret? What feelings if any did she have for him, and would she still think of him as her friend or enemy, or maybe both?

"How long have you been awake?" she asked.

"Awhile."

"How long have you been watching me?"

"Long enough," he said in a coarse tone, as if he was mad at her for betraying him with her secret, a secret she kept so close to her heart. "We're leaving," he told her, and then picked up her clothes and threw them at her on the bed. "Get dressed."

Not knowing he had seen the ring, not understanding his drastic change in demeanor, Dagmara said nothing as she closed the door to the bathroom. She put on the new shirt the old woman had given her, and after she finished getting dressed, they went downstairs. Mrs. Beart greeted them and handed Colin some money.

"For your journey. I would like to give you more, but I'm afraid this is all I can spare."

"We couldn't," Colin said, pushing the money back into her hand.

She closed his hand around the Francs.

"If you're headed towards the train station, look for Mrs. Carlton, tell her I sent you, and she'll give you a place to stay for the night. She'll take care of you."

"Thank you," he replied.

"You take good care of your sister, there is nothing more important in this world than family," Mrs. Beart told Colin, as his eyes widened by her statement. "My glasses may be thick, but I'm not blind. I heard you last night, I hope you both get to where you're going. It's safer if you don't take the main roads," she told them with a friendly smile.

"Thank you," Colin said to Mrs. Beart again, and grabbed Dagmara's hand and they left, leaving the old woman who watched in despair and hope, wishing them both a safe journey home.

CHAPTER 17

Screams deafened in the halls as doctors amputated legs and arms of wounded soldiers, severing the limbs from their desecrated bodies. Countless blood transfusions were performed on the operating table, as the brave soldiers who had survived the sneak attack, only survived to live through another kind of excruciating pain. Rows and rows of beds were filled with injured soldiers who had not died in battle. The room looked more like a blood bath, as nurses rushed in tired step, trying to help each patient who called to them in a tearful cry.

If a soldier was lucky enough to have survived the ambush, then he was in for another torture, the sharp blade of the doctor's knife. Which of the two evils was worse?

In the long line of wounded soldiers one man lied still, unconscious from a head wound, sustaining massive trauma from the blast. A bandage was wrapped tightly around his forehead; blood had seeped through leaving a stain. When the soldiers had found the wounded man, they presumed William Cavill was dead, as they searched the ground for bodies and survivors. When they found his body under the pile of debris and dirt, they found that he was still alive. Miraculously he had survived the deadly explosion, and as they tried to take William's weapon from his hand, he grabbed onto the soldier's arm, not letting go.

They carefully carried his body to the truck, and he was taken immediately to the nearest hospital. The doctors worked on William for several hours, stabilizing his heartbeat, trying to save his life. The massive contusion on his cranial had caused William's body to suffer severely, and at one point in the intricate procedure, his heart rate had plummeted so rapidly, the doctor and attending nurses thought they were going to lose their patient. But something fortuitous had brought William Cavill back from the clutches of death, giving him the strength to live, the will to survive, and that something was Dagmara Morrow.

The doctor finished stitching up the side of his head, leaving a permanent scar, and the pain was alleviated in William's body. Dagmara had given him the will to want to live, in the hope that she was still alive. In the hope, that they would see each other again.

After several days, William opened his eyes regaining consciousness, and looked all around the unfamiliar room. He saw nurses and doctors attending to patients, and then he looked down the long row of injured soldiers, there was more than he wanted to count. The sight was awful. The smell of fresh blood made him nauseous, and as William tried to sit up, he felt an acute pain shooting straight through his head from the injury. He felt the bandage, his heart beating fast, sweat pouring down his face. The enormous shift of pain coursed through his aching bones in silent torture.

He looked all around the room enduring the discomfort, as he searched for his friends among the wounded men, but William could not locate either of them. Stuart and Henry were not there. They were nowhere to be found. And suddenly William started to panic, unable to find his friends. A nurse came by to check on his status, and William asked about his friends, wanting to know their whereabouts, if they were injured.

"You must help me," William said, raising his voice, impatiently wanting to get out of bed and go look for them. "My friends, where are they?"

"You must calm yourself. Now tell me, who are your friends and I'll see if I can find them for you?" she said, wanting to help the wounded soldier, taking an immediate interest.

"Their names are Stuart Shelton and Henry Taylor," he told the cute young nurse with auburn hair.

William grabbed his head in pain, as the nurse gently caressed his forehead, trying to relax his body, not wanting him to go into a convulsion. Then she left his side for a few minutes, as William watched her talk to an older woman who was the head nurse on duty. As he watched the young auburn haired nurse talk to the woman, he saw her eyes widen, her face turn pale.

The young nurse inquired about William's two friends. She found out that Stuart Shelton was found dead, and that Henry Taylor was badly wounded when they found him. The doctors operated, trying to save his life, but they had lost him during the procedure, and he died on the operating table like so many other wounded soldiers who came before him.

Not wanting to relay the devastating news to the handsome soldier, the nurse with auburn hair sat down on the chair beside his bed, and softly told William Cavill without going into great detail that both his friends were dead.

"NO. Stuart, Henry, they can't be dead, they were right behind me!" William shouted, tearing the sheet from his chest, wanting to go search for them.

"Please, you must calm yourself," she told him, as fresh blood started seeping through the bandage, adding pressure to his wound.

She tried to keep William in the bed as he pushed her hands away from his body, trying to get up.

"It's not good to upset yourself, there's nothing you can do for them now. They're in a better place," she said, trying to alleviate his grief with words of comfort, as William wrestled in the bed, not wanting to hear her words, not wanting to hear the truth.

The young nurse placed her hands firmly around his body, restraining him, as two other nurses rushed over to help, and immediately they injected a needle in his arm, giving him a sedative to relieve the pain and quiet his outburst. Slowly William fell back onto the small bed, as the potent drug moved into his bloodstream. His eyes became clouded, his strength decreased, and suddenly his body lied still.

Blinking several times, William felt the pain subside in his body as his eyes closed and he drifted off to sleep, dreaming of his friends.

"You better keep an eye on him, he won't be able to sustain another outburst like this," the head nurse told the young auburn haired nurse who looked upon her patient in despair.

When William awoke a few hours later, the young nurse with auburn hair was sitting beside his bed. He looked over at her, seeing the pretty smile on her pale cheeks, and then looked down at his hand, feeling something between his fingers. The impressionable nurse had found the crumbled picture in his jacket pocket, and had placed the photograph in his hands. William had forgotten all about the picture, thinking only of his friends, the torture they had gone through, their deaths. All three men had known one another since private school, and now, William Cavill was alone. His two best friends in the entire world were gone.

He looked at the photograph in his hand, looking at the distorted image of Dagmara Morrow between the crinkles, and suddenly his eyes became sad, his heart sank in unbearable pain.

"Is that your girl?" the nurse asked him.

He looked at Dagmara's face, and thought back to the moment when they were alone together in his hotel room the night before he left. He slid his finger down the picture's edge, as if he was outlining her naked body with his hands. Dagmara was so beautiful. He remembered how soft her lips felt, the warmth of her touch, his hands gliding down her smooth skin, lying next to her naked.

William reminisced back to the pleasurable memory. The precious moment would be forever cherished in his heart, as a tear slid down his cheek, capturing every detail perfectly in his mind, although it seemed so long ago. The scent of her perfume, the entrancing look in her eyes. The way she made him feel when he was with her. He remembered everything. Not forgetting a curve on her body. Imprinted in his mind. Burned on his soul.

Remembering as Dagmara slid the picture into his hand that morning, and kissed him goodbye, and now William Cavill wished at this very moment, that he had married her. That he had made love to her. That he simply could be with her now. Then he remembered seeing her name on the list, presumed dead were the words written next to her name, and all hope of a promising future had vanished.

The nurse handed him a tissue wanting to ease his pain, as he pushed her hand away.

"Her name is Dagmara," he told the cute auburn haired nurse who looked no more than eighteen. "We were … I mean … we are to be married," he said, instantly crushing the young nurse's dreams that one day she could warm not only the handsome soldier's heart, but also his bed.

"She's very beautiful," the young nurse replied, slightly feeling sad for her own misfortune, hoping that the girl in the photograph was his sister.

She saw the truth expressed by the love in William's eyes as he looked at the picture, pressing his finger against the woman's image. The young nurse was laboring under a misapprehension that would never come to pass.

Like an addict burned with the initial infliction upon contact, the pleasure distorting the brain, tattooing the skin with pain, the flame never died in the ignite. William Cavill's heart would never stop loving Dagmara Morrow. He would never stop wanting her, yearning with an unyielding passion. He would never allow her to leave his thoughts. He would never stop searching for her.

Brady and Cillian waited impatiently at the train station, pacing up and down several times. The Irish friends had arrived early, and found no evidence of Colin and Dagmara, anywhere. They searched the entire place, wandering all around, but they were nowhere to be found.

"We're early give them time, I know Colin will show," Cillian reassured Brady, trying to convince him or rather himself that they would make it.

When they found themselves trapped in France, the four Irish friends had come across some rebels. Colin traded what money they had left for four tickets to England, enabling them to get one step closer to home. Not fully trusting the men who had sold them the tickets, not knowing if they were thieves who had robbed the rightful owners of their possessions, they did not ask questions, receiving four tickets, making a pact of secrecy in return.

Now the fourth ticket was going to be used by Dagmara Morrow and not Mark Quinn, and the four friends were suddenly separated, and their original plan was broken. Brady hated leaving his brother, and he wished they could have all stayed together, and while he and Cillian safely made their way to the station, staying clear of the police and German soldiers, keeping to their route, Colin had impulsively split the group apart, taking a different, unknown path.

At the time, Colin believed it was the best course of action. By dividing, it gave each party a better chance to get to safety. Brady did not know Colin purposely led the German soldiers after he and Dagmara, allowing them to get away. The soldiers had not seen four people, and were hunting only two, giving Brady and Cillian a chance to slip away in the opposite direction. And while Brady and Cillian escaped, Colin had gotten shot, pushing them back an entire evening, possibly two. Colin and Dagmara were lost, and now there was no chance for them to make their way to the train station in time.

"He doesn't even know where he's going. They could be walking in circles or worse," Brady panicked, elevating his voice, afraid for Dagmara and especially his brother.

A couple walking past them looked over in their direction, overhearing Brady's part of the conversation, bringing unwanted attention.

"Colin knows what he's doing, he always has," Cillian said in a lower tone. "Believe me Brady, I know he and Dagmara are safe somewhere, and have eluded the soldiers."

Cillian's words made no impact upon Brady's thoughts, as they sat silently on the bench, their minds flourishing with images of Mark Quinn's death. His body lying on the ground dead. The knife stuck in his chest. His blood on Colin's hands. And what of Dagmara, they had become close with the beautiful young stranger in such a short amount of time. How they found her lying on the ground beneath Mark Quinn. His hands clasped tightly around her throat with intent to kill. If Colin had hesitated a few seconds and not run after them, knowing what his friend was capable of, Mark Quinn would have killed her. Dagmara Morrow's body would be the one lying on the ground. Her body would be the one found by the German soldiers and not his.

Both Cillian and Brady thought back upon that terrible night. Neither of them spoke about it since and the darkness that harbored on their consciences, unable to make the images of the horrid events fade away.

They sat together side by side, and Cillian looked over at his friend. Colin's words repeated through his head like a never ending record, bringing a cold chill to his body. He gave Colin his word that he would get Brady out of France. He promised him that he would get Brady on the train, no matter what, even if it meant leaving without them, leaving Dagmara and Colin behind.

Cillian looked around in desperation, watching the people move on the departing trains, knowing soon that time would catch up with them. Time would turn out to be an unmerciful predator, and not a friend. He would have to keep his promise, even though it would kill him inside, and he wished he had never seen this place, or the war, as he held onto the secret, alone, carrying the burden of such a horrible, tormenting task.

CHAPTER 18

The German soldiers had taken Mark Quinn's body, and now the French police were in search of two young men who were spotted near the corpse. There was a loud knock on the front door of Mrs. Beart's bed and breakfast. Another pounding knock followed, until the old woman wearing thick glasses opened the door. Immediately she was pushed aside by several police officers. They stormed through her establishment without invitation or permission, looking around the downstairs rooms without consideration or consent from the owner.

"What do you want?" Mrs. Beart asked.

A short, thin man with a cruel mouth stepped forward, and the old woman knew he was the one in charge of this disturbance. She limped towards him, as he looked over her run down house, looking over the old woman with no indifference in expression.

"If you have not heard, we are searching for two young men, early twenties, they were heading in this direction," the man said in a commanding tone, carrying his small frame within a powerful presence.

"No, I know nothing," Mrs. Beart protested.

"I didn't ask if you knew anything, I only asked if you saw them, or perhaps gave them shelter for the night?" he said, seeing the woman's hesitation, her nervousness, believing she knew more than she was admitting.

"No, I have not seen them. You can search my rooms if you want, they are not here," the old woman answered, scared by the presence of police officers in her home.

She knew whom he was talking about, the young man and woman she had harbored and given shelter to for a night. Not knowing they were on the run from the police, that they were fugitives, she had helped them escape like many others who came before them, and she would do it again.

"I believe you are lying to me Mrs. Beart. Go check out all the rooms," he commanded to his men, and they obeyed his orders immediately and started searching every room, closed door, tearing up the entire establishment until they were completely satisfied with their findings.

Men raced up the stairs throwing around pieces of furniture, books, pictures, anything that got in their way of the investigation. They did not care about leaving her house in ruins, as they cared nothing for the feeble old woman.

"They're not here," a young police officer stated.

"Where are they," the short Frenchman demanded, looking the old woman straight in the eyes, knowing he could intimidate her.

Frightened by his domineering presence, by the visible weapon placed at his side, Mrs. Beart tried to keep calm and not give in.

"Why are you so interested in them. What have they done?" she asked, knowing she had already sealed her fate with this man from the moment he stepped foot inside her door and she lied to him. He could see right through her untruthful words.

"Murder," he said in a loud tone, trying to shock her, as her eyes opened wide. "Now where are they!" he demanded again, badgering the old woman, as he grabbed her arm and she shrieked in pain as he applied more pressure.

"You're hurting me."

"I'll do more than this if you don't tell me what I want to know," he threatened, and then struck the old woman with a hard hit to the face, and she fell down to the floor in pain.

She looked up at her attacker. The violent man commanded his officers to trash her house, and they started breaking everything in sight until she would relinquish control and give in, and give him what he wanted. Mrs. Beart got herself to her feet and tried to stop the men from destroying her house, but her efforts were futile. They broke mirrors, dishes, anything they could get their hands onto, and when that did not work, the venal man started moving closer to her. The fear inside swarmed over Mrs. Beart's body, as her heartbeat tripled in speed.

"I guess we'll have to do this the hard way then," he said with a vehement gleam in his eyes, and punched her in the stomach.

He dragged her body across the floor to the couch, as she twisted and screamed, pleading with him to let her go. Viciously he tortured the old woman, berating her with questions, hitting her several times in the face and stomach. Unable to withstand the pain, Mrs. Beart started to surrender as her mouth began to swell. She started coughing, choking on her own blood, as he punched her in the ribs, again and again, and she began to bleed internally from the hard hits. His fist bruised, as he repeatedly hit the old woman in the face, knocking out a few of her front teeth, as blood gushed from her lips onto his hands.

And when Mrs. Beart could no longer sustain the abuse, she gave in, and answered the man's questions with truth. Unable to take the brutal beating upon her fragile body, the malicious man with the cruel mouth who enjoyed his job, had broken her arm and crushed the knuckles on her left hand, until she told him everything, more than he knew.

And when the old woman finished telling him everything he wanted to hear, he not only found out where his fugitives were headed and who they would be staying with, he also found out one important and very surprising detail. That the young blonde boy was actually a girl.

Now they would be searching for a boy and a girl, and when the man was done, and he had retrieved all the information he could get from the old woman, he left her on the floor bruised and bleeding with broken bones and gashes that would turn to scars from his violent tirade. He used this type of force in his position gaining what he wanted, as the man felt absolutely nothing for the battered woman.

"Your establishment is now closed!" he shouted, and then took out an expensive white handkerchief from his pocket, and cleaned off the blood from his hands.

The short Frenchman stormed out of Mrs. Beart's house, as the other men followed, leaving her for dead.

Upset from the previous night's events at Mrs. Beart's house, Colin moved alongside Dagmara at a quickened pace, intentionally, unintentionally taking out his feelings of frustration on her. They walked for hours moving along the back roads, trying to avoid the German soldiers, the police, anyone who might bring recognition to their appearance. Not knowing they were being followed, that the French police were after them, searching for them in connection with Mark Quinn's murder, heading in their direction.

Tired and hungry, Dagmara started to move slower as the wind whipped up, tossing her short blonde curls. She brushed a few strands away from her face, as Colin moved her faster along the uneven, rocky path. He grabbed her arm tight to keep up with him, dragging her at times, making her go further. He kept his fast pace, pushing Dagmara harder and harder.

At times she stumbled, as he dragged her, pushing her along, and all the while she remained silent, moving quietly, trying to keep up with him in step, allowing herself to be treated in such a rough manner.

The more she did not resist, the more he pushed her, having her walk faster, as the only thing that Colin Murphy could think about as he trudged down the road, was the diamond ring on her necklace, the small, shinny stone she kept hidden from him, from everyone. It consumed his thoughts, taking control, as he looked over at her, angered by what had transpired between them. The sensuous encounter.

Like a forbidden fruit once sampled he ached deeply inside to devour, Colin yearned to kiss her lips again, placing his mouth all over her sultry skin. The desire coursed through his loins, wanting to soil her body with his vigorous embrace.

Then suddenly Dagmara tripped over a few rocks and fell, as her hands moved out in front of her to brace her fall, hitting her face against the ground. Rapidly Colin rushed to her side, kneeling down on the ground. He lifted her chin up, and saw a patch of dirt on her cheek, a trickle of blood on her bottom lip, and his heart immediately softened. Gently he brushed the dirt from her face, and sat down beside her. The innocent, sweet look in her eyes made him feel horrid for the way he had treated her, pushing her so hard.

"I'm sorry. I don't know what came over me," he apologized. Hurting Dagmara was the last thing in the world that Colin Murphy wanted to do. "I hurt you every time you come close to me. I push you away, and I don't know why?"

"It's okay."

"No, it's not okay … I don't want it to be okay," Colin said, raising his voice.

Dagmara saw how guilty he felt for her fall, for last night, for Mark Quinn, and his reaction to their first kiss. She knew then in that moment, she could see the look in his eyes, he cared for her. The torment about last night's aggressive, lustful encounter ripped at his heart, because … he was secretly in love with her. Colin Murphy had fallen in love with her.

"I understand," she told him, placing her hand on his.

She knew in her heart he was telling her the truth. She felt his pain, his loneliness, his longing desire to be with her. He took out a cloth from his pocket and wiped off the blood from her lip. Colin could not stand to see Dagmara hurt, especially if he inflicted the wound, and she allowed him to push the dagger, drawing the blood, not once telling him to stop.

The way he was looking at her now enticed her whole body, luring her with his seductive stare. Suffocating the very air she breathed. The attraction intensified, as Dagmara felt compelled in overwhelming temptation to kiss his lips again. Her heart trembled with fear and excite becoming closer to this man, closer than she had ever imagined possible.

And before she knew what she had done, Dagmara impulsively leaned forward and kissed Colin Murphy on the lips. He placed his tongue inside her mouth as their lips vigorously became one.

Then abruptly she pulled back, placing her fingers on her mouth, her pulse racing, her skin moistened, becoming dangerously attracted to Colin Murphy. Tasting her sweetness inside his mouth, Colin yearned for more, wanting to place his mouth over every inch of her naked body.

She brushed the dirt off her clothes, simmering his pain that had slightly been relieved. Silently harboring his feelings, Colin now saw the same look in Dagmara's eyes, knowing the lustful way he felt towards her was not unrequited. The desire coursed through her veins like his, and the sudden burst of passion as she kissed his lips, captivated them both inside.

Colin helped Dagmara stand up, and then heard footsteps approaching, and before he could turn around to see who it was behind them, they suddenly found themselves surrounded by several men and women who were part of the French resistance. The small group had been hiding out in the woods when they saw the strangers walking down the road. Immediately they were suspected as spies, working with the Vichy government, and guns were aimed at their heads.

Rapidly Colin and Dagmara were bound at the wrist. Colin resisted, one of the men hit him in the back of his head, and he fell down to his knees. Dagmara struggled to go to him, as two large men kept her steady within their strong grip, tying her hands behind her back.

Swiftly they dragged Colin and Dagmara roughly off the road. The rope dug into her wrists, as the tightness clasped around Colin's hands, trying to get free. They rushed them into the woods with force, as Colin kept looking over at Dagmara, her face radiant with intrepidness.

They were pushed to a halt after being brought to their leader. A Frenchman in his thirties stepped towards them, and looked both of his captives up and down, noticing their ripped, dirty clothes, noticing everything.

"We found them on the road Alex, they were just sitting there. They must be spies," a young man stated with conviction.

"Or working for the Germans," another man shouted.

"Let's kill them!" a woman yelled, as they rallied together against their captives, and the woman pointed her gun directly at Dagmara's head.

"They look harmless," an older man intervened, as Alex assessed the situation, taking in all their comments, considering what to do with the suspicious strangers.

"We can't trust them!" the woman yelled again.

Colin struggled to untie his hands. Alex looked over at Dagmara, and then stepped forward towards Colin.

"Who are you?" Alex asked.

The Irishman looked all around, seeing the violent faces of the people that surrounded he and Dagmara, their guns pointed at their bodies, ready to kill.

"We're just passing through," he answered.

"You boys alone?" Alex asked him.

"Yes."

"Heading back to Ireland?" Alex commented, noticing Colin's Irish accent.

"We were on our way to meet up with my friends. We can't be late," Colin told him.

"I don't trust them," the woman said again, taking an instant dislike to them. "Especially this one," she added, keeping her gun aimed directly at Dagmara's head.

"We bid you no harm," Dagmara spoke, as Alex swiftly looked over at her, intrigued by her articulate British accent. Alex realized that the young boy with short blonde hair was not a boy at all, but a girl, now knowing there was more to these two strangers.

"And we should take you at your word," the woman said unconvinced, as she moved closer to Dagmara. "Sounds more like British than Irish to me."

"They call you Alex, right?" Colin said to the leader, distracting their attention away from Dagmara. "You must believe me, we are not spies of any kind."

Just as Colin finished his last word, a bullet flew straight past Dagmara's head, missing her by an inch. Several more bullets followed, surrounding the entire group. Deadly, fiery pellets swarmed around their bodies through the woods, as Colin instantly jumped on Dagmara, smashing their bodies to the ground, placing his body on top of hers for cover. As they hit the ground, the resistance group started firing back, and Colin and Dagmara kept their heads down low. Trying to free their hands, a bullet tore through Colin's coat, as he shielded Dagmara from the massive gunfire.

"I knew they were spies, they led them straight to us," the woman shouted.

"We should have killed them!" another man yelled, as the gunfire deafened in the ambush.

Colin's eyes opened wide, as he suddenly looked up and saw Alex standing over them, his gun pointed straight at his face like an execution. That second as he looked up into the barrel of the gun seemed like an eternity for Colin Murphy, his heart beating at a triple speed, before Alex bent down beside him and cut the rope around his wrists, and then Dagmara's wrists.

"This is not your fight," he told Colin. "Here, take this," Alex said, and shoved a gun into Colin's hand. "You might need this where you're headed."

Colin slipped his fingers around the weapon, feeling the gun within his hands, enabling him to protect both of them on their journey.

Bullets flooded the air, flying straight at their bodies in the woods, as Alex fired at the enemy with courage. The resistance group scattered for cover, moving all about, when one of the stray bullets crushed into the untrusting woman's skull, killing her upon contact, and she fell down to the ground beside Dagmara. Her eyes, wide open, as her face lied next to Dagmara, and blood splattered onto her skin. Immediately Dagmara wiped off the tiny red droplets of blood, and lowered her face.

"You must go," Alex said, raising his voice among the gunfire. "It will be too late for you both if you don't leave now."

The enemy approached closer, outnumbering the small resistance group, as the bullets increased in magnitude, gaining in distance within each shot fired.

"Go straight through those trees till you get to the end, and then you'll come to a road. You can take that road into the next town or wherever you're headed," Alex told him, befriending the young Irishman, believing that they were innocent of the crimes that his friends accused them of.

Colin was just about to ask Alex for directions to the train station, when another bullet flew directly past their heads.

"GO!" Alex shouted, and shook Colin's hand. "Good luck," he said to him, and then stood up and started firing fearlessly at the enemy.

Rapidly Colin and Dagmara started running through the woods, increasing in speed as they ran away from the gunfire, distancing themselves farther from the enemy. They escaped unnoticed, as the resistance group occupied the German soldiers' attention. Colin tightened his grip around Dagmara's hand, and around the gun in his other hand, and they kept moving forward through the woods without looking back.

The gunfire started to fade, distancing themselves farther from the deadly battle, as neither of them had stopped running. Dagmara and Colin hurriedly made their way to the road, and kept on moving forward at a quickened pace, not once looking back. Not wanting to see if Alex or his friends had gotten killed, or had been taken by the German soldiers.

Barely escaping with their own lives, both Colin and Dagmara knew the German soldiers and the French police would never stop searching for them, until they were found, killed, or out of the country.

CHAPTER 19

Not knowing if some or any of the resistance group had survived, especially Alex, Colin and Dagmara had no time to think upon their deaths or triumph over the enemy, as they continued to move farther away from the Germans, placing themselves in safety. Colin took a quick look behind him, seeing no one was following, they started to slow down, still keeping to a quickened pace.

They traveled feverishly for hours without stopping, without faltering from being physically exhausted, without letting the cool night air affect their bodies. Darkness was almost upon them, and soon nightfall would intertwine with evening, as they kept moving forward, placing vast distance between themselves and the enemy. Unable to see down the path as the sky became dark, the road they traveled was desolate. Colin and Dagmara were now lost, as every road looked the same, not knowing which direction they were heading, if they were even moving in the right direction.

They kept moving forward, and Colin knew they were not going to find Mrs. Carlton's house, they were not going to make it to that town, and especially they were not going to make it to the train station in time. Brady and Cillian would go without them; they would have to without choice. Cillian made him a promise, and Colin knew he would keep his word, even if it meant leaving without him so his brother would be safe. Brady would fight, resist wanting to leave, but eventually Cillian would convince him, and they would board the train and head for home, leaving both he and Dagmara behind to find their own way. To find a new way to get out of the country. To find the means and people to gain them access to get home.

Colin looked over at Dagmara, seeing her rosy cheeks from the cold, the tiredness in her step as she slowed in pace, and he was unable to tell her what he knew. That they were trapped in France, with no way out. And as her eyes sparkled in the dark, he knew he would be her only chance for survival. All they had now were each other. He would protect her and keep her safe, as Colin felt the gun within his hand, knowing he would do so, even if it meant his life.

Late in the evening, they stumbled upon a town and rented a room for the night, using some of the money Mrs. Beart had given them. They just started to settle into their room, when there was a loud knock on the front door, and several police officers stormed in. The man in charge was the same short Frenchman that had inquired about Dagmara and Colin's whereabouts earlier. The same vicious man that had accosted Mrs. Beart in her home, beating the old woman for lying to him, for helping the fugitives escape. He yelled his questions and demanded answers, as the man and woman who owned the establishment immediately answered him, giving him all the information he requested.

"We are looking for two Irish boys, or rather a boy and a girl. Have you seen them or rented them a room?"

"Yes, they're in the room now," the husband answered, not allowing his wife to speak.

"Thank you, your assistance will be much appreciated in apprehending the criminals."

Instantly the police officers disbursed, and stormed towards the room that Dagmara and Colin occupied. Thrashing in a loud stomp, the men ran down the hall towards the end, and then without announcing their presence, they smashed through the door and moved inside.

Just as they bolted into the room, they caught a glimpse of Dagmara moving out the window as Colin pulled her through from the outside, and they were unable to apprehend the fugitives, as they got away.

"Quickly, go after them," the short Frenchman shouted, as the police officers ran back down the hall and out the front door.

"Stop, you are under arrest!" one of the officers yelled, as Colin and Dagmara ran down the street trying to evade the French police.

Unable to escape, the pursuit heated into a lavish chase. Colin and Dagmara ran towards the corner running through the alley towards the next street, trying to increase their speed, as the men closed in on them gaining in distance. There was nowhere for them to run.

"Shoot them!" the short Frenchman commanded, and the order was immediately obeyed, as several police officers opened fire, aiming their weapons directly at Dagmara Morrow and Colin Murphy.

The deadly bullets flew through the air, speeding like lightening, heading straight towards their targets, when a man suddenly appeared in the dark, standing on the corner of the street. He lit a lighter having the small flame give off light in the darkness, and then whispered in a deep voice, alerting his presence. "Over here."

A bullet sliced through Colin's coat just as they ducked out of the way of the fiery pellets of death, and moved in the direction of the stranger.

He lit the lighter one more time, barely showing his face. "Hurry, follow me," he whispered.

Hearing the ferocious men storming down the street, the guns firing in consecutive order, Colin and Dagmara had no choice but to follow the stranger and allow him to aid them in their escape. The man led them down the street and onto another, as they moved along at a fast pace, eluding the police.

"In here," he motioned, and they followed the man inside.

The stranger took them to his flat. He turned on a small lamp for light, locked the door behind them, and as he turned around, they finally saw his face. The middle aged man was clean shaven and well kempt. Dressed in an expensive suit wearing a long black coat, he wore a hat, gloves and a scarf for warmth, and looked more like a spy than a traveler on his way through Europe.

"Why did you help us?" Colin asked, distrusting the stranger who just happened to appear at the precise moment they needed help.

"You were in trouble, anyone who is running from the police is in need of help," the man answered, as his words flowed smoothly out of his mouth, as if he was trained for this line of questioning.

"I asked you why?" Colin said again, still distrusting the stranger.

Without hesitation the man answered, "I have connections with the government. I heard the police were searching for a young Irish couple, I thought I could help," he told them, as his French accent suddenly disappeared, and his thick British accent immersed.

"You're English?" Dagmara said with surprise, as the man swiftly took his eyes off Colin and looked at her.

"Is she your sister, or your girl?" he asked him, as his eyes shifted towards Colin.

"She's, my sister?" Colin stated, disliking the shady look in the man's eyes.

"Interesting. Your sister must have grown up in England then," he commented, disbelieving Colin, noticing the difference in their accents, noticing more than that.

"She was sent to school in London," Colin told him, disliking the stranger's inquisitive questions, as his own suspension of disbelief sharpened.

The man noticed that Dagmara looked at Colin when he made the statement about being his sister, accidentally giving him the truthful answer to his question without them knowing.

"What exactly do you do sir?" Dagmara asked.

His eyes dark and imperious, as an unsettling feeling swarmed over Colin Murphy's body, as the clever stranger looked at Dagmara. Instantly he knew this man was not whom he pretended to be. A wealthy aristocrat he was not.

"Why don't you both relax and take off your coats," he told them, avoiding the question.

Colin looked at Dagmara, intensely, and she knew exactly what he was thinking, he did not have to say a word, they both were thinking the same thing. The stranger's mysteriousness brought uneasiness to the precarious predicament they found themselves placed in. Danger lurked not only in the desolate corners of the streets, as the police searched for their fugitives, but also inside this room, as the latter of the two deemed darker.

They sat down on the couch together. Dagmara stayed close to Colin, as the stranger took off his coat, opened a bottle of scotch, dropped a few pieces of ice into a glass, and poured himself a drink.

"Would you like some, or perhaps your sister is too young."

"She won't be having any, but I'll take one," Colin replied, as his intrepidness coursed through his words, tightening his mouth.

"Would you like some water?" he asked Dagmara.

"Yes, thank you."

The stranger handed them both a glass, and Colin noticed the man's finger slide suggestively over Dagmara's hand. Dagmara was neither blind to his hand brushing across her skin, the provocative look in his eyes, or the disdain that Colin had for this man, as she herself did not trust him, not knowing if they could believe a single word he spoke.

Colin waited for the man to take the first sip.

"Oh, I see," the man said with a laugh, and took a large sip of his drink. He could read people well; it was his expertise, knowing they thought he might have drugged their drinks. He was cleverer than they presumed.

Colin took a sip of his drink, and then Dagmara followed, as the man watched noticing the closeness between them. Like a predator watching his young prey, he gained insight, waiting for the kill. Observing their movements, the way they looked at each other, their words, the mysterious stranger gained power over his friends and especially his enemies, enabling him to find their weakness, and slaughter them in triumph.

"You never answered the question. What is it you do?" Colin asked, taking another sip of his drink.

"I work for the government," he answered, pouring himself another scotch.

"Which one?" Colin insolently slandered, insulting the man with his question.

"The British government of course," the man responded with no inflection in his voice, disregarding Colin's insolence.

"You're a spy!" Dagmara said loudly, as Colin gave her a look not to say anything further, now knowing they were dealing with a very clever individual.

He laughed. "Your sister has quite an imagination."

"What is it you're doing in France?" Colin asked.

"I'm gathering information, now that's all I can really tell you both," the man answered, looking directly at Colin with a piercing cold look in his eyes, telling him he was no match for him, he would lose. "Now if you're done interrogating me, I have a few questions of my own. Did you kill that boy?"

A cold chill crawled over Dagmara's body, as the man gave her a look like he was looking straight through her, devouring her alive.

"We thank you for helping us, but we have to go now," Colin said abruptly, and grabbed Dagmara's hand, and moved her to the door.

"Wait!" the man shouted in a frightening tone. "I didn't mean to accuse you both of anything, but I had to ask," he said lowering his voice, not wanting them to leave.

"Is that why the police are after us?" Colin asked.

And in that moment, the stranger understood everything. They had lost before they ever realized what they had given him in information.

"You really don't know do you," he answered, seeing the expression on their faces.

They were not spies. They were not even dangerous. They were just two young kids mistakenly lost in a country at war, in over their heads.

"Please sit down, and I'll tell you both what I know," he said to them in a gesture of kindness, motioning to the couch.

The eloquence of his words roared with a thickening façade to the dark underlying of his true intentions. He intimidated them with the domineering look in his eyes, as the more powerful his forceful presence became.

"Colin," Dagmara whispered to him, not wanting to stay.

"Colin, is that your name," the stranger noted, gaining more information on them every second.

Colin and Dagmara moved away from the door and sat back down on the couch, as the stranger noticed Dagmara holding onto Colin's hand not letting go. The unsettling feeling scorched through their bodies like a warning flame of danger, telling them not to trust this man. Not knowing if they could believe anything he told them.

CHAPTER 20

"And what's your name Blondie?"

"Her name is not important," Colin told the stranger, disliking the way he was looking at Dagmara. "What's your name?"

"I mean no harm to you both," he said, as the words flowed smoothly out of his mouth again noticing their apprehension, and the more he reassured them of his kindness, the more suspicious they became. "David Bragger," he replied.

"Bragger," Colin mused, not believing for a second that was his real name, taking the identity for a false cover.

"They found a young man slain in the fields several days ago. The police have been searching for both of you for questioning."

"Then why were they trying to kill us back there?" Colin asked.

"They think you are spies, consorters with the enemy. Clever ones at that, they've been looking for you both for quite some time. And each time you've managed to escape, miraculously."

"We didn't kill anyone, it was an accident," Dagmara said.

"I didn't figure you both for murderers, but that young man, he was a friend of yours?" Bragger asked, as if he already knew the answer to his question, wanting them to reaffirm his suspicions.

"He was my best friend," Colin answered.

"Now I know why you've been desperately trying to get out of the country. You were eluding the police even before you knew why."

"Can you help us?" Dagmara asked.

"We don't need his help," Colin instantly stated.

"I would be happy to help both of you if you want," Bragger replied, smiling at Dagmara.

"How do we know we can trust you?" Colin asked, still unconvinced that David Bragger was not an enemy.

"Do you have a choice," he said to them, knowing they did not. "Why don't you both stay here with me for the night, and tomorrow I'll get you some new clothes, and I'll see what I can do."

"Can you get us safe passage on the next train heading to London?" Colin inquired, wanting and not wanting to believe in this man.

"But what about …" Dagmara started to say.

"It's just the two of us here, no one else," Colin rapidly interjected, overlapping her words, knowing she might mention Cillian and Brady.

Closely David Bragger watched their expressions, as Dagmara understood Colin did not want her to mention his friends, and she obliged him, and said nothing further.

"There's no one else with you?" Bragger asked them.

"No," Colin stated with reassurance, not falling into his trap.

There was something in David Bragger's eyes that Colin did not trust. His suspicious demeanor. Some underlying feeling towards the stranger made him dangerous. This man was not being completely truthful with them, but they had no choice but to believe that he would help them, that he would get them safely out of the country, as Colin looked over at the clock seeing the late hour of the evening. And then he knew, Brady and Cillian would go without him, and now he and Dagmara had no other way out.

"We have to go."

"NO, I'm not leaving without my brother," Brady told Cillian, as he looked at the clock noticing the time.

"The train is leaving, we must go," Cillian urged his friend.

"I told you I'm not going without Colin. I can't. I won't!"

"They're not coming, look at the time, they would have already been here by now. They're not going to make it," Cillian stressed, as the train started to move slowly down the tracks.

A few late ticket holders moved aboard as the train started to leave the station.

"We have to go now!" Cillian shouted.

"He's not your brother," Brady said, raising his voice, intentionally hurting Cillian with his harsh words, knowing Cillian felt as if Colin was his brother too.

"We might not share the same blood, but he's more like a brother to me than I've ever had. You know that Brady," Cillian said, angered by his friends impudent words.

The train started to pick up speed, and Cillian forcefully grabbed hold of Brady's coat.

"This is our only chance Brady, if we don't go now, we'll be stuck here, and Colin wouldn't want that, for either of us. I promised him I would get you on the train, that I would get you out of here. Are you listening to me Brady?" Cillian shouted, trying to impress upon his friend the urgency of the situation. "He wants you to go without him."

Cillian's words suddenly registered in Brady's head, convincing him to leave. He knew his brother, knowing he would have said that, now realizing why they had separated.

"I'll knock you out and drag you with me if I have to," Cillian threatened.

"No, you won't have to do that," Brady acquiesced, knowing Cillian was just doing what Colin wanted, resigning to the fact that he would have to leave without his brother.

Brady had always done what his brother wanted. Colin had been more like a father to him than an older brother. He would comply with Colin's wishes, even though everything inside of him was screaming not to leave. Not wanting to leave his brother behind. Not wanting to leave both he and Dagmara in this place of death, with no means for escape, with no means for survival.

"I'm sorry for what I said, I didn't mean it," Brady apologized, feeling horrid for the things he said to his friend.

"I know, let's go," Cillian urged, forgiving his friend, and both men ran alongside the moving train, racing along the tracks.

They jumped aboard just in time as the train started to increase in speed, and they were the last passengers to board. They watched as the train left the station, leaving France, moving closer towards home. Soon they would be back in Ireland, and as Cillian looked out among the sad and happy faces of the people left behind, Brady was dying inside. Like a knife had sliced his heart in half, leaving the other half behind. He wanted nothing more at this moment than to have his brother by his side. They had always done everything together. Every time they got into trouble, they prevailed as a team. Colin had always looked out for his brother, keeping him safe and out of trouble.

A powerful bond was formed between the Irish brothers. A silent pact that could never be undone. Erased. Changed. Brady felt both he and his brother being torn apart, ripped at the seams like a tear. He had a horrible feeling about Colin and Dagmara being left behind. Why had Colin not shown at the train station? Where were they? They knew this was their only chance to escape. Now both of them were trapped, amongst strangers, amongst enemies, with no other way to get them across the border to safety.

And the longer Brady looked out among the dreariness of the countryside, and the German soldiers that patrolled the roads in fearless force, the more frightened he became, both he and Cillian became, as the alarming question echoed loudly inside their heads, repeating like a shriek of terror. How would Colin and Dagmara now find their way home? How would both of them now make their way out of France … alive?

David Bragger watched as Colin and Dagmara went into the bedroom, waiting for the door to close, and then immediately he turned around and placed a phone call.

Quietly Colin opened the door and peered into the room, watching as David Bragger dialed a number. Dagmara watched in silence, as the peril suffocated them in their unsafe surroundings, feeling defenseless.

"I have them both. They're here with me now at my place," Bragger said to the man on the other end of the line. "I'll bring them both to you in the morning."

Colin's instincts were dead on. His intuition was right. Expecting the phone call, knowing the man who called himself David Bragger, assuming that false identity, was not working for the British government. He was working against them, against his own country, aligning himself with the enemy, as the spy just revealed himself as a traitor. And the danger of Colin and Dagmara knowing the truth, knowing who he was, or rather who he was not, placed both their lives in peril, along with their existence for survival.

They knew too much, they had seen too much, and Colin knew a man like David Bragger would not allow them to leave, he could not afford them to escape, and that notion oppressed heavily on his thoughts as he looked over at Dagmara.

"I'll find out what I can. The boy's name is Colin. I don't know the girl's name, but they are not brother and sister, I can assure you of that. The boy you found in the field was their friend, they wouldn't tell me much more than that … if I have to, I know what to do," Bragger stated, reassuring the man on the other end of the conversation that he would follow orders, and then he took out a gun from his desk drawer, and placed it down on top of the table.

The revealing of the weapon instantly caught Colin Murphy's attention, and the door accidentally squeaked from movement, alarming their captor. Colin knew he was playing in a whole different realm than what he was used to back in Ireland. And as Dagmara gasped in fear, David Bragger immediately hung up the phone, and swiveled his head towards their direction, staring straight at them!

The strength started to return in William Cavill's body, regaining feeling, healing at a quickened pace. The doctor and nurses had taken excellent care of the courageous soldier, especially the young auburn haired nurse who took an instant fancy to William. She sat by his side almost every day, helping her handsome patient recover. She brought him food, she read to him, she even sneaked him special treats when the head nurse was not looking.

Knowing fraternization with patients was strictly prohibited; she broke the forbidden rule and engaged in many long, late night conversations with the soldier, keeping William company, having him keep her company in return. Lonely, the auburn haired nurse playfully imagined that William Cavill was her fiancé. That when he was better, she would return home with him. But it was just an unrealistic thought that faded through her heart, knowing his heart belonged solely to another. And it made her sad at times seeing his pain and devotion. She could never tell him. He would never know how she truly felt, knowing he would never feel the same.

When William was strong enough, he got permission to make a long distance phone call to his father. The special privilege came as a favor to him or rather to his father from one of the doctors who had gone to college with Jonathan Cavill. William was taken to a private room where the auburn haired nurse left him alone to place the call. Wanting and not wanting to speak to his father, William knew no one else he could call to ask for help.

He and his father had not parted on the best of terms. Words of anger were left unsettled, disputing over his dangerous position in the war. If his father could have had his way, he would have placed his son in a safe zone. Some desk job where he would be out of reach from the enemy, and no harm would come to him. But William would not allow his father to call in special favors for him, while both his friends were placed in peril.

Going against his father's wishes, refusing his help, William took his place alongside his two best friends Henry Taylor and Stuart Shelton, who were now dead, as he almost took a third seat right next to them in death.

Miraculously William had survived, knowing it was not his time to die. He knew he had been saved or rather spared to save Dagmara. His father would be pleased he was alive. That he had survived the violent ambush, but he would also chastise him for going, for leaving England. William would never convince his father otherwise, and he stopped trying the day he left, knowing he would never change his mind. But now after everything he had seen and gone through, losing his best friends in a bloody, vicious attack, William Cavill somehow felt his father was right, and maybe he should have listened to him after all.

Now it was too late, it was too late for a lot of things, but not to set things right with his father. Jonathan Cavill would be furious, but he would forgive his son. He would help his son. He would look forward towards his son's safe return home. William had not written to his father, he had only called him once from Venice before he left on his assignment, and the heated words exchanged in the conversation had angered him not to write.

The anger had ceased, subsiding in fallen history. William had forgiven his father, succumbing to his own rebellious defeat, and their argument no longer remained important. Not wanting to fight anymore, the only thing that still worried William about his father's powerful presence was the fact that he had not mentioned anything about Dagmara.

He had written to Dagmara earlier telling her that he had told his father all about her and their engagement, but that was not true. Jonathan Cavill knew nothing of their relationship, that they even had one, and he especially knew nothing about their engagement. William had not asked permission from Dagmara's father or from his own to marry her. Without acknowledgment from either family giving consent, they had followed their own impulsive hearts and gotten engaged. Dagmara Morrow had accepted his ring, his vow of marriage, accepting his sweet proposal before he went off on his deadly mission.

William would ask his father to send someone to search for Dagmara, to bring her back to him. He knew his father employed many men, having extensive connections. His power and wealth would secure a man who could get passed the heavily guarded border and sneak into France. That man would go undercover with false papers, allowing him access to files regarding the investigation of the crash. He would find out everything, whether she had escaped the disaster or was buried somewhere unseen in the debris.

This man his father would send would find out if his future wife was still alive. Then they would know either way, because nothing could be worse for William Cavill than waiting with no means to an end, not knowing if Dagmara

Morrow was dead or alive. William would not rest until he knew, until he saw her body and they brought her back to him. He would not let her go without a fight, even if it killed him.

Jonathan Cavill would recruit a man immediately, as William knew his father would do anything for him, he always had. He had always given his son everything in the world; anything he wanted William got, and if he knew how much Dagmara meant to him, Jonathan Cavill would do whatever was in his power to help his son.

Once Jonathan Cavill heard about Dagmara Morrow, her background, her family, her beauty and sweetness, he would be pleased with his son's choice, even if he thought he was marrying too young. He would not call off the engagement. And the more William thought about the conversation he was about to have with his father, the more he realized how much his father really loved him. Through all their arguments and disagreements, through all the rough patches while growing up, school and college, and especially the war, William now realized his father only wanted the best for him. And at that moment, he could not have been more proud to be the son of Jonathan Cavill.

After the death of his mother when William was only eleven, his father had brought him up the best he could without help from a woman. His father had several mistresses, but not one did he marry or bring home to spend the night. He did not want to inflict pain on his son by dishonoring his mother's home, and especially her bed.

Blinded by the rage of not having a mother, hating his father for the women he took to bed, defying his mother's remembrance by the lust he craved, William realized for the first time, that it was only a hunger for companionship that his father longed for, and nothing more. And as William dialed the number, waiting for his father to pick up, the fear inside strengthened. His pulse raced as the operator clicked over and placed the connection, listening to the echoing silence for his father's voice.

There were two rings before a deep voice answered on the other end of the line. "Hello."

William could barely breathe hearing his father's voice. "Hello father," he answered.

"William is that you!" his father shouted into the phone, happily surprised to hear his son's voice, knowing he was still alive.

CHAPTER 21

Dagmara slid across the table hitting the wall hard as the gun went off, as Colin and David Bragger struggled violently for possession of the deadly weapon. Bragger punched Colin in the stomach, as the Irishman fought with his fists, used to street fighting and bar brawls back home. He was not trained like David Bragger, but his worldliness, fist fighting, and youth, gave him a slight advantage over a man of his caliber.

Colin's mouth was bleeding, as the blood dripped down his chin to the floor, and a bruise formed around his left eye. Dagmara lied on the ground, her forehead bleeding. She was momentarily knocked unconscious from the heavy hit against her head, as David Bragger slammed her against the wall in a vicious attack as she tried to help Colin.

Neither man would let go of the gun, as Colin smacked Bragger in the face breaking his nose with the strong punch. Blood started pouring from his nostrils, as David Bragger shook off the immediate sting, as both men were relentless in giving up their position.

Then suddenly Bragger reached for the letter opener on the desk, and jabbed the sharp end into Colin's wounded shoulder. Colin yelled in pain as the acute object tore at his bandage inflicting enormous discomfort to his body. The puncture reopened the wound, drawing blood.

Colin punched David Bragger in the face again with his powerful strength, and then pulled the sharp object out of his flesh, when the gun went off a second time, as Bragger pulled the weapon towards him. He placed his hand around the gun and aimed it straight at Colin's chest, as Colin forcefully punched him in the nose again and ripped the gun out of his hands, and the weapon fell to the floor, spinning towards Dagmara.

Bragger punched Colin in the stomach, again and again, with repeated robust hits to the ribs, as blood gushed out of his nostrils, and he withstood the pain, as he kicked Colin down to the ground. Then he picked up the letter opener, and violently moved towards his throat. An image of Colin's past flashed before his eyes, his father beating him, kicking him, overpowering him in strength. Now that same attack was being carried out by another man, but with the same malice.

Suddenly a bullet was fired into the air, and David Bragger rapidly looked over and saw Dagmara holding the gun, aiming it directly at his body.

"Drop it!" Dagmara demanded, as she slowly stood up, holding the gun tight within her hands, momentarily stopping David Bragger, as he let go of the weapon and stood up. "Move away from him," she ordered.

The vile David Bragger moved away from Colin, and then instantly he reversed his attack, and placed his full attention on Dagmara. He wiped the blood from his nose with his hand, smearing the redness on his torn shirt, and then he started walking towards her, undauntedly, moving closer and closer towards her and the gun.

"Stay where you are," she shouted, but he did not listen to her authority, and kept moving towards her, towards her shaking hand that was holding the weapon.

For a brief second, Dagmara shifted her eyes and looked at Colin lying on the ground. Bragger took that opportunity, lunged forward towards her, and before Dagmara knew what had happened … she fired the gun.

Her pulse raced as if her heart was going to jump right out of her body. Silence deafened inside the room. Slowly Colin stood up and moved towards her. He grabbed his bruised ribs in soreness, took the gun from her hand, and pointed it directly at their assailant. The bullet had sliced through David Bragger's right thigh, momentarily immobilizing him from movement, as he winced in excruciating pain, his hands full of blood.

Colin destroyed the phone with a single shot, and then walked over to the desk and opened the drawer. He threw the contents onto the table and hurriedly looked through the papers. He grabbed an envelope that had a government seal and a clip of money, and slipped them into his coat pocket. Then he walked back over to Bragger, smacked him in the back of his head with the gun, and the traitor fell down to the ground unconscious from the hard hit.

"That should keep you quiet for awhile," Colin said to him.

Then he grabbed Dagmara and they ran out of the flat leaving David Bragger, leaving with a pocket full of stolen information and money. Hoping they had slowed him down long enough not to catch up with them, as they raced towards safety in their electrifying, perilous escape.

They made their way on foot through the night, knowing they could no longer stay with Mrs. Carlton. If they ever reached her house, that would be the first place their trackers would be searching for them, so they were forced to find another hiding place. A place where they could seek shelter, time to rest, think upon their next course of action to get them out of the country, before the French police, the German soldiers, and especially David Bragger found them.

And the farther they distanced themselves from the danger, the farther they were from getting home, and the closer Dagmara and Colin became. The closer it brought them together as companions, more than just a brother and sister. A relationship sparked by peril, lust, and powerless, dominating fear.

Their trackers would be looking for them at every hotel, every bed and breakfast. They could not go to any of them. Nowhere was safe. Colin and Dagmara roamed like vagabonds, wearing ripped clothing, looking less like aristocrats and more like thieves. They knew David Bragger would wake up shortly and inform his contacts in the Vichy government, and they would start tracking them, if they were not already. Bragger would be searching beside other powerful, ruthless men who were looking for two Irish boys, or for some, a boy and an English girl.

And all Dagmara Morrow and Colin Murphy had now was each other, and no one else. They only had one another to rely on for survival, to count on for comfort, some type of solace from the terror that surrounded them in every direction. That notion not only scared Dagmara, but brought them closer, closer in a way neither of them ever imagined.

Several days they traveled together, hiding in places David Bragger nor the police would ever think to look. They took a room at a small overlooked bed and breakfast that had been turned into a café. They signed the register under the name of Mr. and Mrs. James Caulfield. They were just passing through they told Mrs. Bronchet, the middle aged woman who ran the establishment. Her hair turning gray before time, haggard by her exhausting, exuberant children who ran wild through the halls while her husband was off fighting in the war.

They had come across this place when they stopped to get something to eat. The woman's misfortune turned into a fortuitous one for both Colin and Dagmara, and no one, not even David Bragger would think to look for them in this café.

The woman seemed harmless, she would not be a threat to them, they felt confident she would not call the police and turn them in. She had no idea who they really were, or that they were wanted for murder, and hounded like fugitives. Mrs. Bronchet chased after her five-year-old son who had stolen a doll from his younger sister who sat on the floor crying. The eldest daughter who looked older than her eight years remained silent, sitting in the corner looking at Dagmara and Colin with her large black eyes, watching their every move. Watching as they paid in cash for the room, handing over several Francs to her mother, giving her extra money for some food.

They used the money Colin had taken from David Bragger, and the woman's eyes widened seeing the large bills, wondering how two young people could be so well off, when she was so poor. Not knowing that the money was stolen, she gladly accepted the cash, as Colin and Dagmara watched her place the Francs into her pocket, and not in the cash drawer.

Slowly Dagmara and Colin walked up the stairs towards their room. Towards the place where they would spend the night together. Towards the room where they would share one bed. As they moved along the stairs, moving closer to the bedroom, they both fell silent, trapped in their own deciphering thoughts, moving closer to the danger that lurked behind the closed door. That lied within the bed.

Neither of them was able to forget for a second the savage desire that consumed them the nights before in a weakened moment of lust. An attraction that now deemed more dangerous than the men who were hunting them. An intoxicating fire of trouble that scorched through their bodies with insatiable hunger, taunting them in untamed yearn.

Colin grabbed his ribs, feeling a slight discomfort, as Dagmara helped him take off his coat and shirt. Bruises had formed on his lower abdomen from the hard hits he received earlier from the fight with David Bragger. Dagmara cleaned his shoulder, rewrapping the wound with a fresh bandage. The letter opener had torn into his flesh, enlarging the wound, increasing the damage, as Colin suffered silently in pain.

Drawn to the Irishman, Dagmara was unable to look away; her body feeling aroused just being near. They had flirted with the attraction, igniting the initial flame, conflicting them inside. A searing temptation lured Dagmara to him, wanting to kiss Colin's wound, his lips, to feel his hands upon her skin again, unable to control the want. Her entire body elevating with warmth, and the longer she stood next to Colin Murphy's body, staring at his chest, the harder it was for her to move away.

Colin had already fallen in love with Dagmara, even before he knew he was in love with her, he wanted her, he wanted to make love to her. The ache consumed him, longing to feel her lips upon his mouth again, his hands upon her luscious thigh, the lust mounting, as he felt her body brush against his.

The connection intensified by the events that occurred over the past weeks, and especially over the past several days. The rush of escaping death had placed them both in a very precarious place, exciting them instead of succumbing to the emotion that should have been provoked. Seduced by Colin Murphy's vigorous presence, he was a man who had saved her life more than once, and that notion equally scared and allured Dagmara at the same time. Her heart confused by every passion filled kiss he stole.

Slowly Dagmara unbuttoned her coat and took it off. Then she started undoing her shirt as Colin watched in silence. As she took off her shirt, undoing one button at a time, moving her hand down her chest, the thin material of her slip immediately incited him, and then she took off her pants and stood in front of him.

Neither of them said a word in the tantalizing moment. Her aggressiveness enticed him, as Dagmara moved her hands to his pants, and started unbuttoning them. He allowed her to do so without saying a word, wanting and not wanting her to stop. Her sexual forwardness speeded up their heartbeats, as the seductive look in Colin Murphy's eyes pierced through her propriety, shattering her virtuous innocence.

He felt her fingers undoing the buttons, moving the zipper down. Her breathing doubled, her pulse raced, and then forcefully Colin grabbed her hand stopping Dagmara from going further.

"Stop it Dagmara!" he shouted, angered by her provocative behavior.

The roughness of his grip frightened her.

"I thought this is what you wanted."

Surprised by her audacious actions, stunned by her words, the vivacious young woman who stood before him was full of passion, waiting to be unleashed. He wanted to ravish her, to place his hands upon her naked body, his lips over every inch of her skin, again and again. She was offering him everything he had silently yearned for, ever since he had kissed her lips and felt her soft skin beneath his fingers. But Colin did not want her in this way, not wanting Dagmara's most intimate embrace because she felt obligated to him for saving her life. It took everything inside of him to push her away, pushing away the one thing he wanted most.

"Why are you doing this?" he asked, angered by her forwardness.

"Isn't this what you wanted?"

"Not like this," Colin said, getting more upset, as his arrogance hardened through his words. "I'm not charity!" he shouted insolently.

"No, you're wrong," she told him, wanting to say more, but unable to get the words out.

No longer did Dagmara Morrow care about their different upbringings, or their different status in life. All of that was forgotten after what they had gone through together, after their magnificent kiss. A kiss that overshadowed all other kisses. At one time Dagmara did feel superior, but now, none of that mattered anymore. She thought of Colin as her equal, even better than her in ways, and his impudent statements hurt her, having him think she regarded him in such a degrading manner.

"You feel you owe me," he said, raising his voice again, intentionally hurting Dagmara with his harsh words. His pride bruised by his own prejudice of her and the upper class. "Why would you think I would ever want you!" he yelled, as his contemptuous words and impetuous reaction burned through his tongue the moment he said them to her.

Abruptly Colin grabbed his shirt and coat and stormed out of the bedroom, running down the stairs, wanting to get as far away as possible from Dagmara and the room. And as Dagmara watched him leave, watching Colin Murphy run away from her, she slowly sunk down to the floor in the middle of the room. She did not want to argue with him, she just wanted them to be friends, not enemies, anything but that. She regarded Colin's friendship highly, whether he knew it or not, and all she really wanted from him now, was for him to like her, accept her, and possibly even someday, love her.

"I've ruined everything," she whispered sadly, as a tear slid down her cheek, not wanting to be left alone, not knowing when and if Colin Murphy would return.

Colin had no idea how much Dagmara needed him, wanted him, and now desired him with her whole body. She might never make it home. She might never see her family and especially her fiancé, ever again. And all she longed for now, was for the man who had saved her life, countless times, to walk back through the door so she could tell him how she felt.

He was wrong about her. She was not like the other rich, spoiled aristocrats he classified her with, she did what she wanted, she lived the way she wanted, and not by anyone's standards.

Could Colin Murphy not see that? Could he not see the sparkle in her eyes every time he looked at her, the way her heart speeded up every time he got close? Had all this time together not shown him how much Dagmara Morrow truly cared for him. How much she fancied him. How much their friendship meant, how much he meant to her. Could he not see ... that she was beginning to fall in love with him.

CHAPTER 22

Hours later, the handle turned on the outside of the bedroom door, and Dagmara looked up, still sitting in the same position on the floor. As the door opened, Colin walked into the room with an insufferable look on his face. Slowly she stood up, and one word described the picture of what Colin Murphy saw as Dagmara Morrow stood in her sheer slip by the lamp. Stunning. Her lashes flickered, her mouth slightly open, her eyes had changed to turquoise in color from the tears. She looked unbelievably lovely as he walked towards her. Her body trembled with each step he took.

And there he could see for the very first time the look in her eyes, she was in love with him, as he was with her. And Colin Murphy found himself in another night, in another bed, but this time with the same girl. A smile crossed her lips, happy to see him. Colin walked closer, she moved to him, and simultaneously they started to talk, his words overlapping, forcing his words to dominate.

"No, I'm the one who must apologize. I was unforgivably rude and … I'm sorry," he said with sincerity, his heart aching with torment, knowing he had caused her pain.

"It's all right."

"No, it's not, it's not all right. You let me hurt you; you let me criticize you, and you said nothing, not once. And I don't know why I keep hurting you, pushing you away; because I don't want to … can't you see … I'm dying for you Dagmara!" Colin confessed, finally telling her how he really felt.

Then Colin swooped Dagmara into a passionate embrace. Engulfing her mouth, he kissed her vigorously on the lips, kissing her with such lustful intensity; she almost fell off her feet, throwing her off balance. The feeling was absolutely wonderful. The pleasure Colin Murphy bestowed upon her mouth was sensational. It was simply irresistible, as Dagmara kissed him back, putting her entire body into the kiss.

"Where have you been?" she asked, momentarily breaking their lips apart.

"Just walking around trying to think."

"When you walked out that door, I didn't know if you were coming back, and when you did … I realized how much you mean to me."

And Colin realized for the first time how innocent she really was. The delicate flower, her sweet ripeness, how special Dagmara Morrow was to him. He had never met a girl like her before, and she had never met anyone like him, which explained the sexual attraction. He knew in his heart that she loved him; he did not have to hear her say the words.

As if she was living in a dream, a surreal realm, Dagmara Morrow found herself in love with two men. Both from vastly different backgrounds, so different in character, and it seemed she was so far away from her life, William, her former self when she was with Colin.

"I want you," he said to her.

"For how long?" she asked him.

"It doesn't matter," he replied.

And then Colin kissed Dagmara fervidly hard on the mouth. As oil mixed with fire, their passion ignited deep within the burning flames of their lustful embrace, as Dagmara defied her promise to William. She was about to engage in a night of unbridled ecstasy with a man other than her fiancé, and in that one, but ever lasting moment, she had betrayed the small, round object that lied hidden next to her heart.

Aggressively Colin tore off his coat and shirt, and then moved Dagmara towards the bed.

"I want to make love to you," he said to her inbetween their kisses, barely able to control himself. He had been deprived of having her long enough.

Then suddenly Dagmara stopped moving her mouth as Colin kept kissing her, and then he felt her mouth become cold.

"You've been with many women before?"

Seeing her hesitance, Colin sat down on the bed next to Dagmara. Her face, flushed. His pulse, racing. He yearned for more. His mouth wanting to lunge at her lips being so close to her body, just within reach.

"You've never been with a man before," he said, realizing the meaning of his words.

Dagmara did not have to say a word, the look in her eyes told him everything, and Colin knew her answer even before she spoke. Dagmara thought back to the time when she and William were alone in his hotel room, their naked bodies lying next to each other in bed. She had said no to his sexual advances. She had said no to sleeping with him before he went off on his dangerous assignment. The war had separated them, splitting them up, and the longer they stayed apart, the farther they were from ever reaching each other, silently drifting in opposite directions.

She remembered every detail of that night, captured perfectly in her mind. The way his naked body felt next to hers. The softness of William's touch. His lips moistening her skin. His debonair style. The dimple that protruded inward in his chin every time he smiled. The look in his eyes as she took off all her clothes. William Cavill was the first man to ever see her naked, and Dagmara Morrow remembered every feeling, every moment of that pleasurable experience, and now she was about to taint that beautiful memory, and say yes to another man.

"You're my first," she told him.

"Your first."

"Yes, my first."

Colin had slept with several women before. All the young, attractive women in his hometown in Dublin were in love with him, wanting him, lusting for his exquisite lovemaking techniques. Colin had gotten a huge reputation for being an insatiable lover, having older women wanting to experience such vigorous stamina. He knew his way around the bedroom. He knew the exact places on a woman's body that gave them monumental pleasure, and in return, he would receive a lot of pleasure back. His tough edgy presence mixed with his raw sex appeal was a dynamite combination, making him the envy of every man.

And now he wanted to make love to Dagmara Morrow. Wanting to take away with delight the one gift she would give her husband, taking away her virtue from their wedding night. Colin would soil her body, taking that away from her rich, aristocratic fiancé, and he would enjoy every minute, knowing he had her first. But at the same time, Colin knew what she was giving him, and he found himself overwhelmed as if he could barely breathe. Dagmara would give him her most intimate embrace, hoping one day to have her heart.

"I've been with a woman before," he told her.

"Then you're more experienced than I."

"I wanted you even before I got to know you, the real you. And now, I want you even more."

His words conveyed what her heart was unable to say. She could no longer deny her true feelings for this man. Not wanting to fight the temptation, anymore. So she gave in, giving into the lust, the desire that consumed her thoughts, her body becoming uninhibited.

Colin moved Dagmara down on the bed, placing his body on hers. She trembled with excite feeling him on top of her. He could feel her sultry breasts against his bare chest, increasing the stimulation. His tongue licked her mouth, outlining her lips, and then he lavishly kissed her, swallowing her whole.

The immediate arousal to Dagmara's body moistened her skin. Slow, savoring kisses that speeded into fiery hot, passionate, deep kisses, showering her with delicious rapture. Hard and forceful, gentle and sweet, they swirled their tongues together, as she moved her leg over his, moving her hands around his back. The softness of her fingers caressed his skin, as he pressed his body down on top of her more, their bodies started to warm.

The intimate position pushed them closer together, connecting them, moving Dagmara farther away from William, separating their souls. Her body now became the conquest of another man, succumbing to the Irishman's seduction.

"I've wanted to do this since the first moment I saw you," Colin told her, as they immersed themselves deeper into the intoxicating kiss, a kiss that pleasured them both for several hours.

Each of her kisses tore into his loins, wanting more. Wanting to taste her entire body inside his mouth with lustful longing. The strength of his kisses invigorated Dagmara in an erotic way. He had touched her in places; no man had ever touched her before, as the enticement coursed through her bones, aching for more.

Colin moved her slip off her shoulders, entranced as the material moved down over her breasts, falling down around her waist. Her half naked body illuminated her magnificent beauty. His breath deepened as he looked at her neck, the bruises, remembering the terrible thing his friend had done. Slowly Colin slid his fingers down her arm, wanting to erase that painful memory. Then he moved her down on the bed, and gently started kissing her neck, moving his lips down her chest.

His tongue tenderly moved around each nipple, immediately giving her arousal. Then his mouth moved down lower on her navel. His mouth moved upon her luscious thigh, as he ripped off each of her silk stockings with his teeth. He pulled the rest of her slip off her body, and removed her underwear, as Dagmara lied on the bed completely naked.

Colin looked at her naked body for a long, mesmerizing moment, memorizing the image in his mind. Her slender figure was curved perfectly. The look in her eyes, captivating. Her underwear had lace trim, and Colin Murphy had never seen such fine undergarments before. His eyes opened wide as he stared at the lace, feeling the silk texture in his hands. None of the girls back home in Ireland had worn underwear like this, but none of the women he had bedded were of Dagmara Morrow's stature and wealth.

"You're so beautiful," he said to her.

Dagmara did not know how lovely she really was, till she saw the look in Colin Murphy's eyes as he stared at her naked body. He was completely enamored with her. Then he took off his pants and removed his underwear.

As Colin took off his clothes, this was not the first time Dagmara had seen a man naked. Contrary to what he believed, William in that sense was her first. Colin's naked body looked like Williams, except he had a few scars on his skin, and his build was more like an athlete. His chest flexed in the cool night air, and Colin Murphy looked absolutely gorgeous in all his nakedness, the moonlight shadowing over his perfectly sculptured body.

An inviting smile crossed her mouth. Her body trembled as Colin moved near. He was the second man to ever see Dagmara completely undressed, in all her nakedness, and both times each man had said she looked absolutely beautiful. Their comments elevated her vanity with their admiration for her. She was everything a man like Colin Murphy desired, and so much more, more than she knew.

Gently he laid his body down on top of hers, feeling her soft skin beneath him. The coldness of the night surrounded them, but the small area circling the bed became increasingly hot. Colin kissed Dagmara passionately on the lips, as she moved her hands around his back, feeling his naked body. His fingers moved down her skin, as Colin pressed his body down on top of her more. The fervor shared that night between their souls erased all memory of previous sexual encounters Colin had with other women.

Their forbidden love affair was very sexual, as Colin vigorously ravished Dagmara with lust. His mouth was like an enormous suction device. His stamina was incredible. His luscious lips covered every inch of her smooth skin, giving her body extraordinary amounts of pleasure. Their bodies glistened, as Colin moved his lips down to her neck, her chest, to her inner thigh, making his fervid way down her body and back up again. His tongue increased in strength. His kisses, heavenly, watering into the depths of perfection.

"I'd rather make love to you, than with anyone else," she told him.

That was all he wanted to hear. Her words elevated his vigor, as Colin complied happily with her wishes and kept enthralling Dagmara, wriggling in motion, contorting her body with exquisite, circular rhythm.

Knowing exactly how to please a woman, Colin pressed his body down on top of Dagmara, harder and harder, moving into her. She grabbed him around tight, tighter, breathing hard. And at that precise moment she opened her eyes looking straight into his; he engulfed her mouth … and made love to her.

And in Dagmara Morrow's eyes, the virile Colin Murphy was everything she could ever want in a lover; he was the perfect embodiment of a man. He was exciting, but dangerous. Seductive, but arrogant. His erotic love making technique was wonderful, inducing Dagmara to go further and further each time.

The art of seduction, Colin Murphy was an apt pupil.

They surpassed each other's expectations, fulfilling every desire within their lustful ways. The enormous amount of pleasure that Dagmara felt within her body intoxicated her with ecstasy, ruining her for all other men.

His endurance, incredible, her lips became red, suffocating with delight, as they made love over and over without stopping. Infatuated with him, Dagmara allowed Colin to dominate the situation, as he was completely infatuated with her. And each time they made love, the more aggressive he became. The slow, gentle approach soon turned into a voracious, powerful thirst. A thirst that heightened the intense pleasure of each intimate embrace. And soon the love overpowered the lust; increasing the passion he drew out of her body, stealing it away from another.

Dagmara had never been with a man before, and although she loved the incredible experience she shared with William Cavill that night, it could not compare to what she was feeling and experiencing this very moment.

The pleasure ripped her up inside with torment, knowing she had betrayed William, allowing herself to endure the pain. She let herself be carried away, feeling for the first time since she left London, that she was lying in the grass again as a child, her hair blowing in the soft wind, feeling the ground beneath her. Dagmara felt at peace, cherishing the memory, feeling as if she was lost in a world all on her own.

Colin Murphy was very vigorous, as their bodies became one, intertwined perfectly with each other. Their naked bodies warmed with each embrace. They could not get enough of each other, straining for breath, not wanting to stop. Never wanting to leave the room, each other's arms, wanting to perpetuate the moment.

They gave each other everything that night, holding nothing back, giving each other what they both greatly needed after what they had gone through together, after what they had witnessed and survived. A warm bed. A place of safety. A moment of peace. A memory that would last forever.

Dagmara and Colin immersed themselves deeper within each enamoring kiss, devouring each other like two strangers passing in the night, never to meet again. As you only get a couple of moments, sometimes only one that defines your whole life, and then it is gone, forever. And their unforgettable, sexual encounter would be forever burned in their souls, upon their bodies, for as long as they lived.

For hours they made love that night, intertwined like a pretzel, staying in the heated throws of blissful passion for as long as their bodies could last. They were like honeymooners, or just two people who knew they would never see one another again after this night. After they made it home, they would be torn apart, and Dagmara would be placed back into her world, and Colin would be placed back into his. Cillian and Brady would be waiting for him, and William and Dagmara's friends and family would be waiting for her. Their steamy sexual night of passion would be just one of lust, loneliness, and love, bringing them both solace in a time of war.

As they made love that night, they knew it would be their first, last, and only time they would ever be together, shimmering in the twilight, and Dagmara Morrow embraced carpe diem fully, letting the pleasure overtake her body, thinking only of this moment.

And as they immersed themselves deeper in the ecstasy, the peril of the contents of the stolen envelope from David Bragger's desk drawer remained unopened, unread, slightly hidden away in Colin Murphy's coat pocket.

CHAPTER 23

Enfolded in his arms, their bodies were completely exhausted from the rapturous night of passion and pleasure, pleasure that would satisfy them for a long time after they had parted ways. The evening seemed like a stolen moment, coming and leaving too quickly, and soon the next day would be upon them, and so would the predators that hunted them ruthlessly without qualms of conscience.

They lied together in intoxicating ecstasy, as if they were hooked on a novocaine drug, their bodies would never feel the same in completion, ever again.

"You were incredible," Dagmara told Colin with a mischievous smile, as he slid his fingers down her cheek, gently caressing her moistened skin.

"You were wonderful," he told her with a devilish grin, and then kissed her on the lips.

"Even with all those girls back home to amuse you?" she said flirtatiously.

"Not one of those women is as special as you. You were perfect."

Dagmara kissed Colin passionately on the lips, charmed by his words. She felt completely comfortable with him, lying naked next to his body, uninhibited. Invigorated, Colin never had a more enjoyable experience making love to a woman than he did with Dagmara. Their bodies were aligned perfectly with one another, making each other complete. They were each other's half. The missing part that every person searches for endlessly through life, they had found that elusive element in each other. But she had also found that element with William. Who is to say you cannot be the missing half of two different people, making all three complete.

Colin looked at Dagmara's naked body, focusing on her neck, and he realized what it was that was missing. He had disregarded it while making love to her, seeing only her bruises, but something he had first noticed when he took off her slip and kissed her chest had eluded his thoughts until now. Her necklace. The diamond ring. It was not around her neck. It was gone, and he finally remembered it.

Dagmara had taken off the one thing that meant the world to her, hiding it secretly within her clothes. She had removed the symbol of William's love she kept so close to her heart. She had removed all evidence of her fiancé, and Colin did not know if she had done so for him, for her, or perhaps for them both?

And the more he stared at her neck and the missing piece of jewelry; Dagmara knew what he was searching for. On purpose she had removed the necklace, taking the ring away from her heart, breaking her promise to William that it would never leave her body. She had defied her heart, and broken her vows to William Cavill even before she lied in the arms of another man, naked, in betraying warmth. Before she soiled her body with pleasure, Dagmara had removed the necklace after Colin had left, placing the diamond ring in her pants pocket.

And at that moment, as she looked into Colin Murphy's eyes, Dagmara Morrow feared she was lost to William Cavill.... forever!

"Why did you remove it?" he asked, as she was still such a mystery to him.

Dagmara moved closer to him on the pillow.

"What's his name?"

"William Cavill, perhaps you've heard of him."

"No, should I?" Colin said with a slight arrogance to his tone.

"His father is Jonathan Cavill. The Cavills are well known around London, and other parts of Europe," Dagmara told him in an eloquent manner.

"He's wealthy and well educated," Colin stated with contempt in his voice, immediately disliking William, wanting to know more about the man who kept a special place within Dagmara's heart.

"William comes from a long line of aristocrats and money," she said, trailing off the last word in almost a whisper.

"Is he your husband?"

Instantly Dagmara distanced herself from Colin, and moved back from him in the bed. "William is my fiancé. He's an RAF fighter pilot. He proposed to me the morning before I left Italy ... before he went off on his dangerous assignment ..."

Colin could see the sadness in her eyes.

"Do you love him?" he asked her.

Dagmara looked away from him for a moment, looking out the window. Colin moved closer to her, gently turning her head to look at him.

"Does it matter?" she replied, not wanting to hurt him, but at the same time, not wanting to hurt William.

Colin wanted to press her further on the subject, but he did not, as he could see the look in her eyes when she looked at him. Dagmara did have feelings for this other man, perhaps she even loved William Cavill with her whole heart, but Colin could also see her pain, the agony tearing her up inside, as he looked deep into her soul. She was also very much in love with him. Colin Murphy had captured Dagmara Morrow's heart. He had stolen her love away from another man. He had captivated her with his seductive, arrogant, rogue like manner, and she allowed him not only to enter her life and her bed, but also her heart.

"Does he treat you well?"

"William has been wonderful to me. I met him in Venice while on holiday with my two best friends," she started to tell him, suddenly remembering her friends Kate and Amelia, wondering if they had made it home safe? She had not thought about them until now.

"Where did you go just then?" he asked, caressing her face.

Her eyes momentarily closed feeling his touch upon her skin. Feeling his warm hand upon her cheek. Feeling safe within his arms. Dagmara did not want to think about the past or the future, the present was agonizing enough.

"We had not known each other long, and William had to leave urgently on a secret mission. He asked me to marry him before he left," Dagmara confessed, remembering back to the moment of their departure at the airport. Reminiscing back to the moment in his hotel room when William proposed, asking her to be his wife. "I have not seen him since."

"I'm sorry," Colin said with compassion, even though everything inside of him loathed this other man.

He hated William Cavill without even knowing him. Hating him because he loved Dagmara. Because he was wealthy, upper class, and he was not. He especially hated him, because he was her fiancé, and he had her love. Dagmara loved William like a woman should love a man, except Colin Murphy wanted to be that man.

Dagmara saw the look on Colin's face, and she wished things could have been different. Perhaps if she had met Colin before William, before the war, before now, things would have been different. Maybe they would have had a future together, and she would be wearing his ring and not another mans. Maybe she could even love Colin Murphy with her whole heart, and maybe he could love her back the same.

Colin wanted to tell Dagmara how much he loved her, how much their time together has meant to him. How much he wanted her, wanting her not to marry William Cavill. Wanting her to run away with him, and emulate the same connection she shared with this man. But that was just a beautiful, unrealistic thought that shimmered through his heart, knowing she could never be his. Dagmara would not hurt William and shatter his world; she would keep her promise of marrying him, and make him the happiest man in the world.

"Where are your friends?" he asked.

Dagmara had not said goodbye to either of them before they left. She had reassured Kate and Amelia she would be safe, she would take the next flight out of Venice and join up with them later in London. She remembered telling them she would stay behind, and she also remembered that she had not mentioned to either of them her engagement to William. Stuart and Henry knew, William happily told them, but Dagmara had not gotten the same chance to tell her friends, let alone her parents. How excited Amelia and Kate would be, especially how happy her parents would be for her marrying into the Cavill dynasty.

"They left before me. They wanted me desperately to go with them, but I refused. I wouldn't go, I wanted to stay with …" Dagmara did not finish her thought, as Colin finished the rest of her sentence for her.

"You stayed behind for him."

"Yes."

And Dagmara wished in part that she had not stayed behind and left with her friends, than she would be safe back home in England with them now. But at the same time, she was almost thankful she had not left with Kate and Amelia. If she had not stayed and taken the later flight, she would never have met Colin. She would never have met him or his friends. She would never have had this incredible, perilous adventure that almost killed her the moment she survived the plane crash. Mainly, she would not be lying next to Colin Murphy now, in ecstasy, soiling her body each passion filled pleasurable second.

"And I would do it all over again, just to have met you," she said to him with sincerity.

Her words not only surprised Colin, but also enamored him with elevating devotion towards her endearing qualities. And as the love immersed inside his heart, he could not help but feel anger and agony at the same time.

"You don't know what you're saying. You'll go back to William, to your life, and you'll forget all about me … as I will with you," he said to her, hurting both of them with his truthful words.

"How could you say such things? I could never forget you. I would never want to forget you. I could never forget what you've done for me," she said to him with conviction, as she moved towards him, and this time he backed away.

"William will be waiting for you," he replied arrogantly.

Colin was full of envy, dying inside each second having to let Dagmara go back to her fiancé. Having another man touch her in a way he had all night long. Tormenting him, wanting his body alone to be the one that ravished her with ecstasy. Making love to her all the time, anytime, anywhere, how many times he wanted. His lips alone to give her pleasure.

The jealous creature overpowered Colin, and Dagmara dismissed his hurtful remarks and asked him point blank, "Is that what you really want?"

The innocence of her words, the expression on her face, tore him up inside with deep seeded frustration. She was unconsciously naive, as he was anything but that if not cynical. Colin had lived a much harder life than her, and was forced to become a man before he was one. But he could never honestly forget about Dagmara, nor would he ever want to.

He could never forget the smell of her perfume, the light fragrance that infiltrated his senses the first time he was close to her body. The softness of her touch against his skin. The passionate hours they spent making love. How sweet each of her kisses were that she bestowed upon his lips. And her face, her beautiful face, even if he tried to put her out of his mind, he could not. Dagmara Morrow would be forever imprinted in his brain within lustful memory, burned into his skin like a flame that would never die out.

"No," he answered, and then passionately kissed her, moving her down on the bed beneath his body, putting an end to their unpleasant discussion.

If he was to be deprived of having her after this night, never to share his bed again with the woman he loved, than Colin would make the most of their few, precious, stolen moments, and capture the memory in perfection, to one day fantasize about on a lonely, starry night in Dublin.

He did not need her love, but he silently yearned for it now.

And as their bodies intertwined again as one, the lust engulfing them with rapture, the big question was, how could Dagmara Morrow be in love with two men at the same time? How could she love two men that were vastly different, from completely different backgrounds? One would give her the world, the other, would make her his world. And as she contemplated which she wanted most, oppressing her thoughts and her heart heavily, she also contemplated which she desired and needed most?

William Cavill would give her the world. He was everything she thought she ever wanted in a man, a husband, a companion in life. But Colin Murphy would make her his world, and up until this moment, she had not realized that maybe what she desired most for in life was not actually what she needed, let alone wanted anymore. Finally Dagmara had gotten everything she wished for, but now, she was not sure if her heart felt the same?

CHAPTER 24

When morning rose the next day and the sun started to slowly rise in the sky, both Colin and Dagmara were fast asleep. Their bodies entangled, lying naked in exhausted, satisfied warmth. Their night of passion exceeded Colin's expectations of their forbidden love affair. He dazzled Dagmara with sexual pleasure. His youthful endurance awakened every bone in her body.

And slowly as the sun rose higher in the sky to the wake of the new day, the light shined in through the window's curtain, and Dagmara and Colin opened their eyes and stared at each other in complete silence, knowing what they had done. Their fingers clasped tightly in each other's hand, not wanting to let go.

After making love, Dagmara was radiant. Her sultry skin illuminated, and she looked even more beautiful if that were possible. Colin's hair, messed, his skin, moist, his lips, red, as she licked her chapped lips that were also red in color. Her eyes sparkled, her body felt sore, so did his, and Colin had forgotten the pain of his bruised ribs, as the immense pleasure he felt inside his loins overshadowed the discomfort.

The night of passion was not a figment of their imagination; it was real, and the hand on her thigh and the softness of her breast upon his chest, made the realization all the more real. The night was exquisite, the hours of savage desire glistened over their naked bodies that were still warm. Colin could still taste her inside his mouth; her sweet ripeness flowed through his veins like ecstasy.

Dagmara had changed him. She had broken down his tough exterior. She had penetrated his heart, and his dislike for her from the beginning was now unjustified. She was not some silly girl, nor was she an upper class English brat; instead Dagmara Morrow lived by her own rules, no ones stereotype, and saw through Colin Murphy immediately.

She had stayed with him through his arrogant behavior, his harsh, insolent words. She had stayed by his side through everything, and he had hated her for all the wrong reasons, because in actuality, he hated the unfair world in which they lived. He hated William Cavill, the man she was going to marry. He hated the war, but mostly, he hated himself for loving her, especially for her loving him back.

If only she had said no. If only she had stopped him. If only she had resisted his sexual advances, than maybe the ache he felt in his heart would not be so painful. The acute feeling tore into his chest, and Dagmara was the one who inflicted the wound.

Colin had lost his best friend and had separated from his brother because of her. And each time he looked at Dagmara, every time he was near her body, he had pushed himself away from the alluring, innate feeling, only now to be betrayed by that lustful element. Love was the ultimate dagger, the game that both of them now played.

Colin would not apologize for what transpired, nor would he regret what they had done. Nobility was long gone. He had in a way ruined her, soiled her for her wedding night, and he did not care, he was almost happy by that darkened thought, that he got to have her first, before any other man. He had stolen her virtue from her future husband, and he felt empowered and awful at the same time. Stealing her away from William, the rich aristocrat that he held in contempt, Dagmara had given herself to him. She had given Colin her most intimate embrace. Her sweet, long kisses, bestowing them all upon him.

The smoldering seduction, the layers they ripped from each other, tearing at their souls, enamoring him closer to her, and Colin did not know why she had done so, giving him what he desired most. How could she love him? How could someone like her, of her status and upbringing, love him? The real question was, how could someone of his upbringing and poor surroundings, love her?

And in the end, Dagmara had not saved herself for William. In a moment of impassioned weakness, lust overpowered, dominating the love within her lonely heart, within the dark, bloody world that surrounded them, and she gave into temptation, giving into the desire she had for Colin Murphy. He was everything she had turned away from. Arrogant, lower class, impudent at times, but he was also intrepid, chivalrous, and very, very passionate.

Colin was an amazing lover, incredible in bed, his stamina never ending. Exquisite were each of his intoxicating kisses, overwhelming her with his vigor, as her lips felt numb. Rapture culminated her inside, coursing through her body, as Colin devoured every inch of her with his potent lips. Pleasuring her for hours, not once did Dagmara think about William, the war, or the consequences of her actions, immersing herself deeper into the infatuating, intimate connection.

And thinking upon her actions, knowing Colin Murphy was the man she had made love to and not William Cavill, her future husband, a silent tear slid slowly down her cheek from the realization as she looked into Colin's eyes.

Dagmara did not regret what they did, what she had done, as she only regretted in life the things she did not do, but it seemed so long ago that she was with William, in Italy, in his room. The moment of him proposing with an offer of marriage, sliding the ring on her necklace, feeling his naked body next to hers. The first time she met him on the street, captivating her with his piercing stare. The memory was fading, and the promising future she once looked forward to, now seemed unclear. The moment that seemed only like yesterday was so far away, but still within reach.

Now her actions had tarnished her propriety, distancing herself from that special time and place, from her former self, and especially William. Proper. Naïve. Pure. She was no longer that girl. The innocent young woman that smiled while William Cavill took off her clothes and kissed her, that moment now seemed like a lifetime ago, but Dagmara still kept the feeling so close to her heart.

As if it never really happened, the only thing that felt real, that felt alive, was this moment. Dagmara thought she would never fall in love, and fortuitously she met the dashing William Cavill, and he was everything she could possibly ever want. Everything she had desired and more. But now fate had stepped in again, a second time, and intertwined her destiny with Colin Murphy, such an unlikely pair. Never would Dagmara Morrow have guessed she could have met two men, so different, and have both of their love. And the future that lied ahead for all three of them was now rewritten. Sometimes the greatest journey two people travel is finding their way back into each other's arms. Because in love, there are no boundaries.

Her future was now unknown. The path that lied ahead for all of them, no one knew, not Dagmara, not Colin, not even William. William had no knowledge of what she had done and with whom, and while he was trying to complete his deadly assignment and stay alive for her, for a future with her, she was desperately trying to get back to him, to London, to home. And somehow in the middle of all the peril and disaster, the blood and the killing, the delicious

Colin Murphy came into her life. A man who risked everything including his life for her. He had now become an inconvenient man.

And as the tear slid down her cheek, both Colin and Dagmara realized in that moment, their vigorous love affair was dead before it ever started. It was over with before it ever began. Completed, and yet never to be forgotten by either.

Colin wiped the tear from her face and asked Dagmara in a serious tone, "If I asked you to come home with me, could you?"

Never did he think he would ever ask her that question, but Colin found himself unable to turn away, he had to ask and know the answer, even if she said no. He could not stand by and watch her marry another, especially William. He could not stand by and just be her friend when he wanted to be so much more than that. Maybe one day to even call her something more special, like his wife.

And for a brief but fleeting moment, Dagmara actually found herself considering such a proposition, contemplating her future and with whom. When she had said no to sleeping with William, she thought she had her whole life ahead of her, to look forward to, wanting to wait until they were married. She had said yes to Colin, because tomorrow they could be found, taken, tortured, and killed by the enemy. William might never make it home. Nothing was certain in life.

The only thing Dagmara knew for sure was that she did love Colin, but not in the way she loved William. She was hot for the Irishman, and Colin did love her, it was not just lust anymore, it had become real. They had become close after the time they spent together. Saving each other's lives had brought them even closer, closer to the emanating attraction that had been there from the start. But she could not hurt William. Even though she had broken her vows to him before she had given them in ceremony, she could not go back on her promise to him in marriage. She loved him far greater than Colin knew, than she herself knew until now.

And there it was, she had made her decision. Dagmara had made her choice before Colin asked her to choose between them, and she hated the circumstances, being placed in such a horrid situation, not wanting to hurt either of them. Not wanting to turn away from love, from a man who might turn out to be the one true love of her life.

But Dagmara Morrow could not run away from her past, from William, or her life, she had responsibilities, so she did the only thing she could. She would have to let Colin Murphy go. He would have to let her go. It could never be between them. She would have to sacrifice his feelings and hurt him, even though it would kill her inside with every breath. And she would be forever in silence and aching wonder, wondering if she had made the right decision and not followed her heart.

"You can't can you?" he said, seeing the look on her face, the long hesitation, knowing he should not have asked her to go with him.

"You don't know what you ask."

"I should have never asked you then," he said, getting upset.

"I don't want us to argue," she said, and placed her fingers on his cheek.

"You want us to stay as we are now, but we can't. I can't do that Dagmara," he told her, elevating his voice.

"Neither of us has a choice."

"You want me to stand by and watch you marry William, even though you know it's a mistake," he said to her with conviction.

"It's not a mistake," she said, coming to William's defense.

"I can't do what you ask of me. I won't!"

"Let this be what it was and nothing more, as I promise you, I will always yearn in my heart to be placed back in this moment with you, for as long as I live."

And as he looked at her sad but radiant face, what could he say to her? Those words were more beautiful than he ever imagined hearing from a woman, and now he loved Dagmara Morrow more than life itself. So he would promise this to her, for her and her alone, as she in turn had ultimately ruined him for all other women.

"For you," he told her, as he moved his hand onto hers.

And not a day would go by for either of them without one thought about this night, about the passion, the peril, their secretive love for each other, and maybe one day they would find their way back together again. Maybe their destined encounter was just that and nothing more, and their worlds would keep them apart, separated by status, longing for their other half. Maybe Dagmara Morrow could never live in Colin Murphy's world, and he could never live in hers? Maybe it would never be possible to sustain what they have.

The morning hue began to break, and they wanted to remain in the pleasure of each other's company, to stay in the moment for as long as they could, before it was lost, and one day stolen. Slowly like a shadow that was taken from their bodies, the moment was over and had finally come to pass. And as Colin Murphy looked at Dagmara Morrow now, she had changed right in front of his eyes. She was not the same person he first met on the streets. She had cut off her hair, worn men's clothing, and had survived a brutal attack. She had escaped the German soldiers, and eluded the French police. She had even shot a man, and made love to a stranger.

"I believe in two things in life," he told her. "Destiny, and the beauty of impulsive acts."

A smile crossed her face.

"You believe in carpe diem," she said.

They were both so alike, more than they knew, yet so different.

"Is that your secret?" she asked him with a flirtatious look in her eyes.

"We all have secrets Dagmara, mine are just more darkly hidden than yours," he told her, as her smile slowly disappeared from the tone of his voice.

"I told you mine before you asked."

"Yes you did," he said, changing his attitude, as a seductive grin flourished over his face thinking about her secret. That he was her first.

"You know, you're the best time I've ever had Colin Murphy."

His eyes widened.

"No one has ever said that to me before," he replied, flattered by her compliment.

"Then I could be your first in that."

"I know I would have missed you if we had never met," he told her.

"That is the sweetest thing anyone has ever said to me."

And with that said, Colin and Dagmara kissed, enfolding her in his arms, one, last, memorable time. Their inexplicable encounter, much like their friendship, would be forever locked in silence, just like their passion, taking it with them to their graves. Holding onto the hopeless dream that there would be a tomorrow for them, and a day after, knowing it could never be.

CHAPTER 25

After his intense and very pleasant phone conversation with his son, Jonathan Cavill immediately got into contact with a man who worked for the British government. Then he was put into contact with a man who had several connections in Europe, especially France.

William would be unable to return home until his injury had healed better, but the wound in his head was not the only thing that was keeping him from coming home. He would not go back to England, to his father, before he found Dagmara. He would not leave her. He would not leave without her. William would search endlessly for her, and he would not stop searching until she was found, until he could be with her again.

Dressed in an expensive suit and wearing a long black coat was the mysterious stranger who sat across the table from Jonathan Cavill.

"I need to employ you," Jonathan Cavill told the man whom he secretly met with at a secluded café twenty minutes outside of London.

Robert Langton watched the handsome, illustrious gentleman as he took a sip of his drink. Langton scanned the entire room, observing everyone with his trained eyes.

"Do you have the money?" Langton asked, and Jonathan Cavill handed him an envelope stuffed with hundreds of Pounds.

"The people I spoke with said you are the best."

The man did not insult Mr. Cavill by looking through the envelope to see how much money was inside. He knew of his wealth, he knew by reputation, and when he received a call from the aristocrat, he knew their dealings would make for a profitable union. The down payment he received would only be a trifle of the money that would exchange between their dealings if he came through on his end of the deal.

"What is it you need from me Mr. Cavill?"

"I need you to find a girl."

"Why is she so important to you?" Langton asked his employer, curious to the nature of their secrecy.

"She's my son's fiancée."

"What's her name?"

"Dagmara Morrow," Jonathan Cavill answered, and took out a picture from his pocket and slid it across the table.

Langton picked up the small photograph and looked at the image of the young woman.

"She's very pretty, I can see why your son would want to find her."

"It's the only picture I could get without contacting her parents. They believe as I do that Dagmara … that Dagmara is dead. You see Mr. Langton, she was headed for home when her plane crashed somewhere over France."

"Then why do you need my help if you have already resigned yourself to the fact that she is dead. To confirm it?" Langton inquired.

"My son believes she is still alive. She was listed on the dead or rather presumed missing list of passengers. They have yet to find her body, but they are no longer searching. That's where you come in. I need you to go there and find out what you can. To find out if she's still alive, and if so … bring her home."

"You ask for something you do not believe in," Langton questioned, seeing the expression on Jonathan Cavill's face, the look in his eyes, knowing he was doing this only for his son. "I'll see what I can do for you Mr. Cavill," Langton said without any indifference in expression. Not giving him hope, or taking any away from his lack of emotion. Not being plagued by that weakness.

"Do you have children Mr. Langton?"

"No."

"Well then you do not know what it is like to have your son or daughter die before you. It's tragic for any parent to have to go through. You see Mr. Langton … I love my son. He might not always think that highly of me, but he's my only child … and I would do *anything* for my son."

"Yes, I believe you would Mr. Cavill. As I said, I'll see what I can find out. I'll do my best," Langton replied.

"I leave everything to your discretion then," Mr. Cavill said, insinuating that Robert Langton should use any means necessary to get into France, attain the information, and if possible, bring Dagmara home.

"That's what I'm known for, being discreet," Langton said with a sly grin. "You came to the right person."

They shook hands.

"Thank you."

"We'll be in touch Mr. Cavill," Langton told him, and then got up from the table and walked out of the café, leaving behind the shadow of hope that he would find Dagmara Morrow, as Robert Langton knew he would find the young woman, he just did not know if he would find her alive or dead?

Instead of traveling by night where they would be less visible, Dagmara and Colin left in the late morning hour. Before they left, without Dagmara knowing, Colin had opened the envelope with a government seal, the one taken from David Bragger's desk drawer. And after reading the contents, knowing of its importance, knowing what they now held within their possession, Colin knew the danger this placed them in.

Well rested, having eaten breakfast before they were on their way, they were refreshed towards the long day ahead of them. The vigorous night of passion had fueled their bones. They were renewed in a heightened manner. And as they moved feverishly on the open roads keeping to themselves, they were unknowingly being tracked each step of the way.

Unknown to them, the tracker was the deadliest of all the predators that hunted them. This man was more ruthless than the vicious German soldiers. The French police were not as clever or dangerous as this man, because he was not only searching for his two, young victims, he desperately needed to take back into possession the envelope that had been stolen from his belongings. The important papers that held the key to his secretive, treacherous dealings with the enemy. And if it were to fall into the wrong hands, it would mean immediate death for the traitor. David Bragger would not allow that to happen. He could not allow either of them to get out of the country with those papers. He would kill them first!

A thin line of smoke moved slowly through the man's lips as he took another puff off his cigarette standing at the crash site in France. The man looked around the disaster area. The bleak surrounding had given him little information on his investigation, as he threw his cigarette to the ground and walked away. The trail was getting cold, as Robert Langton assumed the identity of a tourist, moving along unnoticed with other bystanders.

Dagmara Morrow's body was not found among the dead. Her name was still listed under missing, presumed dead by the officials who were satisfied with their findings, not searching for any survivors. To them, everyone on board the flight was dead, even if they could not locate every passenger's body, they believed the fire had burned up the remains, and did not want to investigate further into finding a single survivor they had already cast off among the dead.

Robert Langton would not give up so easily; he had just begun his search. His private investigation funded by a very wealthy client kept his case alive, so he would keep looking further, not satisfied with the findings and forged paperwork. If William Cavill's fiancée was still alive, and had somehow miraculously survived the plane crash and found her way into the nearby towns, Robert Langton would find her. He could find anyone, but this time he had little if any leads to go on, and the longer he searched, the harder it would be to find Dagmara Morrow by the elapsing time inbetween. As if he was searching in dead end circles.

Money shuffled between hands, strangers offering little if any information on what they had seen or heard. No one wanted to talk. No one wanted to get involved. And the more Robert Langton investigated, digging deeper into the botched cover up of the plane crash, the more evidence leaned towards the fact that Dagmara Morrow had not walked away from the disaster.

A second cigarette was lit, as an attractive woman sat down at a table, smiled to the stranger who sat across from her, and took a sip of his coffee. She crossed her legs as she sat down, and a glimpse of her stocking protruded from her skirt. Well kempt, she was one of the few people in France who had not been horribly stricken by the devastation and starvation that war brought to the country. Her curly brown hair, the red lipstick, her fine clothes smothered in money by a rich boyfriend, as the man took a puff off his cigarette, noticing the absence of a ring on her forth finger. It was the only thing missing from the picture. She traded secrets for money, power for wealth; trading anything she could, including her body to stay alive, to keep her in her accustomed, comfortable lifestyle.

The man watched as the woman took off her coat, revealing a low cut dress. Her sultry appearance was the envy of every woman sitting in the café. She took one of his cigarettes, waited for him to light it, and then settled back in the chair.

"So you have what I need?" the man asked skeptically.

"Yes," she answered in a husky voice.

"You know where they are?"

"That's why I'm here," she said, and took another puff off her cigarette.

She looked over at the man behind the counter, and waited for the gentleman to buy her a drink. Nothing from her would come free. The man bought her a drink, refilling his cup with coffee, and then they got down to business.

"Where are they?" the man asked, enjoying the view, the attractive company, but his mind was set on business, not allowing the woman's physical beauty to distract him.

She motioned to see the money, and he passed an envelope to her under the table. She felt the bills within her fingers, taking a quick peek at the large sum of Francs, and then slipped the envelope into her stocking.

The man watched as she lifted her skirt higher up her thigh.

"That's one place I wouldn't have thought of."

The attractive woman smiled at the compliment, indicating there was more where that came from if he was interested.

"The two you are looking for have taken a room at Mrs. Bronchet. It used to be a bed and breakfast, now she's turned it into a cafe."

"Are they still there?"

"I am just the messenger, I only know what I'm told."

The missing link to the puzzle, she had given him the key before he discovered it.

"Do you know where they are now?" he asked.

"No," she answered.

"You've been slightly helpful then," he said, mildly insulting her, knowing her true talent lied within a bed and not in conversation with single word answers.

"Is there anything else you want Mr. Bragger?" she said with a provocative look in her eyes, and crossed her legs again.

"Maybe some other time," he told her.

Their secret meeting did not arouse suspicion among any of the patrons except for one, one lone stranger who sat in the corner observing everyone. He specifically watched as the money changed hands under the table, the information traded for what was inside the tiny envelope that lied hidden in the woman's stocking. Trained with a sharp, suspicious eye, the man became increasingly interested in their conversation, and decided to do a little investigating of his own.

CHAPTER 26

❀

A tall man wearing a long black coat visited Mrs. Bronchet. Her three children were loud and rambunctious, as they ran through the front room chasing after each other with mischievous smiles on their faces. The view was refreshing for the man, especially after witnessing such devastation from the previous days journey. He smiled at the children as they ran past him in joyful play.

"Oh, I'm so sorry sir, sometimes they can be a handful," Mrs. Bronchet said to the gentleman.

"Children should be happy," he replied.

"Are you wanting something to eat?" she asked, looking the man over, seeing his clothes, knowing he was wealthy.

"Actually, I'm interested in some information you can provide for me."

Her eyes widened, her heartbeat quickened, as she looked up at the stranger with a frightened look in her eyes, thinking he was working for the Vichy government.

"I know nothing sir, I have three children, please …" she started to say in a hysterical panic.

"No, you have mistaken me. I bid you and your family no harm. All I want are some answers I believe you can provide for me," he told her, trying to put her mind at ease.

The look on her face did not change, and as the stranger moved closer to her, she immediately felt threatened by his intimidating presence.

"Are you with the government?" she asked.

"No Mrs. Bronchet, as I said before, I'm not here to harm you."

He reached inside his pocket to grab something, when simultaneously the woman shook in fear thinking it was a weapon. Slowly as his hand moved out from his pocket holding a photograph and not a gun, the woman breathed again.

"My name is Robert Langton, I'm searching for this girl," he told Mrs. Bronchet and handed her the picture. "Some very important people are looking for her back home in England."

The woman took a look at the photograph, and then looked up at the stranger and shook her head. "No, I haven't seen anyone who looks like this. I would remember her. In fact, I don't get too many customers in here nowadays. The last two who stopped in for some food stayed the night, but they were from Ireland. A young couple that was married."

"Ireland?" Langton mused. "Has anyone else been around here today asking about them?"

"Well yes now that you mention it, earlier this morning, how did you know?"

"Lucky guess."

"Are they in some sort of trouble? I hope not, they seemed so nice," Mrs. Bronchet said.

"Did you get a good look at them?" Langton asked.

"I don't know what you mean."

"Did the girl have blonde hair, very pretty, maybe she was dressed in different clothing?"

The question stumped the woman, not fully comprehending what the stranger was asking.

"What I mean Mrs. Bronchet, could the couple you saw last night, could the girl have been the one in this picture?"

"I don't believe so."

"It's very important I find her, please take another look at the photograph. Is there any possibility that this girl could have been the one that stayed here last night?"

The woman looked at the picture of Dagmara Morrow again.

"Did they happen to sign a name in the book?" Langton asked.

Her eyes opened wide. "Yes, it's right here."

Mrs. Bronchet pointed to the name on the ledger.

Mr. and Mrs. James Caulfield

"Does this help you?" Mrs. Bronchet asked.

"No, I'm afraid not," Langton answered.

"Wait, I just thought of something Mr. Langton, I don't know if this will help you, but …"

"What is it?" Langton interjected, not letting her finish her sentence.

"I didn't think of it until now, but it did seem strange at the time."

"What did?"

"Well, it's probably nothing, but they did ask for a bottle of orange juice, and the girl was wearing pants, like men's clothing, and her hair was cut short, like a boys."

"Anything else you can recall," he pressed further.

"Yes, he called her by her first name. I don't know why I didn't remember this before. I only mention it now, because I've never heard the name. It didn't sound Irish to me, but then again, I've never been to Ireland."

"Can you remember her name?" Langton asked.

"It was very unique, very pretty though, I think it started with a … D … Dar, no … Dag …" she started to say, trying to remember the girl's name.

"Dagmara!" Robert Langton shouted.

Mrs. Bronchet looked at him in amazement. "Yes, I believe that was it. A very unusual name."

"This is Dagmara," Robert Langton said, and pointed to the girl in the photograph as his eyes widened, his voice exhilarated by the information he just found out. Dagmara Morrow was alive, or at least it seemed that way.

"I couldn't say for sure Mr. Langton," she told him honestly looking at the picture. "The young woman in this photograph looks so beautiful, maybe if you took away the clothes and the long hair, but I couldn't say for sure."

"Did they say where they were headed?" Langton asked.

"No, I did not ask."

"Thank you Mrs. Bronchet," Langton said, and handed the woman one hundred Francs. "For your help."

Her eyes opened wide as he handed her the large sum of money. "Thank you," she replied most graciously.

"You've been most helpful Mrs. Bronchet."

And then Robert Langton left in a hurry, as he placed the photograph back inside his coat pocket. The information he just received was not expected, and he was surprised that his lead had turned dramatically from cold to warm, becoming hot.

Dagmara Morrow was alive. She had survived the crash and was moving about somewhere in France. But where, where was she going and with whom? Who was this young man that pretended to be her husband? Why were they moving about together, and where were they headed? Especially, why were they hiding? The big question that Robert Langton scrambled around in his mind was whom were they hiding from?

All those unanswered questions formed in his thoughts, and he realized that if he knew of this information, so did the man sitting at the table in the café. The man who had exchanged money with the attractive woman was also looking for them. And Langton now knew he was not alone in his search. Someone else was hot on their trail, ahead of him by several hours, and by the look in the man's eyes, and the stack of money that crossed hands under the table, Robert Langton knew he had to find them first.

As the sun slowly started to set in the sky, nightfall would soon be upon them, and Dagmara and Colin started to move in a more hurried pace, distancing themselves farther from their enemies. But each time they turned onto a road, or stopped for a moment to catch their breaths, they heard a faint movement in the distance. Someone was following them; the same person that had been tracking them for hours was still behind them, moving in closer. Each time the footsteps were less silent, as if the predator wanted his prey to know of his presence without knowing of his intentions.

Both of them could sense danger lurking at every corner, behind them, surrounding their every move. They were not alone anymore on their journey, and Colin knew as soon as darkness was upon them, the violent hunter would show his wicked face, and unleash whatever he had planned for his unwilling captives. And the only weapon they had between them was the gun Colin kept at his side, leaving them wide open for attack. Their only defense was each other. They would either save one another, or die trying in their courageous, deadly fight for survival.

In the late night hour, they stopped to take a short break by a stream of water they had stumbled upon. The coolness of the night brought about a light breeze that sprinkled Dagmara and Colin with the moving water.

"Do you think we'll make it?" she asked, looking for Colin to give her the answer she knew he could not provide.

"If we keep heading in this direction," Colin started to say, trying to give her some hope, trying to give himself hope in a desperate, almost futile situation.

"We missed the train, didn't we," she said.

"A long time ago," Colin finally told her.

"Why didn't you tell me?"

"What good would it have done," he replied.

"Do you think they made it?"

Colin reminisced back for a brief moment remembering the conversation, telling Cillian to get his brother on the train, to leave without him, to get Brady to safety. He remembered the look on his brother's face not wanting to leave him, hoping it would not be the last time he saw his friend and his brother. Hoping it would not be the last words spoken to either of them.

"I'm sure they both made it," he told her.

Gently she placed her hand on his for comfort.

"I'm sure Cillian and Brady are both safe. They are both smart and brave … just like you," she told him with a smile, trying to ease his pain.

And then Colin realized why he had stayed behind, why he had not listened to Mark Quinn as he looked into Dagmara's eyes. Colin would not have traded this moment; he would not have traded their night of passion … for anything.

Then suddenly Dagmara spotted something in the bushes down by the stream. "What's that?" she asked, and pointed to what looked like two dead bodies on the ground.

Slowly they moved towards the bodies with caution. Colin bent down next to one of the corpses and turned the man over. Rapidly they moved back from the bludgeoned sight. The man's face was pulverized. Bugs lied heavily within the blood, and the ghastly sight made Dagmara nauseous as she looked away. The stench was thick. The bodies were still fresh in their own decay, as Colin turned the other man over and saw the same gruesome image.

"Who could have done such a thing?" she asked.

"Germans," Colin stated with loath, as he moved his hand in the dead man's pocket, seeing if he could find any identification on them to see who they were.

As Colin leaned over the man's body, looking through his pockets, Dagmara was suddenly struck with a horrid image, the remembrance of the crash. The vile German soldiers sifting through the pockets of the dead passengers, and the haunting images slammed through her mind, as she felt paralyzed from the memory.

Colin found a wallet hidden inside the coat pocket of one of the men. "Look what I found Dagmara," he showed her. "Dagmara," he said to her again, waking her from the suffocating images. "Are you okay?"

"Yes, what did you find?" she asked, pushing back the terrible memory, as she blinked several times and took a few deep breaths.

Inside the wallet Colin found the identification of the two slain men. They were English, most notably spies, and as Colin emptied the contents, his eyes suddenly opened wide. He opened the piece of paper. It was a letter of transit. He could barely believe his eyes, as Dagmara moved closer and saw what he was holding in his hands. Two letters of transit, there was another one underneath. She looked at Colin with a huge smile, knowing what this meant, overwhelmed with their serendipitous find.

"I don't believe it."

There were several hundred Francs mixed between the letters of transit, and now they had a way out. A way out of France and the war. A larger smile crossed Dagmara's face as she hugged Colin with happiness, and just as they found a glimmer of hope intertwined with all the blood and peril, footsteps forcefully crashed down on the ground behind them. And as they looked up, they found themselves completely surrounded by over a dozen armed men, all aiming their weapons directly at their heads.

One of the men stepped forward.

"Stay where you are!" he shouted at his captives, as Colin clasped his hand tightly around the letters, trying to hide them, as his other hand tightened around the gun.

Colin looked at Dagmara, as she looked at him with fear, and then the armed man moved closer from the cluster of guns, moving straight towards them from the hidden shadows of the night.

CHAPTER 27

"Get up!" Jarred shouted at them, and slowly Dagmara and Colin stood up.

The dark haired man, who looked no more than eighteen, saw the desecrated bodies lying on the ground beside his captives. The vicious manner in which the unidentified men were killed sickened the young man with disgust, as his eyes sharpened in tightness looking at his two prisoners.

"You did this?" Jarred shouted, already condemning his captives."

"No, they were already dead, we found them like this," Colin explained, but Jarred did not believe him, nor did he want to listen to their explanation, as he saw Colin trying to hide something in his hands.

Jarred moved to grab the wallet from Colin's possession, and Colin pulled out his gun, and instantly the men that surrounded them stepped forward ready to fire.

"Wait," Jarred commanded, as Colin pointed his gun directly at his head. "We have you outnumbered. Give me your weapon!" he demanded, showing no fear, showcasing his blind confidence of youth.

"No," Colin replied, showing him the same fearless quality.

"You'll get one shot off before my men kill both of you," Jarred stated with confidence.

"But that one shot will be in you!"

Jarred looked Colin directly in the eyes like a showdown. Neither one willing to give up their position, when Jarred swiftly grabbed hold of Dagmara, and placed his gun against the side of her head.

"Let her go," Colin demanded.

"Drop your weapon or I'll shoot her," Jarred demanded.

Colin could see the look in the young man's eyes; he believed he would kill her.

"All right, just don't hurt her," Colin replied.

Slowly Colin started to place his gun down on the ground, when Dagmara bit the man's hand and he yelled in pain. Simultaneously Colin moved back up, but it was too late, as one of the men hit him in the back of his head, knocking the gun from his hand, pushing him down to the ground.

Jarred slapped Dagmara in the face, hard, as the force of the hit knocked her off her feet, and she fell down to the ground beside Colin. Then Jarred kicked Colin in the ribs and placed his foot on his back, keeping him pressed into the ground. His face eating the dirt, as he stripped the gun away from Colin, and placed it in his pocket.

Jarred looked down at Dagmara. "Take them," he ordered, and immediately the men moved in and grabbed Colin and Dagmara as she struggled to get away, pushing the men as they took hold of her by force.

They were overpowered by the men's strength, as two men grabbed Colin and dragged him into the bushes, as another man grabbed hold of Dagmara, and she kicked and screamed.

"Where are you taking us?" she shouted. "Let go of me!"

Instantly she was silenced as the man placed his hand over her mouth, as another man helped drag her into the bushes, and both of them were taken by force and rapidly carried away into the dark before a blink of an eye.

The men took their prisoners to a secluded hideout where they were greeted by several more men and women who were part of the French resistance. They threw Dagmara and Colin down on the ground as the men surrounded them again with their guns, aiming their weapons directly at their heads, ready to kill on command. Treated like criminals, Colin was still somewhat dazed from the robust hit to his head, as Dagmara felt the sting of the young man's hand against her cheek.

"What's this?" one of the women asked.

"We found them by the stream. They killed two men, and we found these on them," Jarred replied, and held up the wallet full of money.

The man in charge of his rebels walked out of the house hearing all the commotion, and as he moved down the steps, one foot at a time, Dagmara slowly looked up, and her eyes opened wide seeing the man's face. As if she had seen a ghost.

"Alex!"

"Take them inside," Alex ordered, recognizing the prisoners.

"But …" Jarred started to say, angered that his leader was taking a liking to the two strangers he had captured.

"I said take them inside," Alex commanded.

Immediately his orders were obeyed, and Colin and Dagmara were taken inside the house.

"Why, we can't trust them, they killed two people. Alex, you're making a mistake!" Jarred insisted, raising his voice, wanting his leader to see his point of view.

"Leave us," Alex told him.

"But …" Jarred protested again.

"I'll be fine, don't worry Jarred, I know them."

"I'll be right outside," the young Frenchman said, looking at the strangers, not trusting them, and begrudgingly left, storming out of the house like a child not getting his way, slamming the door shut.

"I hope he didn't hurt you both too much. He can be rough at times, but Jarred is a good kid."

Colin rubbed the back of his head. "Alex, we thought you were dead," Colin said with surprise and great delight, having him rescue them for a second time.

"The German's can't kill me that easily," he said with a laugh. "But what are you both still doing here?"

"We didn't kill those men," Dagmara explained.

A smiled crossed Alex's face as he looked at both of them knowing they were not murderers, they were harmless.

"I believe you, but what were you looking for?"

"We stumbled upon the bodies on our way, and we found what you're holding. We need those papers, they're letters of transit, they can get us out of the country Alex. You can keep the money, but we must have those letters," Colin stressed, knowing he was in no position to demand anything.

Alex disliked Colin's commanding words. "I'd watch your tone my friend," he cautioned his visitors, and looked through the contents of the wallet, seeing the letters of transit, the money, and placed them down on the table. "These are worth a fortune, do you know how much I could sell these for."

"You must give them to us. We found them," Dagmara protested.

Alex looked at her with a domineering look in his eyes. "You're hardly in a position to demand anything."

Suddenly there was a loud knock on the front door, and Jarred walked in interrupting their conversation.

"The men and I wanted to know what you're planning on doing with them?" he asked, upset that Alex had befriended them.

Alex looked over at Dagmara and Colin. "They are my guests, they'll be staying with us for the night," he answered.

Jarred saw the money on the table, his face filled with anger, and he stormed out of the house disapproving of his leader's orders.

"As I said to Jarred, you are my guests this evening, you are welcomed to stay," Alex told them, and swooped up the letters and money in his hand. "You make a good argument, or perhaps I just want to see two people get home in one piece," he said, looking straight at Dagmara, and handed over the letters of transit to Colin.

Delicately Colin placed them inside his coat pocket, treating the papers as if they were gold.

"Thank you," Colin said graciously, thanking Alex for his generosity, for not only giving him back the letters of transit, but for giving them a warm and safe place to stay for the night.

"What kind of man would I have become if I kept them, no better than the enemies we fight."

"You're a good man Alex. We appreciate this, immensely," Colin told him.

"I'm not that good, I will keep the money," he said with a sly grin, placing the Francs inside his pocket.

They heard laughter coming from outside from a few of the men and women who were drinking and singing a song in French. Dagmara looked outside and saw how happy the people were at such a dreary time, wondering how they could act in such a blithe manner?

Alex saw the look of puzzlement on Dagmara's face. "Today was a small victory for us, we killed six Germans so we celebrate, because we know each time we go out, could be our last," he told her.

The horror of his statement hit Dagmara like a ton of bricks slamming into a wall that had been shielded from the outside world. The realization of how these people live day by day opened up her eyes to a whole new way of thinking. A world in which she had been heavily guarded from, only now to be plagued by that hindrance.

"I understand. These men and women live each moment as if it was their last, because one of these days … it will be," she commented, trailing off the last few words deep in thought. "What valor."

Colin noticed how affected Dagmara was by watching these people. The compassion she expressed only made her more beautiful to him, connecting them closer, as she felt sadness within her heart.

"Yes," Alex agreed. "But both of you have also been extremely brave and lucky. She must be your lucky charm Irish boy," he said, smiling at Colin.

Later that night, Dagmara started twisting and turning in her bed, wrestling with a nightmarish dream that flourished in blood and death. A light sleeper, Colin heard her movement and woke up, noticing her discomfort from the bad dream. Her eyes twitched as if she was struggling to get free and run away. He went over and placed his hand on her forehead. The nightmare was lavish, colorful in dramatic flair. Her skin was moist; her heartbeat was racing, as he caressed her face, trying to calm her down with the comfort of his hand.

A slight scream woke Dagmara from the nightmare, as Colin sat down beside her and caressed her body, as she twisted in the blanket, feeling his hand upon her skin.

"William," she said softly, speaking the name of her fiancé.

Slowly she took a few deep breaths and then fell back asleep holding Colin's hand, feeling safe by his presence beside her. The name she spoke was one he had heard before. She was calling out to another man, perhaps even dreaming about him. It was William Cavill who invaded Dagmara Morrow's dreams and not Colin Murphy he thought. Hearing William's name slightly angered him, as he waited several minutes to see if she would be okay, knowing Dagmara must be having a violent dream, as he had the same.

Colin bent down and kissed her on the lips. "You'll be all right Dagmara, I'm here with you now. No one can harm you. You're safe," he whispered.

He moved the blanket up over her chest to her neck, tucking her in the bed, and then lied back down on the small couch. He watched Dagmara for several more minutes till his eyes became droopy, and he fell back asleep.

Early the next morning, Dagmara and Colin ate breakfast with Jarred and Alex. Jarred still disliking the strangers, resigned himself to Alex's wishes, and let go of some of the contempt he originally had for them. He disliked foreigners, even if they were on his side. They were all his enemies he felt, but sometimes the least likely people would turn out to be his allies.

"I'm sorry about roughing you up before, and for hitting you," Jarred apologized, looking straight at Dagmara. He had never intentionally hit a woman before.

"Jarred will take you up the road for a few miles, but after that, I'm afraid you're both on your own. We cannot jeopardize going farther without compromising our position here," Alex told them.

"I understand. I have money …" Colin started to say, and reached inside his pocket taking out the Francs he had taken from David Bragger.

"Keep your money, you both will need it, and I won't ask where you got it," Alex replied.

"I wouldn't tell you," Colin said, as Alex smiled, liking the young Irishman's feistiness.

Alex would love to have Colin stay and fight alongside him, but he knew his place was not here; he had another path in life, one that did not include his war with the Vichy government. Alex knew Colin Murphy's path was with the young woman who sat beside him. He could see it in the young man's eyes every time he looked at her. He would never leave her, not for anything, or anyone.

"I wish you both safe passage home," Alex told them.

"Thank you," Dagmara said with a smile.

"Thank you Alex. I won't forget what you've done for us," Colin told him, and shook hands goodbye, thanking him for his benevolence.

Alex hugged Dagmara. "Be safe," he whispered in her ear, knowing this would be the last time either of them would see one another again, and she gave him a small kiss on the side of his face.

Her smile would be the one thing he would remember most about Dagmara Morrow, as he gently rubbed his cheek feeling her soft lips press against his skin, and then he watched them drive away in the truck.

"I hope to never see you both again," he said, taking in a deep breath, wishing for their safe passage through France, and then Alex placed his gun at his side and began to get ready for a new day's bloody battle.

Silence immersed inside the truck as Jarred drove down the road, driving them away from his hideout, and then abruptly came to a jolting stop at an ending point in the road. Their ride was over; he could take them no farther. The rest of their journey would have to be traveled by foot.

"You have to get out here," Jarred told them, looking all around making sure they had not been followed.

Colin helped Dagmara out of the vehicle. Jarred got out of the truck, walked over to them, and extended his hand to the Irishman.

"I might not agree with what Alex did, but I respect him, and if he trusts you, than so should I," Jarred said to them, and reached inside his pocket and took out Colin's gun. "I believe this is yours. You'll need it."

"Thank you," Colin said, and shook hands with the man who once regarded him as an enemy, and now offered his hand in friendship.

"Good luck," Jarred commented, and then jumped back into the truck and drove away.

They watched the truck move farther away from them. They watched as the dust twirled around in the road, leaving them behind, alone. They were on their own again, with only each other to rely on, momentarily helped by two men who believed in a cause greater than themselves. There were several hundred men and women who were part of the resistance in France, and they came across two, courageous men with integrity who had befriended them and aided their escape.

And as the dust settled to the ground and the truck and all signs of Jarred, Alex and the resistance were gone, Colin and Dagmara looked down the long, desolate road that lied ahead, that would lead them on their path to freedom.

"It will soon be over with now. We'll soon be home," Colin reassured Dagmara, as the dreariness darkened on the long, narrow road.

"Yes, we'll soon be out of here, and forget all about this place and everything that ever happened," Dagmara added, as she looked down the road and then at Colin with a slight happiness and sadness to her eyes, as she realized what she had just said.

Colin took Dagmara's hand in his, and they started walking down the road together. He felt the letters of transit in his pocket, and he hoped they would make it to the airport without coming into contact with anymore resistance groups, Germans, and especially the man who would never stop searching for them no matter where they hid in France. He would always be one step ahead of them. He would eventually find them. David Bragger would track them down, relentlessly, hunting them, searching for his document, the key that held his life, his very existence within a piece of paper. An envelope they now held within their possession.

They could destroy him with the papers. They could ruin him and prove he is a traitor to his own country, and it would mean certain death. They held his life within their hands, and as Colin and Dagmara moved down the road together, moving closer towards home, they also moved closer towards peril within each step they took.

David Bragger among others would kill for what Colin kept inside his coat pocket. And there would be no escape, no turning back. There would be no other way out, as they could only move forward, and had to keep moving in that direction, and find their way home.

CHAPTER 28

They traveled till nightfall, keeping to themselves, heading in the direction Alex showed them. The sun had set, darkness closed in around them, and then they stopped for a short rest when they heard a vehicle in the distance, and hurriedly moved behind a tree for cover. They shielded themselves from eyesight as the truck full of German soldiers thrashed down the road at a fast speed, kicking up dirt, and then was gone.

Dagmara and Colin stayed hidden for several minutes in case another truck followed, and then they decided to take a short rest before heading back down the road again. They would make it to the next town before they would stop for the night, and then continue on again in the morning.

They sat down together and took a few deep breaths. Colin took out the small container full of water and offered it to Dagmara. She took a large sip, and then he took a few gulps, wanting to conserve the liquid until they could get more. The sorrow in her eyes thickened as she thought about her nightmare, about what Alex had said to them. The words she spoke earlier.

"What are you thinking about?"

"Nothing," she said with an unconvincing lie.

"Was it the dream you had last night?"

She looked at Colin, surprised that he could read her so well.

"Yes, how did you know?"

"You were having a nightmare."

"Did I say anything?"

Colin thought back for a moment, remembering her saying the name William. Remembering her calling out another man's name, and not his.

"No," he answered, wondering what she thought she might have mentioned unintentionally to him.

"It was awful, I've never had a nightmare like that before. It seemed so real, like I was really there in the moment, and everything around me was happening."

"Do you want to tell me about it?"

Everything inside of Dagmara wanted to tell Colin about the dream, but she could not, she would not tell him what she saw. How could she tell him she dreamed his death, William's death, and her own.

She dreamed they were all sitting together at a table in a crowded upscale restaurant, their table leading out towards the dance floor. They were laughing, drinking champagne, enjoying each other's company. Dressed in a long, silver, form fitted gown with long gloves to match, Dagmara had long hair again, her curls falling down over her shoulders. Red lips, long black lashes, she looked more beautiful than she had ever seen herself look before.

William was dressed in a black tuxedo, his hair slicked back looking incredibly handsome. The twinkle in his eyes, his dimple protruding from his chin, she had missed him. And then there was Colin; he was seated on the other side of her. He was also wearing a tuxedo, clean shaven, his hair cut short, smoldering in sexiness.

They were toasting, celebrating some happy event, when suddenly German soldiers stormed in and started shooting up the establishment, sporadically killing every person that crossed their path.

People were screaming, running in panic for their lives. And then she saw the woman who was viciously raped and murdered at the plane crash being dragged across the ground by two soldiers, screaming for them to let her go. Blood was everywhere. The dance floor looked like a pool of death, and as the enemies approached their table, William and Colin tried to defend themselves, but they were powerless.

They were both shot, several times. The deadly bullets piercing their flesh, slicing into their bodies, as Dagmara screamed with terror, unable to help them. She saw William fall over onto the table dead. Then she witnessed Colin taking a bullet in the forehead, his body falling down to the ground dead. And she was left sitting alone, having watched both men she loved killed right in front of her eyes.

Stricken with indescribable horror, she was unable to move, paralyzed by the amount of blood all over their bodies. Then she looked down at herself, and saw a large hole in her stomach, blood all over her hands. She looked back up into the enemy's cruel eyes, and saw him point his gun directly at her face … and fire.

She closed her eyes, trying to shake off the disturbing, violent dream, not wanting to relive the traumatic events, not wanting to see the bloody images in her mind. The faces of William and Colin, reliving the pain, reliving her own death. Her chest moved rapidly with several deep breaths, and then she opened her eyes feeling Colin's hand upon her arm.

"Was it that horrid?" he asked.

"Even though I know it was just a dream, it seemed so real … as if … of events to come," she answered.

Dagmara was trembling, as Colin held her around in his arms, enfolding her body closer to his for comfort.

"I'm frightened that what I saw might come true," she told him.

"It was just a nightmare Dagmara. Dreams are never what they seem to be, usually they're the opposite," Colin told her, trying to simmer her fears.

She looked up at him, wanting to tell him, but she could not. She saw the look on his face, and knew she never would. How could she tell Colin she saw him being killed? That she saw all three of them die, including William. How could she tell him what she dreamed might be more than a nightmare. That it might be a premonition in some eerie way?

"I want you to know that what I said back there before about forgetting everything … I didn't *mean* everything. I don't want to ever forget about you … about us," she said.

"I know. I too want to forget about things that happened here," he said, regarding his friend Mark Quinn.

"I know you must be hurting," she said and gently touched his hand.

Softly she caressed his fingers, as both of them wanted to be banished from this hell, the darkness that surrounded them in every corner. But at the same time, they equally wanted to move once more back into that fiery warmth of passion, that layer of lust and love that thickened within each kiss. Forbidden to ever feel that pleasure again.

Dagmara started to hum the song she once heard on the dance floor in Venice. And for a brief moment she could hear the music playing perfectly in her head. Her heart swaying in feverish remembrance hearing the torch singer sing the enchanting song. She had loved that song ever since that night, which now seemed so long ago, but in her heart, it was only a moment ago.

"What's that you're singing?" he asked.

Suddenly Dagmara was back into the present moment, feeling as if she had momentarily left this place of death. The moment had seemed so real, as if she could feel William's hands upon her skin, twirling her around the dance floor, leading up to their very first kiss.

"Just a song," she replied.

"It sounds nice, what's it called?"

"I don't know, but it was beautiful," she said, as a smile crossed her face. Her eyes radiant with happy memories.

Then the smile on her face slowly disappeared as she let go of the memory and looked into Colin's eyes, the Irishman who made her heart flutter like butterflies on a warm spring day. She would never sing that song again, it would be too painful, as she saw the look in his eyes, knowing she could not give him what he wanted, what he needed, and especially desired.

"I can't give you what you want. You must know that. You must try to understand …" she told him, wanting to say more but unable to get the words out, not wanting to hurt him.

His fingers moved down her cheek, and the roughness of his hands felt gentle across her face, as he caressed her smooth skin. She closed her eyes feeling his sensual touch, wanting to give him what he yearned for, but could not.

"I can't help how I feel. You must know that," Colin stated with passion, as she opened her eyes. He desired to devour her body like a block of ice melting down the cold, hardened exterior of his heart.

"Part of me is afraid to go home, for what will be waiting for me."

"And the other half?" he asked.

"Wants to stay with you," she told him, and then a cold chill crawled over her body. "Why do I have this feeling … that I will never see you again."

Colin leaned towards her mouth, her breath deepened, her lips slightly opened, and rapidly in voracious momentum he kissed her. Passionate, the fiery lust scorched through the cold air, as he placed his hands around her face, connecting them closer. The kiss was amorous, connecting their souls.

Then suddenly they heard footsteps approaching, broke their lips apart, looked up, and saw a gun aimed directly at them. They saw the shine off the deadly weapon from the moonlight's glow as the man stepped forward from the shadows.

It was him, the man who had been tracking them since they left. The man who was ruthless in his endeavor to recover his stolen papers. The man who was left wounded in his flat. Dagmara and Colin stood face to face with their assailant, as David Bragger moved closer with a vicious, determined look in his eyes, tightening his finger around the trigger.

"Well what do we have here?" Bragger said, as he walked closer, motioning for them to stand up. "Brother and sister, I suspected not. I've never kissed my sister like that," he said in a condescending tone.

They both stood up.

Quietly Colin started to move his hand towards his gun.

"Don't move, stay right where you are!" Bragger shouted, and Colin obeyed, moving his hand away from the concealed weapon. "Now slowly, take out the gun, and place it down on the ground," he ordered.

Slowly Colin moved his hand towards the weapon, and as he pulled out the gun, he contemplated for a brief second about firing a shot, deciphering if he would be quicker than David Bragger, knowing he would have only one chance to find out.

"I'll shoot you before you even get a shot off," Bragger told him, anticipating his move. "Go ahead, try it," he said, taunting Colin to pull the trigger, wanting him to take a shot, as Colin felt the gun tighten within his hand.

Then feeling the power slowly slip away, Colin placed the gun down on the ground. He stood back up and looked David Bragger directly in the eyes. Intrepid, Colin showed no sign of fear as their captor aimed his gun directly at his chest.

"Ah, the blind confidence of youth," Bragger mused, admiring Colin's fearlessness. "Now where is it!" he demanded.

"What are you talking about?" Colin answered.

"Don't try to play games with me, you know exactly what I'm referring to. Where is the envelope!" he yelled.

"You mean the papers that will prove you're a traitor to your own country," Colin stated brazenly, disgusted by his treacherous actions.

The boldness of Colin's words upset David Bragger, figuring out who he really was. He was not a spy for England; he was a double agent working for the Germans. Colin Murphy had now become a liability to him, they both had by knowing the truth.

"I don't think you both realize the danger of the situation you are in," Bragger told them, as Dagmara looked at Colin, and a cold chill moved over her body.

"I promise to give you your papers if you let us go," Colin said, trying to make a deal.

"I think you fail to see what has to be done here," he told them with no qualms of conscience.

"Let her go, and I'll give you what you want," Colin stated, wanting to sacrifice himself for Dagmara.

Colin Murphy's uncommon valor drew Dagmara Morrow closer to him, knowing what he would do for her.

"No, you can't. I won't let you do that for me," Dagmara said, shaking her head no, not wanting Colin to sacrifice his life for hers.

"How sweet, now give me the envelope, and I'll give you both a ten second head start," Bragger said with a vicious grin.

"I don't have it. I've already mailed it to England. So whether you kill us or not, your life is already over. *You're already dead*!" Colin stated with impassioned conviction, prevailing in the deadly predicament his words placed them in. Now knowing David Bragger had no intention of ever letting them go.

"I don't believe you, I'm calling your bluff Colin," Bragger responded, and pointed his gun directly at Dagmara. "You have five seconds to produce the envelope, or I will kill her!" he stated with deadly intent.

David Bragger was excellently trained, he could see through a lie, as Colin Murphy's suspension of disbelief had failed him for the first time. He had found a man cleverer than he, in every aspect. And as David Bragger started counting down to one, strong in his murderous plan, Colin instantly took out the envelope, producing evidence of his failure. Failure to bluff the man who was a master at this game, who held their lives within his deadly, treacherous hand.

"Now throw it over to me," Bragger demanded.

Colin looked at Dagmara, and then at the gun that lied beside his feet, and as he threw the envelope towards their captor, Colin simultaneously reached down for the weapon and grabbed it in his hands.

The envelope flew through the air towards David Bragger, but he anticipated the young Irishman's move, and as Colin grabbed the gun in his hand, David Bragger simultaneously fired a shot. The bullet was aimed directly at Colin's chest, and as Colin stood back up, the bullet was already flying through the air, straight at his body, in accurate, deadly, precision!

CHAPTER 29

David Bragger reached his hand out to grab the envelope, and before Colin could move out of the way of the flying, deadly bullet, Dagmara suddenly moved in front of him, placing her body as his shield; and the bullet sliced through her like a flame of fire. The bullet pierced her flesh with enormous force, as her whole body shook from the robust impact, and Colin was unable to push her out of the way in time. It happened so fast. Dagmara had stepped in and saved Colin Murphy's life. And in the end, she was the one and not he who had sacrificed her life for the other. She sacrificed her life for him.

Dead silence swarmed over them in the darkness of the night, as Dagmara fell weightless in the air towards the ground. David Bragger was momentarily dazed from witnessing her heroic act, as Colin was paralyzed from movement watching the bullet pierce Dagmara's body. Neither of them breathed in the climatic moment.

Colin caught Dagmara in his arms as she fell down to the ground. The bullet sliced through the side of her stomach, leaving a large hole, and it was as if her nightmare had somehow come true. Blood flowed out of the wound. Her body lied still. Her eyes staring up at him, as he was speechless, unable to comprehend what she had done.

Fury immersed within Colin's body, his strength becoming the violent weight of two men, as he looked down at his hands that were full of blood, her blood. Rapidly he got to his feet, and forcefully charged towards David Bragger. Like a man on fire gunning for vengeance, he moved so fast that Bragger could barely see him, as Bragger fired his gun at the moving, unstoppable, target.

The bullets flew passed Colin, not stopping him from moving forward. Fearless with strong conviction, not caring if he was shot let alone killed, he attacked the man who had shot the woman he loved. He jumped on David Bragger, both men fell down onto the ground, and the gun was knocked out of Bragger's hand.

Blinded by rage, Colin punched him in the face, whaling at him with incredible force, as anger fueled his venomous strength. Colin kept hitting and hitting him, as Bragger tried to defend himself as he punched Colin in the eye, hitting him in the ribs that were already injured from the last time they fought. But his hard hits were no match for the fierce anger that lied within Colin Murphy's hands, as he kept seeing the image flash before his eyes of the bullet slicing through Dagmara's body, distorting his vision to see and think clearly.

Bragger's face was bleeding, the blood dripping down his nostrils and through his mouth, as Colin smashed his face ferociously with his fists. Bragger got in a few strong punches, as they wrestled on the ground, tearing at each other viciously like two animals in the wild. The enormous strength the young Irishman had within his hatred overpowered the strength of his enemy, as Bragger lied pinned on the ground beneath his body. His fist clenched with force, his knuckles bleeding, Colin emerged into an uncontrollable, unstoppable, machine. He felt hollow within his heart, not wanting to stop.

David Bragger's strength started to give way to the brutal beating. Unable to defend himself, the wild animal attacking its predator, the violent beating seemed endless for the man who had killed the animal's mate.

Then abruptly Colin stopped, stopping himself from killing Bragger. It took all the strength in his body not to kill this man, as he looked over at Dagmara lying on the ground, covered in blood, not moving. His hands were bleeding, his face bruised, his ribs broken, as Colin moved off Bragger's body, and started walking towards her. He felt his heart aching in agony, the torment seeing her body lying there. Each step felt unbearable as he moved towards her and wiped the blood off his lip with the back of his hand.

Slowly Bragger opened his eyes, spitting out blood, trying to move himself off the ground, when suddenly he reached for his gun, and Colin instantly turned around. This time anticipating his move, being one step ahead of him, Colin fired his gun, getting off the first shot. Transformed into an unmerciful killer, Colin's eyes almost glowed in the moonlight, as he fired a bullet directly at him.

And before the smoke even cleared, the bullet hit David Bragger straight in the forehead, killing him upon contact, killing him before he had a chance to fire back. His body fell down to the ground, his head hitting the rocks, his hand letting go of his weapon.

Feeling no remorse for his victim, feeling no qualms of conscience for killing the vile David Bragger, a piece of himself, of his soul was taken within that second as Colin fired the gun. And as the bullet hit its target, and the enemy fell down dead, Colin Murphy stepped back into that darkened place, *and lied with the devil once more.*

And Colin wished he could do it over again as he rushed to Dagmara and held her in his arms. Her body felt comatose. Feeling no life within her, drained by the blood loss, taken from him by a fiendish traitor. The bullet had sliced into her body, tearing her flesh with excruciating pain, as her warmth started to fade. Blood gushed from the open wound, all over their clothes, as he pressed her body against his chest.

"NO!" Colin shouted. "You can't die on me Dagmara. I won't let you!" he said, and kissed her on the lips with love, as the pain engulfed his heart, feeling as if the bullet had pierced his chest. It was killing him inside to see her like this.

The blood on his lips smeared onto her mouth, as he kissed her with his entire body. The force of his kiss was so powerful; he felt his hands almost crushing her frail body in the embrace. He kissed her and kissed her again.

"You have to be okay, you have to, because … I'm in love with you. Do you hear me Dagmara … I love you!" he told her, and as he said those three words, a tear slid down his cheek, sliding onto her face, as he enfolded her in his arms, smothering her face.

Never having said those words to another woman, not even in the throws of passion, Colin Murphy pronounced the love he truly felt for Dagmara Morrow. And he wished one day that she would say those three words back. It was the first time Colin Murphy had ever shown his emotional side, showing he was just like everyone else, having a weakness in his tough exterior. Love was his weakness; she was his strength, as he held Dagmara tightly in his arms. He closed his eyes for a brief moment; the agonizing feeling ripped him apart inside, as if he was silently dying.

"Why her?" he shouted, as anger fumed in his bones. Then he looked up into the sky and said, "I should have been the one to die, not her. It should have been me!"

Colin closed his eyes again, as his words of love and devotion swirled around them in the open wind, and the forces that lie hidden to why some people live and others die, had been silently awakened. The moonlight shined down upon them and Colin slowly opened his eyes. He looked down at Dagmara, and suddenly he felt her hand squeeze his. It was not her time to die. Dagmara Morrow had not completed her journey yet.

She had been saved a second time, rescued from the clutches of death by the love of two men. One who held her in his arms, the other, who lie wounded in a hospital bed. But it was the first and not the latter of the two men, the one who was the closest to her that fate had heard, honoring his request.

But this time her body was badly injured, as the bullet held her life's existence within its deadly rapture, and Dagmara could barely move let alone speak, choking on her own blood. The oxygen was not flowing properly through her damaged, weakened body. Her lungs started filling with blood, and Colin desperately needed to get her to a doctor in order to save her life. He had to get her to someone before time ran out. Before the irreversible was done. Before it was too late.

He would not let that happen to her. He would not let her die in his arms if it took every breath inside his body to get her help. Colin Murphy would not allow Dagmara Morrow to die.

"It's going to be all right Dagmara," he whispered in her ear. "I'm going to get you help."

Dagmara tried to speak, but he placed his finger on her mouth telling her to save her strength. Slowly she moved her hand onto his, pushing it aside, and spoke in a barely audible tone. "Is he dead?"

"Yes, he will never be able to hurt you or anyone else, ever again," Colin told her, and then he asked her the question he had to know the answer to, the question that plagued his thoughts, haunting him in image. "Why, why did you do that Dagmara?" wanting to know why she had placed herself in front of him, taking the bullet that was meant for his destruction.

She touched his cheek with her hand, sliding her fingers over his face, feeling his swollen lip, his left eye that had already started to change in dark bruised color.

"Because ..." she started to say, feeling the enormous, acute pain in her body, the bullet draining her of strength. And then he understood perfectly why she had done so, because of him, for him ... because she loved him. Dagmara Morrow truly loved him.

Angry that Dagmara had sacrificed herself for him, Colin felt not worthy of her love, hating himself for ever treating her with mean intentions. He once had said he would not sully his hands with the likes of someone like her, he could not have been more wrong. His arrogance was gone. The rogue like layers had been stripped away. The sexy Irish charmer had immersed into a soft spoken, compassionate man. His prejudice was no longer there within her ripped layers of pride, no longer separated by classes of birth.

"Tell me you love me," she said, as blood seeped through her lips.

"I love you."

"Dagmara."

"I love you Dagmara," he told her, as she gasped for air, wanting to hear those words before she died, before she would never hear them again, as her body became cold, numb, feeling less of his touch upon her skin, and more of nothing at all.

Then Colin kissed her on the lips with incredible passion, sealing their fate, as if it was the long kiss goodbye. This time the blood on her lips smeared his mouth.

"Please don't let me die here," she told him in excruciating pain, barely able to breathe, gasping for air. "Please don't leave me alone."

"I won't. I promise you, I'll never leave you Dagmara. Just stay with me, stay awake. Try to keep your eyes open," he told her, his heart filling with love, holding back the tears that formed in his eyes. He wanted to be strong, for her, for himself, not wanting to succumb to that weak element in a time of emergency.

He was going to leave Dagmara and get help, not wanting to move her body, but Colin had given her his word against his better judgment, and he would not go back on his promise, so he would take her with him. Colin looked down at her face; her eyes had closed again as he shook her body to keep her awake, and she reopened her eyes looking up at him. The glossy look in her eyes was one of pain, love, intertwined into one. Her light was slowly being extinguished, fading in time, as the passion they felt towards each other was inexplicable for anyone else to fully comprehend.

He told her he loved her, and he did. Colin Murphy loved Dagmara Morrow more than anyone else in the world at that very moment. He loved her more than life itself. He would give his life for her. He would die for her. Enamored with her vivacious presence, her fervor, her intrepidness, and especially her cute little smile, which was her most endearing quality. The way she looked at him with her entrancing eyes. The way her naked body felt next to his. The softness of her hand against his skin.

He loved everything about her; almost to the point that he wished William Cavill was here with his money and power to help her. But all the money and power in the world could not help save Dagmara if he did not get her to a doctor in time.

The envelope had David Bragger's blood on the outside as Colin slipped it into his pocket, and gently picked her up in his arms. And as he carried Dagmara in his arms, her head resting on his chest, her hands wrapped around his neck, he looked down the long, darkened path that lied ahead. Seeing no light in the distance, Colin courageously started to walk down the desolate road. He knew there would be no going back for them. He had killed a man, an enemy, a traitor, but in favor of the Vichy government, and as long as they were in France, nowhere would be safe.

Now more police of higher rank than the short, cruel Frenchman would be searching for them, adding another murder charge to their names, adding to the countless list of treason. It would mean certain death for both of them if they were caught. If they could not escape and make their way out of the country, eventually they would be found, and that notion pushed Colin with determined conviction to move as fast as he could carrying her in his arms, desperately trying to find someone who could help, someone who would help them, and save her life.

CHAPTER 30

Colin Murphy walked feverishly in the dark, rapidly moving along the narrow, empty roads, pushing himself to go further, not wanting to stop, as time became a deadly predator, not knowing how many hours if any Dagmara had left. He carried her in his arms, shifting her body in different positions, trying to keep her awake, as the cold temperatures of the night chapped his lips, weakening the warmth he felt within his limbs.

Physically drained, Colin persevered forward unwilling to give up, as his eyes started to blink several times wanting to close. His pace started to slow down, his arms and legs felt numb, and suddenly he stumbled, losing his footing, and both of them went tumbling down to the ground. Dagmara did not even feel the crash as Colin fell on top of her; her eyes had closed awhile ago, and her body lied still.

It seemed that all hope was lost, futile in his effort that he would ever find her help, to find someone to take them in. But the hunger of love felt within his heart kept Colin Murphy alive, determined not to falter in his devoted conviction. He turned her body over, she was not moving, as he placed his fingers on her neck trying to feel her pulse. Unable to breathe, choked with panic and fear, his heart started beating at a quickened speed, as he pressed his head to her chest, hearing a faint heartbeat.

"You're alive! You're alive!" he shouted, as a tear slid down his cheek in happiness, instantly freezing on his face.

He licked his lips trying to warm them up, thankful that Dagmara was still breathing. That she was only unconscious and not dead, as his heartbeat started to slow down in rhythm, feeling a slight relief, but knowing the urgency. He had to get her to a doctor immediately if she was going to survive the night.

"Stay with me Dagmara. I don't want you to leave me, ever. I couldn't survive without you. I couldn't go on if anything happened to you," he told her, hoping she would hear him, as he kissed her gently on the lips.

He picked her up in his arms, and started to carry her farther down the road. Half dead himself, unable to feel his legs from the cold, his lip swollen, his eye blackened by the fight, Colin Murphy persevered, not willing to give up.

Then suddenly he saw a light up ahead towards the side of the road, and rapidly his pace increased, his legs feeling refreshed, as he rushed towards the light with renewed hope.

He knocked on the door several times, finally the door opened, and an old man and woman peered through the small opening. Waking them from sleep, the man grabbed for his glasses and looked outside seeing the strangers more clearly. Seeing a young man with a blackened eye, dried blood on his mouth, holding a young woman in his arms with blood all over her clothes.

"Please sir, you must help us. She needs a doctor," Colin stated strenuously.

The old woman looked up at her husband, afraid to take in strangers and give them shelter, knowing what the penalty would be for harboring fugitives.

"She needs a doctor, she's been shot," Colin repeated in a loud, desperate tone.

"Hurry, come in before you're seen," the old man replied, motioning for Colin to come inside, showing benevolence to two strangers in a disastrous time of need, as he shuffled them in and closed the door quickly behind them. "Here, put the girl on the couch," he said, and Colin placed Dagmara down, putting a pillow underneath her head.

"I have money, whatever you want …" Colin started to say in a state of panic, his pulse racing as his emotions ran rampant seeing Dagmara lying on the couch not moving. Seeing the blood, the dark red color all over her clothes. He would trade his life for hers; he would do anything in the world for Dagmara Morrow, as Colin Murphy was beside himself, not knowing how to help her.

"Go get my bag," the old man told his wife, and sat down beside Dagmara. He opened her coat, and started tearing at her shirt.

"What are you doing?" Colin yelled, as he grabbed the man's arm.

"I'm trying to save her life," he said, as his wife handed him a small black bag. "I used to be a doctor. It's been several years now since I've last practiced, but I still know what I'm doing," he told the young Irishman, as he opened his bag and pushed his glasses on tighter.

The old man in his mid sixties was still competent to be a licensed physician, but by hospital standards he was regarded as past his prime, too old to operate on people, and was pushed into retirement before he was ready to leave.

Hurriedly the doctor ripped open her shirt, saw the blood seeping through all over her white slip, and then looked up at the young man.

"What happened here?"

"She was shot … saving my life," Colin explained. "You must help her sir. You must!" he shouted at the old man.

"Calm yourself," he told Colin, as he moved his hand down to Dagmara's stomach seeing the bullet wound, his fingers full of fresh blood. "She needs to get to a hospital, she's lost too much blood," he diagnosed, as he took her pulse, feeling the slowness of her heartbeat starting to fade.

Just as the doctor started fumbling through his bag, all three of them suddenly heard footsteps approach the house. They immediately looked towards the windows and saw shadows lurking outside. They could see the outline of several men carrying guns.

"You must go, we'll take care of her," the old man said.

"NO, I won't leave her!" Colin shouted.

"You must, you can't help her now, especially if you're caught. I don't know what you both are involved in, but you don't seem threatening. I'll think of something to tell them, just go," the old man urged Colin, thinking they were both part of the French resistance.

"I can't," Colin said, raising his voice again, looking all around, seeing the shadows moving closer to the door. "I won't leave her!"

"We'll see she gets help. I'll take care of her. I promise you."

"Do you have another way out of here?" Colin asked, thinking he could take Dagmara with him.

"Go through the back. Hurry!" the old man yelled.

Just as Colin was deciphering what to do, not wanting to leave Dagmara, but knowing he could not be caught, especially with the important papers he carried inside his coat pocket, the front door slammed wide open and several armed men rushed in.

Rapidly Colin raced through the room into the kitchen, darting through the rooms towards the back door, and as he opened the door, he immediately came to a shattering halt. Several flashes of light blinded his vision, as he put his hand up to his eyes trying to see, he was instantly struck in the face by a weapon, and forced up against the wall by several armed men.

His face hit the wall hard, as the rough measure in which they apprehended their captive was forceful. Before Colin had a chance to speak let alone defend himself, he was frisked, his gun taken from him, and so were the contents of his pocket containing David Bragger's envelope, their money, and most importantly, the letters of transit.

They removed his belongings, and Colin forcefully struggled trying to stop them, grabbing at the papers that were being seized, as one of his hands got loose, and he punched one of the men in the face. Swiftly Colin was struck with a robust hit to the ribs, causing enormous pain to his lower abdomen that was already badly injured, breaking another rib. Then they smashed his body down to the floor, tying his hands behind his back, keeping control of their prisoner, as two men held him down on the ground, and several others covered him, aiming their guns directly at his body.

"If he moves, shoot him," the man in charge commanded, as he took a look at the envelope, noticing its importance, and placed it inside his coat pocket along with the money and letters of transit, and then walked into the front room.

Both the old man and his wife had their hands raised in the air, barely breathing, as three armed men pointed guns at them. The man in charge walked over to the body lying on the couch, and saw it was a young woman. He swiped his finger through the redness on her clothes, placed it to his nose, smelling the fresh blood, and his face turned ferociously cold with anger.

"Did you do this?" the man shouted, and the old couple shook their heads no.

"The young man brought her here for help," he tried to explain, barely getting the words out, as his wife squeezed his hand in fear.

"Are you a doctor?"

"Yes, well … was," he answered, trying to control his shaking hands in the presence of all the guns.

"Looks like you didn't do a very good job doc," the man in charge stated, as he walked back over to Dagmara, infuriated at the bloody sight.

Then the man motioned to his men to keep an eye on the old couple, and walked back into the other room to his prisoner. He motioned for them to pick him up, and they pulled Colin up off the ground to his feet. The man in charge stood tall, taller than Colin, as he looked down at the Irishman with a dominating look in his eyes that would induce fear in the most courageous of men.

"Who are you?" he asked his prisoner.

Colin did not answer him, and then the man in charge motioned to one of his men standing alongside his captive, and they hit Colin in the ribs again, this time even harder. The enormous hit tore into his body like a crashing bolt of lightning, and he started to cough up blood. Colin spit the blood in the man's face, and then the man punched him in the mouth with a forceful hit, took out a cloth from his pocket, and wiped the blood off his cheek.

"Take him," the man in charge ordered, and the armed men started dragging Colin into the front room past Dagmara.

"She needs help!" Colin yelled. "She must get to a hospital right away. You must help her!" he shouted, as he struggled to get away, but he could not unleash the powerful grip the two men had on him, as they pushed him unwillingly through the front door.

"Bring her," the man in charge ordered, as one of the men picked Dagmara up in his arms and carried her through the front door.

"She needs a doctor," the old man concurred.

"I'm sure she does," the man in charge stated, as he walked out of the house, having his men follow behind.

They loaded Colin into a car, pushing him in as he struggled to get free. "Where are you taking me?" he shouted, and then he saw them load Dagmara into another car. "Where are you taking her?" he yelled.

Colin demanded answers, protesting being treated like criminals, as they locked him in the vehicle and drove off down the road, as he watched the man in charge get into the vehicle with Dagmara.

Not knowing where they were being taken, having lost their only chance to get out of the country, their fate now lied within the hands of the man who held their letters of transit. The papers to their freedom. To their journey home. Their fate lied within the man who had taken them by force. The man who asked questions and gave no answers, as the vehicles followed one another in unison, racing down the desolate road at an accelerated speed.

CHAPTER 31

"Quickly get her on the table," the doctor ordered his staff, as several nurses rushed around the young woman and lifted her body carefully onto the operating table.

Instantly a nurse fitted the doctor with a mask and gloves, not expecting another patient at this late hour. Immediately the doctor cut open Dagmara Morrow's slip, as the nurses moved about and removed her undergarments and sterilized the opened wound.

"We don't have much time, she's lost a lot of blood," the doctor told his staff.

The operation would take over an hour, as the doctor prepared himself for the long haul, hoping it would not take several hours, knowing the risk of losing this young woman was high. The danger of the intricate procedure in removing the lodged bullet in her body had to be perfect in precision; otherwise the bullet might shatter, if it had not already.

There was more blood on Dagmara's clothes than it seemed in her body, as the middle aged doctor with a steady hand made a small incision, and slowly moved his long, silver instrument into her flesh. The doctor had seen hundreds of patients in the past several months, but none had been a fair headed beauty as the one that lied before him on the operating table. He had seen all types of bodies, but he had not seen a woman in a long time, operating mostly on soldiers wounded in the war.

"Her heart rate is plummeting," a nurse said, monitoring her vital signs.

"I have to keep on going," the doctor replied, moving the long, skinny instrument deeper into her body, piercing her flesh with force, as he searched for the bullet.

More blood seeped through the opened wound, the incision increased in size, adding pressure to the injury, which caused a reaction that was common.

"Doctor we're going to lose her," a nurse shouted, as her heart rate rapidly decreased.

"You must stop!" the head nurse stated strenuously, urging the doctor to stop the procedure.

"If I don't continue, we're going to lose her anyway," the doctor told his staff, as he continued searching for the bullet, moving the instrument farther into the wound.

Blood continued to flow to the surface as he pierced her flesh with more force. Unconscious, the fever had taken over, and Dagmara felt no pain at all.

"Doctor," the first nurse yelled, as her heart rate started to lower, her body lied completely still.

Suddenly the doctor was forced to make a quick and dangerous decision. A decision, that would either save or kill his patient.

"Give her another dose," he ordered.

"It will kill her," the head nurse intervened, disobeying the doctor's orders, as she believed he was making the wrong choice.

"I don't have time to argue with you Marnie, she will die if I don't find the bullet. Now give it to her," the doctor commanded loudly, frightening the other nurses.

"Yes sir," the head nurse replied, acquiescing to the doctor's orders, and injected the patient's arm with a needle, as Dagmara felt no discomfort from the sharpness.

The doctor waited a few seconds. He knew the deadly repercussions of his actions, but he believed he had made the right judgment call, knowing the patient would die if he did not keep going, knowing she would die if he stopped. It was a two way dead end, and both ways seemed futile. The young woman was teetering on the brink of death, lingering between the shadows of darkness and light.

Oppressed with the enormous pressure, her life was solely in the doctor's hands, and whether she would live or die, he did not know, as he began searching for the bullet again. When his patient started moving into a comatose state, and the head nurse Marnie started shaking her head at the doctor, he knew he had only seconds to find the bullet and either save or kill this young woman. He held Dagmara's survival within his hands, and in a way he was like a god, having the power to save people's lives. The doctor desperately wanted to save this patient, but felt compelled to give into reason, acquiesce to Marnie, and not listen to himself.

As Dagmara began to lose all signs of consciousness, and drift off into the hollow existence of forever darkness, the doctor clamped onto the bullet with his instrument, and pulled it back through her flesh, through the opened hole in her body.

Marnie's eyes opened wide, and so did the other nurses, as they were in complete surprise that the doctor was able to find the bullet in time before he lost another patient. Amazed at his fortuitous find, the doctor immediately examined the bullet to see if it was intact, all in one piece, and no fragments had broken off in her body. If the bullet had shattered and lied hidden in her flesh, the complications would be too severe, and he would never be able to find the tiny fragments in time. To his delight, the bullet was completely in one piece, as he moved back over to his patient, and started sewing up the wound.

Her vital signs started to rise, almost to a steady heartbeat, as the doctor gently moved the needle and thread in and out of her skin, trying to make the stitches small, not wanting to leave a large scar. He did this not only for the young woman's vanity, but for the man who would make love to her nightly, who would look upon her naked body. For him, he kept the stitches small.

The nurses cleaned and sterilized her body again. The wound was closed. The stitches seemed small to the naked eye of an observer, but the scar would be noticeable to his patient, leaving a permanent mark on her stomach. For now, his patient was stabilized and in fair condition, but the worst part was far from over, knowing the wound could reopen and she might have complications from the procedure. She needed to be monitored closely the entire night.

"I'm sorry I doubted your decision," Marnie said to the doctor, congratulating him for saving the girl's life. "Perhaps you will want someone else now as head nurse," she said, feeling embarrassed, angry with herself for questioning his orders at such a critical stage in the operation.

"No Marnie, you did what you thought was right at the time. I myself was beginning to think you might be right," the doctor told her, not blaming her for disagreeing with his decision.

"I'm glad you didn't listen to me."

The doctor moved closer to Marnie and said in a softer tone, "I'm always interested in what you have to say. You're a very good nurse," he told her with a slight smile, still wanting to keep their personal and professional lives separate without clashing in the operating room.

Everyone knew of their late night assignations, but none of the other nurses ever mentioned it in conversation, especially when either the doctor or Marnie was around. Marnie was practical, cynical even, but her confidence exuded not only in the operating room, but also in the bedroom. That was in part why the doctor had taken her as a lover. He could have had someone younger, prettier, but he found himself extremely attracted to Marnie for that specific reason.

"That young woman has you to thank for her life," Marnie stated.

"She has all of us to thank," he told her, looking around at all the nurses who helped in the procedure. "She will need all of our support. I hope she still has the strength left inside to fight."

Marnie smiled at the doctor, as he threw away his mask and gloves.

"Do you want me to tell the two men outside?" she asked.

"No, I think I better do it," he said, hating this part of the procedure, the aftermath, having to report the status of his patient's recovery to their family and loved ones. He loathed having to watch the bereaved faces of the family members of all the patients he could not save. Their pain, the tears, the screams, the faces that would haunt him forever in his dreams.

"They haven't moved from outside the door," Marnie commented, as the doctor looked over at the clock seeing that over two hours had past since they brought the young woman to him.

"You keep an eye on her," he told Marnie.

"Absolutely," she assured him, as the doctor took a look at his patient lying on the table, and then walked into the other room.

The doctor walked towards the two men who waited impatiently for the results of his young patient's status. Simultaneously, Colin Murphy and Robert Langton stood up. Colin felt the pull from his taped, broken ribs. His eye had already turned dark in a black and blue color. A large bruise formed on the side of his cheek, and his lips were slightly swollen from the beating. But still his sexiness was not overshadowed, as several of the young nurses that walked past him smiled in a flirtatious manner, wanting desperately for him to smile back.

"Well doc ..." Robert Langton started to ask, his emotions never fluctuating.

"How is she doctor?" Colin interjected, overlapping Langton's words, his heartbeat racing at an enormous speed. Emotional, the doctor could see how worried the young man was for the girl.

"The procedure went well, she's stabilized for the moment. I found the bullet and removed it. She's very lucky it had not shattered," the doctor told them.

"That's wonderful doctor," Colin said, elated hearing that Dagmara had survived. That she was going to be all right.

"There's more," the doctor started to say.

"What is it?" Langton asked, seeing the expression deepen on the doctor's face with concern.

"You must tell me doctor, is she going to be okay?" Colin asked, raising his voice.

"I'm afraid she's lost a lot of blood. We had to give her a transfusion. We were extremely lucky to find the bullet in time ..." he said, stopping himself before he said too much.

"What does that mean?" Langton asked.

The hesitance of the doctor's words meant unpleasant news, as Colin needed to know the full truth.

"What are you not telling us doctor?" Colin impatiently asked.

"We almost lost her ..." the doctor replied.

"But I thought you said you removed the bullet and she's now stabilized," Colin interrupted.

"Let the doctor finish," Langton said, seeing the concern in Colin's eyes, and it was then at that precise moment when he looked at the young Irishman, Robert Langton understood Colin Murphy's true involvement with Dagmara Morrow. They were not just friends let alone strangers, thrown together in a desperate attempt to get out of France. They were much more than that. His overwhelming concern for her had unintentionally shown how much he cared for Dagmara, and suddenly the missing pieces of the puzzle started to fit together, falling into place.

"Yes as I said, we have her stabilized, for now, but the procedure was very intricate in removing the bullet. She has sustained massive trauma and blood loss, and her body is weak. Her organs strained from the injury, especially her heart. She's in a very critical stage right now. We will be monitoring her status the entire night," the doctor told them.

"In English doc," Langton asked straightforward.

"If she's tough, hopefully she will pull through."

"What can we do?" Colin asked, raising his voice again.

"There's nothing more either one of us can do for her now, other than hope she keeps fighting, and will make it through the night," the doctor told Colin, feeling for the young man, hating this part of the conversation.

"Make it through the night," Colin repeated, as his heart sank in gut wrenching agony. "But she's too young to die doctor ... she can't. She can't!"

Colin shouted, as his words choked him inside, feeling as if the vicious hands of the man who pulled the trigger was crushing his heart.

The torment was unbearable for Colin to withstand, as he looked through the small opening of the door and saw Dagmara lying on the table. Her body lifeless. Her eyes closed. He loved her more than life itself.

Robert Langton felt empathy for Colin, and in a moment of weakness, never allowing himself to get involved in any of his client's cases, always showing no indifference, he felt sorry for the young Irishman, an emotion that was hardly ever felt inside his hardened heart. He placed his hand on Colin's shoulder for comfort, feeling his pain, insinuating to the Irishman he was not alone.

The hand on his shoulder did not make an impact on Colin Murphy. Aching with tremendous torture, the acute agony in his chest had not subsided for a second, feeling incredibly distraught. A feeling he had never felt before. The love that had blossomed in his heart for Dagmara Morrow had broken down the layers of his arrogant demeanor. She was not just some girl, a woman he had bedded and lusted for, she was so much more than that, taking a place within his heart alongside his mother and Brady.

"You have to be strong son," the doctor told Colin, feeling sympathy for the young man. "I'll do everything I can to help her, but I'm afraid the rest is up to her now. It's out of our hands."

"You'll let us know if anything changes," Langton said to the doctor.

"Of course. I've done all I can, if I could do more for her …" the doctor started to say, trailing off his words in thought.

"Thank you doctor, we know you did your best," Langton told him.

"I'll leave you both."

The doctor started to walk away, and Colin yelled out to him. "Thank you."

The doctor shook his head to the compliment, and then walked back inside the operating room and closed the door.

"I'm sure Dagmara will make it. She's young, strong," Langton said, trying to reassure Colin, giving him hope.

Colin looked up at the stranger, his eyes conveying the sorrow of his tortured soul.

"She has to," Colin said, and then Robert Langton reaffirmed his earlier conclusions as he saw the love in the young Irishman's eyes for Dagmara. Whatever they had gone through together, whatever had transpired between them on their perilous, deadly journey, had made them close, closer than Langton first presumed.

CHAPTER 32

The long, endless night seemed to last forever, minutes moved as hours that slowed into seconds. Colin Murphy and Robert Langton sat in silence for the first hour while he watched the young Irishman stare at the closed door to the operating room. Dagmara would soon be moved to another room, and until then, he could not go in and see her, let alone hold her hand.

Oppressing his mind like a thundering bolt of bricks, Colin thought about their time together from the first moment he saw Dagmara Morrow on the street when she looked into his eyes after rescuing her from those soldiers. How she pretended to be a boy, forcing her to cut her long blonde hair, watching as the curls fell down around her shoulders and onto the floor. The first time she kissed him, he had wiped away her kiss, wishing now he could take it back. He remembered how he had mistreated her with disdain for being part of the rich upper class. How they had become close over the past few weeks, and especially the last couple of days, closer than he would have ever imagined.

He remembered the violent way his best friend had treated her. How Mark Quinn's death still weighed heavily on his conscience. The last words his friend spoke to him, and the look on his brother's face when they separated, not knowing if the other would survive. Colin Murphy was not so tough after all; his rough presence had fallen, and he felt weak, not liking the feeling.

He remembered the fall that almost killed he and Dagmara. The old woman's benevolence, and Alex. The bullets that whizzed past their bodies while trying to escape. The loud stomping of the German soldiers, he remembered everything as if it was only a moment ago. The softness of her skin, their night of passion, but mostly he remembered how Dagmara had stepped in and saved his life.

The heroic act had placed her in the hospital among strangers, wounded soldiers, amongst friends. The image of her body moving in front of his, the bullet slicing into her flesh, and the blood as he held her in his arms. Colin Murphy could never forget that terrifying moment as he looked down at his hands that were full of her blood. That blood-drenched image would be imprinted in his memory forever.

Colin stared at the closed door, and wanted only to remember the passion, their night of ecstasy. How Dagmara had given herself to him, giving him her most intimate embrace, and how her body trembled from his touch, as he was the first man she had made love to.

The cherishing moment was breathtaking, as he reminisced back to that pleasurable night, as the ache inside his body strengthened in magnitude, and the lustful memory of how soft her lips felt against his, the touch of her hand on his naked body, had not overshadowed the darkening moment, not being able to succumb to that blissful memory. He could almost feel her naked body lying underneath his; becoming one, and he yearned to be placed back in that heavenly moment, wanting to escape the agony of the present.

Her slow, long, passionate kisses that warmed him inside. Seeing her body naked for the first time. The beautiful, rich pattern of her undergarments. Her sultry breasts that he smothered his mouth in, devouring every inch of her body. The lust invigorating his feverish thoughts, as his heart quickened in pace, his eyes became watery, and he held in the tears, not wanting the stranger who sat beside him to see him so vulnerable.

"I'm sorry those men at the house roughed you up so much," Langton apologized, breaking the unsettling silence.

Colin did not look at him, hearing his words; he cared about nothing but her.

"How did you find us?" Colin asked, keeping his eyes on the closed door.

"I guess I should start by telling you who sent me to find her."

His statement intrigued the Irishman, and Colin looked over at the stranger. "You were hired, by whom?"

"Jonathan Cavill," Langton replied.

"William's father," Colin stated loudly, his eyes opened wide, as Langton looked at him, surprised that he knew of Dagmara's fiancé. "He hired you to come here and find her?"

"Yes, to find out if she was still alive, and if so, bring her home."

"How long have you been searching for her?"

"Awhile, at first it seemed she had died in the crash. I found no evidence that Dagmara had survived other than the fact her body had not been recovered."

"You've been tracking us?"

"Actually the trail came up empty until I overheard a conversation between two people. At the time it was a fortuitous find that I followed up on my intuition and talked with Mrs. Bronchet, the nice woman who runs the café. It was there that I learned Dagmara was still alive, and that the man at the café was looking for you both."

"David Bragger," Colin answered.

Robert Langton could see the loath that Colin had for this individual, and he was justified in his hatred after what he had found out about the traitorous David Bragger.

"Yes, the amount of money that was exchanged in his dealing, he seemed determined to find the two of you at any price."

"Then you know about him?" Colin inquired.

"I've heard about David Bragger, but there was never any evidence that could link him to the whispers and accusations that surrounded him. But when I stumbled upon his body with the group of men I commissioned, rebels you would call them who are part of the resistance, that's when we tracked you down at the house," Langton stated.

"What a clever detective," Colin remarked with a bit of arrogance.

"I understand your dislike for me Colin, but I'm a friend, not an enemy, and much more than that. People hire me because they know I can get them what they want, no matter the cost or the risk. I can go behind the locked gates, and find the shadows where others fail to succeed," Langton told him, slightly boasting about his reputation, understanding the young man's anger.

Colin smirked at his statement.

"I told them to use whatever force was necessary, and at the time, I didn't know if David Bragger was working with someone, and who you were?"

Colin brushed his fingers across his mouth. "You have a hard hit Mr. Langton."

"Again I apologize, if I had known you were helping her …"

"You still would have roughed me up," Colin interjected, and Langton smiled liking the Irishman's audaciousness. "You'll see that the envelope gets to the right people."

"Yes, with this information, we can now prove David Bragger's treachery, and possibly catch the people who aided him. It was brave of you to have gone up against a man like him. He could have killed you," Langton replied, respecting Colin, seeing a part of himself in him when he was younger.

"He almost did."

"Where did you get the letters of transit?" Langton inquisitively asked.

"We found them on two Englishman who were already dead, their bodies had been horribly desecrated by German soldiers. They were supposed to get Dagmara and me out of the country."

"Was it just the two of you?"

Colin looked at Robert Langton without answering him, not wanting to divulge too much information, especially if it was going to be repeated to William and his father.

"Whatever you tell me is in strict confidence Colin, it won't be repeated, to anyone," Langton said, trying to reassure the Irishman seeing his hesitance.

But the precarious situation the stranger placed Colin in was anything but safe. He could not trust this man, not when he in essence worked for the enemy, the man who stood between he and Dagmara. He could not trust what he divulged to this man would stay completely between them in confidence and not leave the room.

"You can trust me Colin, I will be extremely discreet and use my discretion when telling Mr. Cavill and especially his son your involvement with his fiancée."

"I cannot tell you everything, nor would I want to, but I will tell you this," Colin started to say. "Dagmara is a very courageous, smart young woman who went through the depths of hell and back!"

His words were meant to shock Robert Langton, and he knew there was more to the story than Colin was telling. Not knowing the full truth of their relationship, Langton knew half of what they had gone through, and he would not wish that on his worst enemy. How they had ever survived was inexplicable, as he pressed Colin further for more detailed information.

"How did you meet?"

A slight smile crossed Colin's lips, knowing this man would not let up until he knew everything, so he decided to satisfy his thirst for curiosity and tell him the horrid, bloody truth.

"I met Dagmara on the street. Two German soldiers were chasing her when I found her, and took her with me. She was dressed in men's clothing and wanted to pass herself off as a boy, but I could see right away she was anything but that."

"A boy!" Robert Langton said loudly, as two nurses turned their heads in his direction, and immediately he lowered his voice.

"Yes, something so terrible had happened after the plane crash. Dagmara wouldn't even tell me the whole of it, but since then, she was afraid to be seen as a girl, and later on I agreed with her it would be safer for her to be thought of as a boy, if you know what I mean Mr. Langton."

"Yes."

"But I was the one that made her cut her hair, to her protest, wanting to give truth to the image. And we traveled together as if we were brothers …" Colin said, hesitating in his story, deciphering if he should tell Langton about the others, as Robert Langton watched him closely, rapt in his lavish tale. "We traveled with three others, my brother Brady, my friend Cillian, and … Mark Quinn …"

The way Colin mentioned Mark Quinn's name roused suspicion, as Langton watched Colin's eyes, seeing the deep seeded secret he carried with him, desperately trying to move away from, to block out of his mind, and keep hidden.

"We had to separate, the German soldiers surrounded us, we had no choice. Cillian and Brady headed for the train station as planned, and Dagmara and me went in the opposite direction, leading them away as they escaped."

"And what of Mark Quinn?" Langton asked, knowing Colin had purposely erased him from the story.

"There's nothing to tell about him," Colin stated, looking him straight in the eyes.

"Where is he?" Langton pressed further.

"He's … dead," Colin said, finally getting the words out.

"Dead!" Robert Langton said loudly again, and then lowered his voice as another nurse walked past them. "That's why you both are wanted for questioning in a murder, Mark Quinn's murder," Langton realized, understanding everything now.

"I won't tell you anymore about it," Colin replied.

"I think I already know."

Colin's eyes opened wide, surprised that Robert Langton knew about their involvement. "How …" he started to say, realizing that someone of Robert Langton's stature and means of connections would be able to find out anything, including what was going on with a police investigation. "We didn't know at first they were after us until we met Bragger, but I knew from the moment he appeared on the street, there was definitely something shady about him."

"Then you didn't murder your friend?" Langton inquired, pressuring Colin harder to get to the truth.

Colin's silence further instilled what Langton had already assumed.

"You must tell me everything Colin, if I am to help you."

"Why would you want to help me?" Colin asked with caution.

"I'm not the enemy here Colin, but I cannot help you if I don't know what's going on."

"I thought I knew him, he was my best friend since before I can even remember. I didn't know of his true feelings. I didn't think he would ever really harm Dagmara, but I was wrong … and I can never make it right," Colin said, feeling horrid for the way things ended between he and Mark Quinn.

"Then it was self defense," Langton concluded.

Colin looked up at him. "In a way, yes."

"I believe you Colin, I believe what you have told me, and no charges will be brought against you. I promise you that."

"You believe me," Colin said surprisingly.

"Yes, I think you're a good person Colin, you show a lot of integrity for someone as young as yourself. If everything you've told me is true, which I believe it is, than Dagmara owes her life to you for keeping her safe, for keeping her alive in France," Langton stated in words that sounded to Colin as admiration and respect.

"We saved each other."

"Yes, I believe you both did."

Intentionally Colin left out a certain part of the story. He left out one very important detail that made his story incomplete. He would never tell Robert Langton or anyone else what transpired between them in the bedroom that night. He would never tell of their intimate embrace, their lustful behavior, or their passion. A passion so great, it outweighed the peril. No one would ever know the truth, but the two of them.

"It was when we met David Bragger that we came into all this trouble. I believed he was lying to us from the beginning, and when we took the envelope from him, I found out he was a traitor to his own country. That is why he was trying to find us. Why he would never let us get out of France alive," Colin explained.

"And then he found you."

"Yes, somehow he found us, and demanded the papers back, and ... we'll, you know the rest of the story."

"He shot Dagmara trying to kill you, as she saved your life, and in turn, you killed him. And then you made your way to the house, and that's when I came into the picture."

"Exactly."

"And there's nothing else, nothing more that you want to tell me? That you want to add to your story?" Langton asked, knowing Colin was holding back a vital piece to the missing puzzle, a portion that would never be retrieved. The links almost all added up, except for one, his relationship with Dagmara.

"No," Colin answered. "That's it."

Reading people was also Robert Langton's expertise, knowing if someone was lying to him. He could see right through the false story, and up until this moment, he had not doubted what Colin Murphy had told him. But he could see it in his eyes, the way his heart was beating, the heaviness of his breath; there was something else, something between the Irishman and Dagmara that Colin did not want Langton or anyone else to know. Something he would never tell.

They had become close, from strangers to friends, and possibly more. Always assuming the worst about people, Langton wanted to press the young Irishman further, but he did not. Whatever happened between them would stay that way, between them. They had gone through so much together, he did not want to hurt either of them or his employer with assumptions. What good would come of it now? It would only hurt everyone involved.

Robert Langton could see the love in Colin Murphy's eyes for Dagmara. The way he spoke about her. The way he reacted hearing the doctor's news. He loved her, it was evident, and no matter how hard he tried to conceal his real feelings, he could not fool him. Colin Murphy and Dagmara Morrow shared more than just a perilous experience, a deadly adventure, a terrifying journey through the depths of hell. Passion had been shared between them, and not knowing the extent of how intimate they had become, Langton assumed the most intimate of embraces, knowing he would never actually know for sure.

Colin would never reveal the extent of their friendship, how close they had become, nor would Dagmara. Neither of them would defy the other's confidence to anyone, especially to William. And knowing the truth without Colin actually admitting it to him, Robert Langton was satisfied with his findings, and would soon report back to Jonathan Cavill and his son. But at the same time, he knew of this young man's love for Dagmara, a woman who was promised to another man, and perhaps what they shared between them was brought about by the worst possible of situations. The circumstances would be unbearable to withstand if they had not had each other for solace, surrounded in peril, being each other's peace.

CHAPTER 33

The midnight hour ended, and Colin sat in a chair by Dagmara's bed, not moving from her side. They had moved her to one of the beds in a large room with other wounded soldiers. They had put up a small screen for privacy since she was the only woman among the injured.

He watched her sleep. He watched as the nurses checked her status every half hour, making sure she was stabilized without complications. He watched as she lied perfectly still in bed, staring at her beautiful face, holding her hand. The doctor let him stay, knowing he would not leave even if asked, and he felt it would be good for her to have someone she knew by her side.

His eyes closed twice feeling exhausted from the day, emotionally and physically drained. His ribs felt sore, his whole body bruised, as if a truck had run him over, but Colin stayed awake, not wanting to fall asleep. He was afraid that if he did, she would not wake up, so he held onto her hand not wanting to let her go, not wanting her to leave him, ever.

He knew Robert Langton had suspicions about his relationship with Dagmara, but he also knew he would not tell William or his father, and in a way he wished he would, than he could be with her. But he would not sacrifice Dagmara's propriety or disgrace her honorable name with his selfish intentions, no matter how much he wanted it, he could never do that to her.

Robert Langton had left Colin's side an hour ago, and was busy placing calls to Jonathan Cavill and people he knew in France and England. He was clearing up the situation in France with the death of David Bragger and Mark Quinn, and the Vichy investigation. Colin and Dagmara's involvement would be taken care of secretly, and they would be released of all charges and able to go home. He used his connections; he used Jonathan Cavill's money, and the charges would be dropped along with the ones of entanglement with the French resistance.

He contacted Jonathan Cavill and told him of his findings and what had transpired in France. He told William's father about Colin Murphy, intentionally diverting questions, leaving out his real relationship with Dagmara. He would keep their secret. Then he contacted William Cavill and told him Dagmara was alive, but badly injured. He spoke to William and learned of his head injury, and Langton arranged for William to meet him at the hospital. William insisted on coming to get Dagmara himself, to take her home, so Langton knew he had to tell Colin before William arrived in person.

Langton walked back into the room full of wounded soldiers, and found Colin still sitting by Dagmara's side, holding her hand, and as he approached closer, he accidentally overheard his conversation.

"I know you're going to get better Dagmara, the doctor says you're doing great. I wonder if you can hear me," he said, and leaned closer to her ear and whispered, "I wish I didn't love you so much. I wish it didn't hurt so much to see you like this, than I would have the strength to walk away," he told her, and gently kissed her forehead.

The amorous gesture was one of not only compassion, but love, as Robert Langton stood and listened, standing off to the side. Colin knew he would have to give her up, knowing she was not his, nor ever would be. Soon William would come for her, sooner than he knew, and he would have to give her over to him without question, without a fight, and resign himself to the fact that Dagmara Morrow was going home with another man, and what he wanted was just a beautiful, unrealistic dream. A love caught between the shadows. She was not his to begin with, and even now as her life lingered in the twilight, she was still not his.

"There is so much more I want to tell you," Colin said to Dagmara, wishing he had said more to her before, but it was not until this moment that he realized how much he truly loved her. How much she meant to him. How much he meant to her. And he wanted a chance to tell her so, to tell her everything that was in his heart. He especially wanted to tell Dagmara that he did not blame her for Mark Quinn's death, he blamed himself, and now he was afraid he would never get the chance to let her know.

It was tearing him up inside to see her like this, as a tear slowly fell from his eye, sliding down his cheek. He hurriedly wiped away the tear as he heard footsteps coming up behind him. He leaned back from Dagmara, looked over his shoulder, and saw Robert Langton watching him.

"How long have you been listening?"

"Long enough," Langton replied.

"You won't tell them, will you? You can't do that to her," Colin insisted.

"I gave you my word I would not mention your relationship with Dagmara to either of them."

"You contacted them?" Colin inquired.

"Yes, I spoke with both William and his father and briefly mentioned that I found Dagmara, her condition, and what happened. I also made a few calls on your behalf, you and your friends are now cleared of all charges, and when you're ready, you can go home. There's a flight booked for you later today."

"That soon."

"I've already notified your brother Brady and your friend Cillian. I told them you were okay, and that you would be coming home today. They'll be waiting for you when you arrive in Dublin. I took care of everything," Langton stated.

"Brady, Cillian, you spoke with them. They're both all right? They made it safely home?" Colin asked, raising his voice.

"Yes, they're both fine. They were happy to hear that you were all right, and that you would be coming home today. They couldn't stop asking questions, especially your brother."

"Brady," Colin said with a familiar smile, thinking about his younger brother, how concerned he must have been not hearing from him for so long. Colin was so happy they were both safe and at home, that was the most important thing, that his brother was okay.

The imbroglio thickened within Robert Langton's thoughts, as he saw the concern on Colin Murphy's face for Dagmara. Not wanting to tell the young Irishman, he knew he had to tell him of William Cavill's arrival. He would know sooner or later, and it was better he heard from him than from a nurse, or be caught off guard.

"William insisted on coming and taking Dagmara home himself. He'll be arriving shortly. I didn't think you wanted to be here when he arrived."

"You think of everything don't you Mr. Langton," Colin replied, and looked at Dagmara. "I don't want to leave her, you know that. Not until she wakes up. Not until I know she will be okay."

Robert Langton moved closer to Colin and said with empathy, "I know how much you care for her Colin, after all you both have been through together. I wouldn't blame you if you wanted to stay."

He could see the agony in Colin's eyes. The torture tearing him up inside not wanting to walk away, knowing the unavoidable.

"You have to let her go Colin," Langton told him.

"Could you?" he asked, looking him straight in the eyes.

"I can't answer that, and I can't tell you what to do. But I do know that if you love someone more than life itself, you have to allow them the same happiness, even if it hurts you. Sacrifice your own happiness for theirs. I once loved a woman, a long time ago, but I refused to see how I could hurt her. And in the end, I wound up losing her anyway, and she hated me instead of loving me for it."

Colin understood, knowing he would have to make his own decision. He would have to walk away and never see her again, never look back, or stay and fight, and risk having Dagmara hate him. The latter of the two deemed bleaker, and he would rather have her love him than hate him for the rest of their lives, even if it meant they could not be together. Their past was dead, along with leaving this place, and the perpetual memory would only live within their hearts, surviving each day until it was one day lost, but never completely forgotten.

"It will do you no good Colin to dwell upon the past and forget to live," Langton told him, remembering back upon his own regret. "It does no one any good," he added softly.

Colin looked up at Robert Langton. "You know there was a time before this when I first met Dagmara, I hated her. Actually I hated everything she represented. But now I see how foolish I was, she was never pretentious, and she was more like me than I realized … I wish I could have told her how I really feel."

Robert Langton placed his hand on Colin's shoulder. "I believe she already knows how you feel about her," he said, as they both looked down at Dagmara lying peacefully in the bed.

Dagmara Morrow would not have taken a bullet for just anyone. She would not have risked her life, sacrificing herself, if she did not love the other person. And that bullet expressed the love she had for Colin Murphy, what words could not form in its place.

Colin extended his hand to Robert Langton.

"You're a good man Mr. Langton, for helping me, for seeing she gets home safely. For keeping our secret."

Robert Langton shook hands with Colin Murphy, and then he did something he had never done before, on any case. He showed emotion, as he cared about this young man and what happened to him.

"What good of knowing would come of it now," Langton replied, seeing a bit of himself in the courageous Irishman.

"Thank you."

"You're more than welcomed. Just promise me, you'll be on that flight."

Colin looked at Dagmara, and felt he would never love another woman again in the same way he loved her. For the first time ever, he felt as if his heart was breaking. Never loving a woman so much to care about having a future with, he now knew what it was like, and he wished he had never met Dagmara Morrow. It would have been easier. He would not have experienced the lust and the love, but at the same time, he would not have felt the loss, the torment, the loneliness. And was it really better to have loved and lost, than not to have loved at all?

Colin did not know the answer to that question, as he pondered the notion in his mind, over and over, coming to the same conclusion each time. He would rather have the memory of Dagmara Morrow, their night of passion, their friendship, than nothing at all. The ecstasy that now felt like agony, burned in his brain, upon his loins, forever. Never wanting to forget the look in her eyes when she looked at him in the bedroom that night. How she trembled by his touch, barely able to breathe as he came near. He knew now he would never want to erase that beautiful memory. He would not give up that moment … for the world!

CHAPTER 34

A young man sat beside Dagmara Morrow, sitting on the edge of the bed, holding her hand. He had a bandage wrapped around his forehead, a smile on his face, and unwithered love immersing in his heart. His eyes alone expressed how much he loved the young woman. It was apparent to the doctor, every nurse and injured patient. It was obvious to Robert Langton, and soon his attentive affections became known to Colin Murphy, as the Irishman walked towards the room and halted at the door, not walking through.

Colin saw the handsome young man sitting at Dagmara's side, and he saw the look in the man's eyes as he looked at her face. It was William Cavill.

He had arrived without Colin knowing. He was warned earlier of his arrival, but had placed the information aside, and it was not until he saw William that he realized it was not a dream anymore, he was real, and so was his love for Dagmara. Colin watched as William gently caressed her face, his hand sliding down her cheek, and it was only a little while ago that he was doing the same.

Now William, the rich aristocrat had taken his place. He had pushed him aside without even knowing. He had taken his rightful place beside his fiancée, his future wife, the mother of his soon to be children, and the realism of that notion tore through Colin Murphy with heartache. He had always known in the back of his mind, but it was not until he had seen it with his own eyes that made it real.

"I love you so much Dagmara. I thought about you ever day, since that day we said goodbye. I never once stopped thinking about you, even when I got injured. It was you, your love that kept me alive. That gave me the strength to survive. That gave me the will to want to live, to be with you. And not a day went by without one thought of your beautiful face. The way you looked at me with your pretty smile. I cherished the photograph you gave me," William said, as he bent down to Dagmara's face, and kissed her softly on the lips.

And while his heart was increasing with happiness and love, rekindling their romance, another man was having his heart broken, hollowed, torn. The agony Colin Murphy felt was unbearable, as he stood witness watching William Cavill profess his love to Dagmara Morrow. Watching in the distance, listening to every word he spoke. Watching as she was being ripped from his heart, and placed back into another man's arms.

This was the first time Colin had ever seen William Cavill, and he knew it was him the moment he saw him. He was exactly as Dagmara described, but taller and even more handsome. He was wearing his uniform, clean shaven, illuminating with the stench of wealth. William looked the perfect image of what Colin Murphy imagined him to be. The thick bandage around his head was from an apparent war injury, and as much as Colin Murphy tried to hate William Cavill for who he was, his rich upper class upbringing, he could not. Instead he found himself almost feeling sorry for the wounded soldier.

Colin watched William and Dagmara, they seemed perfect for each other, in every way, and his passage home, now seemed so unimportant. He had the thing he wanted most, he was going home, to be with his brother, and now he wanted something else, her. Colin wanted to be the one by her side, holding her hand, taking her home. The one who would warm her bed, and the tremendous ache tore him up inside with the agony of losing her, only this time to another man. Having to walk away, and not look back.

Maybe in another time, another place, who knows, he and William might have even been friends? Maybe William was not such a bad guy after all, he loved Dagmara so much, he flew directly to be by her side. And by that devotion, Colin knew William would treat her well, better than a life he could provide for her. One that would make her happy. One that she would be accustomed to. A life she was meant to live.

Colin knew in that moment, as he watched another man's lips touch hers, he could not break them apart and hurt either one of them. They both had suffered, terribly, and so … he decided to let her go, turning his back on love, on a life that could have been, on a life with the one person he had fallen in love with, as Dagmara Morrow would become the one true love of his life.

Then Colin did the one thing, the only thing he could do. Finally he understood Robert Langton's story. Colin Murphy took one, last, long look at Dagmara Morrow, the image of her and William Cavill, the memory that filled his heart with a saddened smile. And as he turned around to walk away, slowly Dagmara's eyes started to flicker, and she opened her eyes. She tried to focus, but all she could see was a clouded image of a man standing at the doorway walking away. And as her eyes began to focus more clearly, the figure walked away into the hallway, and slowly disappeared.

His steps moved at an even pace, as Colin Murphy did not look back, not once, as he moved farther down the corridor, separating them in distance, heading for home. He had given her up, giving up the dream that they could one day be together, reunite, knowing now they would never see each other ever again.

"Doctor, nurse," William shouted, as Dagmara opened her eyes, regaining consciousness, surviving the dangerous, intricate procedure.

Dagmara looked to her side and saw a familiar face. One she had never forgotten. One she was not expecting to see.

"William," she said, extending her hand to his face, not knowing if he was real.

"Yes, I'm right here Dagmara, and I'll never leave you again," he told her, and kissed her passionately on the lips, as a tear slid down his face.

She touched the bandage on his forehead, noticing his injury.

"Are you hurt?"

"It's nothing, nothing for you to worry about," he said, thinking only of her, as a smile brightened on his face, overwhelmed with happiness that she had survived, that she was going to be okay.

The doctor and head nurse hurried over and checked Dagmara, taking her pulse, checking her heartbeat, delighted with her rapid recovery. The fever had broken. And as they all hovered around their patient, there was one man who stood back towards the side. Robert Langton watched as a joyful reunion ignited, and a silent goodbye took place simultaneously, as he watched Colin Murphy turn the corner and disappear, as if he had never actually been there at all.

"Mr. Langton, she's awake. She's awake!" William shouted, as he hugged Dagmara and kissed her. The smile on William's face overshadowed the pain he felt in his body, his head wound had not fully healed.

Dagmara squeezed William's hand, kissing him back, and then she looked all around the room, but he was nowhere to be found. Her eyes scanned the entire room, but Colin Murphy was not there. And as her heart felt warmth and happiness seeing William Cavill's face, feeling his body next to hers, knowing he had survived his dangerous assignment, equally Dagmara felt sad for gaining one and losing another. Losing a man she had given her most intimate embrace to. A man she had given a piece of her heart to. A man she still wanted and loved.

Colin Murphy did not even say goodbye, and perhaps it was as it should be, parting in silent separation without having to deal with the heartache of words. And as Dagmara tried to sit up, wanting to go after him, only one man knew whom she was searching for. Robert Langton could see it in her eyes; he could see the same connection that he had seen in the young Irishman's eyes when he looked at her. He knew in time she would forget all about Colin Murphy, but he hoped she never would.

After a few days, Dagmara was strong enough to travel, and William took her home to her family, and to meet his father. Robert Langton accompanied them on the flight, making sure they arrived safely in England.

Overwhelmed to see their daughter, Mr. and Mrs. Morrow could not stop smiling for days hearing that not only their daughter was alive, but that she was coming home. Robert Langton had also contacted them, and they in turn had contacted Amelia and Kate. The welcome home was filled with blithe and tears of joy, and so was the reunion between William and his father. Jonathan Cavill hugged his son for several minutes, not wanting to ever let him go.

Jonathan Cavill not only paid Robert Langton the remaining portion of their agreement, he also gave him a thick bonus, almost doubling his fee with a gracious thank you for all his hard work and incredible effort in recovering his son's fiancée, and for bringing her home. Robert Langton's reputation had grown in magnitude after accomplishing his assignment for Mr. Cavill, and now his fee would increase each case thereafter.

Dagmara spent another few days in bed recovering, surrounded by all her friends and family, and then a big party was thrown for their safe return, including the announcement of their engagement. William's father thought Dagmara was beautiful and sweet. Enchanted, he did not object to them getting married. He knew William loved her, and she would make him happy, and that is all he needed to know. She would be a good match for his son, as the Morrows happily accepted William into their family, making Jonathan Cavill feel welcomed at their home, anytime.

Her parents were just as surprised as her friends were to hear the wonderful, unexpected news of her engagement to William Cavill. Dagmara's parents had not even known the extent of their relationship, how close the two had become in Italy. They were completely unaware she had gotten engaged before heading home. When Dagmara got better, William wanted to marry her as soon as possible. Too much time had been lost inbetween, and he did not want to lose her again, having just found her.

Shortly thereafter, Dagmara fully recovered, and was more vibrant than ever. The bullet wound had left a permanent scar on her body. William had not completely recovered from his head injury, but the doctors were hopeful for a full recovery within the next few months. Having the best care money could provide, William was expected to be his debonair self soon again.

Invitations were sent out to all the rich aristocratic friends and family of Jonathan Cavill, including a few royals, and all of Dagmara's family and friends. They had a lavish wedding with hundreds of flowers, just like Dagmara wanted. The perfect dress. The perfect husband. The perfect wedding. She could not ask for anything more, as her heart surrendered to the innovative feeling of being Mrs. Cavill. Dagmara immersed herself into the marriage and being a wife, loving William with all her heart. Rekindling their romance.

And on their wedding night, William never asked Dagmara the one question he longed to ask since he sat by her bedside in the hospital in France. Why she had cut her hair? Not wanting his wife to relive the painful memories she had gone through in the war, William respected her privacy, and never said a word.

William doted on her, spoiling Dagmara with gifts and expensive jewelry. His father purchased a home for them in Mayfair, a posh neighborhood to live in when the war ended, which was closer to his house than her parents. Jonathan Cavill set the newlyweds up with a large sum in the bank, and they had several servants to tend to them at the country estate were they all stayed to keep safe and out of danger during the bombings in London.

Amelia and Kate were Dagmara's bridesmaids, and soon after, they both married consecutively one after the other, and all three were married women, just like they had planned since childhood.

Dagmara never told her friends the real truth about Colin Murphy. The night they spent together in the same room, the same bed, making love. She believed they would not understand unless they had been there. No one, not even her friends would feel she had not slighted William in some way. The night of passion would be her secret alone, to carry with her, locked away in silence, afraid to ever place down in words. Her diary would never betray her heart. No one would ever know, as Dagmara's secret would be kept alive, if only in memory.

She would never tell William, even though they kept no secrets between them in marriage, one secret would have to remain hidden. And therefore, a second secret was formed, as some secrets are meant to remain silent, forever.

A few months later, Dagmara immersed herself further into bringing happiness to both their lives every day. She loved being married, being William's wife, loving the status that gave her. Their romance flourished even brighter, and William was honorably discharged from the service. His head injury had never fully healed, bringing him occasional discomfort, something he would have to live with for the remainder of his life.

The doctors said Dagmara had made a complete recovery from the bullet wound, and she would be able to live a normal life, but every time she looked at her nakedness in the mirror, and saw the scar on her stomach, and the small stitches that would never fade, she turned away. The scar on her body would be a constant reminder of France … of the war … and especially, Colin Murphy.

Dagmara filled in some of the blanks where Robert Langton's story left off, but she had intentionally evaded questions pertaining to Colin, as her friends wanted to know more about the Irishman. That was a secret kept within three people, Colin, she, and the man who had rescued them. She knew if Robert Langton had not mentioned her relationship with Colin Murphy, he never would, and she personally thanked him one day.

Surprised by her unexpected phone call, Robert Langton accepted the invitation, and met Dagmara at a café in London.

"I wanted to thank you in person Mr. Langton. I still don't know how you ever found us, but somehow you did. You exceed your reputation."

He saw her hesitation, knowing the real reason for their meeting. Knowing Dagmara wanted to inquire about Colin Murphy, and Langton would not have mentioned it, if she did not press him on the subject.

"I guess you know why I'm really here."

"Yes, I figured you would contact me sooner or later."

"Is he all right Mr. Langton? Did he make it home safely?" Dagmara inquired.

"I cleared Colin on all charges, and he left the day William arrived."

"I always wondered why, why he had not stayed to say goodbye, and now I know. I guess I always knew, but I don't think it makes me feel any better."

"I have a lot of respect for Colin, he was very courageous, and so were you. His only thought was of you. Helping you. He cared nothing about himself."

"Did he say anything to you before he left. Anything at all … to tell me?" Dagmara asked, hoping he had left a message. A few words. Something.

"I wish I could tell you yes, but let me put your mind at ease if this will help," Robert Langton started to say, seeing her suffering. "I'm not sure I'll ever really know what happened between the two of you, or know what you both had gone through, or that I should ever want to, but it was I who advised him to leave before William arrived, before you woke up. I thought it would be easier on him, on both of you with your fiancé there. But I can tell you one thing Dagmara, he loved you. He probably still loves you. He probably always will."

A slight smile creased in her lips hearing those words. Whether they were true or not, they had made her feel better.

"That's all I guess I really needed to know. Knowing that he is safe, back home in Dublin with his brother and friends and family … as I am."

"Dagmara …" Robert Langton started to say, as Dagmara was overwhelmed with sadness, and her smile disappeared. He was never able to watch a woman cry, as he handed her his handkerchief to dry her pretty eyes.

"Thank you Mr. Langton," she told him, as a few tears slid down her cheek. "I guess I shall not be contacting you further. I should not inquire about Colin Murphy … anymore," she said, choked with emotion. "That chapter is definitely closed," she added softly.

She looked towards the window of the café, and saw William standing in the doorway. He had stayed outside, letting her talk alone with Langton, not wanting to intrude on their unfinished business. He did not ask why. He did not need to know. She would never tell him.

Dagmara turned to Robert Langton, wiping away the tears. "My husband is waiting," she said, and shook hands with the man who had rescued her from the clutches of death, taking her out of that place of hell, bringing her home.

As she walked away, Robert Langton sat back in his chair and watched as Dagmara Cavill as she was now called, moved into the arms of a loving man, turning her back on a fallen dream.

Langton had inquired about Colin Murphy a month prior to his unplanned meeting with Dagmara. He found out Colin was at home with his brother, and that their mother had passed away a few weeks after he had returned home. She had taken ill while her boys were gone. Like everyone else who had suffered and survived the war, Colin was starting to rebuild a new life for himself.

Cillian and Brady were elated to see Colin after receiving Robert Langton's phone call. Colin told them all about his perilous journey with Dagmara after they had separated in France. He told them of how they had gotten involved with the French police, a resistance group, and a spy. How the traitorous David Bragger almost killed them, and how Dagmara had stepped in and saved his life, taking a bullet that was meant for him.

It was incredible. They could barely believe the vivid story he was telling them, knowing he was telling them the truth. Both Cillian and Brady could see the look on Colin's face every time he mentioned Dagmara's name. There was more to the story than he would reveal. There was more going on between he and the English girl than Colin would ever admit. Brady had fancied her, and Cillian thought of her as a little sister, so if Colin had gotten close with her, closer than just friends, who where they to judge. They were just overwhelmed with happiness that he had made it out of France, alive.

After Colin returned home, only once did he inquire about Dagmara Morrow, only to find out she had married William Cavill, and since hearing the unpleasant news, he never inquired further. Not wanting to know if she still thought about him as he thought about her, every night, every night he could not fall asleep.

The terrors of war, the memories of the horrid, bloody images he had seen were not the thoughts that kept him wide awake while Brady and Cillian were fast asleep. It was of her, Dagmara Morrow, thinking upon passionate memories, as he looked over to the emptiness that lied beside him in bed. He felt the coldness of the once lustful warmth.

A few months later, as Colin looked out at the stars one night, knowing he was dwelling upon unrealistic dreams that would never materialize, he remembered what Robert Langton had once said to him. That if he kept looking back, he would miss his whole future and forget to live. Because if he held onto the past, he would die a little bit each day, and as for Colin, he decided he would rather live. To live a life full of happiness and not sadness.

But not a day would go by without one thought about Dagmara, their night of passion, their secret love affair. Her delicate fingers caressing his skin. The touch of her body as he pressed his nakedness down upon her in a night of impassioned ecstasy and weakened lust. Her smile. Her beautiful face. The look in her eyes while lying next to him naked in warmth.

All those memories would be forever imprinted in his mind, burned on his skin, seared upon his bones. Colin Murphy would never forget any of those wonderful, pleasurable moments, cherishing each sensual, intimate embrace. And he would perpetuate the memory that would survive, if only in his dreams.

EPILOGUE

The blonde curls blew freely in the open breeze. The long strands falling down below her shoulders, as Dagmara Morrow stood over a gravesite. Unchanged in her stunning looks, Dagmara was as beautiful and young as the day she left London with her two friends headed for Venice. Well kempt in appearance, the years had been gracious to her in withered, darkened times.

She bent down to the gravestone, and moved her fingers gently over the words. She blew a loving kiss goodbye to the man buried beneath the ground.

"I miss you so much my love. I wish you were here with me now. I think of you, every day. You were so good to both of us. I think you loved me more than anything. I will always remember you and what you have given me," Dagmara said with sadness in her voice, as a smile crossed her face in a happy remembrance of their time shared together, and then a tear slid down her cheek.

She looked over towards the young boy who was playing with a toy airplane, and then looked down at the gravestone.

It read …

William Cavill
In loving memory of a courageous son,
a devoted husband, and a wonderful
father. You will always be in our hearts!

They were once so happy and in love. Soon after William and Dagmara married, she was with child, and neither William nor his father Jonathan Cavill could have been happier. A baby boy was born, and it seemed Dagmara had the perfect life, having everything she had ever wanted, and more. A beautiful baby, a handsome, wealthy, loving husband, and a father in-law who loved and adored her as if she was his own daughter, and all was well for several years thereafter.

William and Dagmara traveled the world once the war ended. William worked alongside his father in business, as he watched their son grow into a handsome young boy. Dagmara would bring her son over to Amelia's house and Kate's house, and all of their children would play together. Even though Dagmara only had one child while her friends had two and three children each; her firstborn meant more to her than any other.

The war had not affected Jonathan Cavill as it did with many other wealthy aristocrats and businessmen, the Cavills still enjoyed the same rich lifestyle and status as prior to the terrible, bloody darkness.

Sometimes Dagmara would dream about France. The woman at the plane crash, and all the deaths she witnessed. The horror of her nightmares awakened her in terrorizing images. Haunting images she wanted to suppress, to wipe out of her mind, completely. But there was one thing she wanted most to forget, which was by far the hardest. She knew she had to separate herself from Colin Murphy, but a constant reminder of him and the time they spent together in France, stared her directly in the face, every waking day.

She could not escape him. Wherever she looked, somehow he was there, and the more she pushed Colin Murphy out of her thoughts, distancing herself from him, the more she felt the connection breaking, not wanting to envision him with another.

Shortly after her son was born, becoming rapt with her son's life and married life, Dagmara slowly felt the bond loosening between she and Colin, as she grew closer to William every day, placing him first.

Soon after, the love she had for her husband prevailed over a forgotten dream. A long ago moment that seemed like a lifetime ago. Dagmara was a different person now. The war and everything she had gone through had changed her. The perilous situations, the violent killings she had witnessed, the bullet wound, Colin Murphy, all of that had changed her, maybe for the better. Amelia and Kate noticed the biggest difference in their friend's demeanor and the person she matured into after returning home from France, losing some of that childhood innocence.

Dagmara was strong, and felt fortuitous for having her life and her family. Her flair for pictures increased and so did her love of art. She would spend many countless hours in the warm spring days painting pictures of beautiful images, images she once roamed freely in when she was a child.

Her vigorous fire had not faded, it only increased within time. William Cavill and Dagmara Morrow were the perfect couple, and they lived life to the fullest, living every moment of every day as if it was their last. That was the way Dagmara wanted it, to live in carpe diem with William Cavill, forever. She wanted to perpetuate the moment, feeling if she did not, it would be stolen, lost, and never return.

And William in essence did give Dagmara Morrow the world. He was the perfect husband. The perfect father. The perfect lover. She never wanted for anything. He denied her nothing, and she in turn gave him her whole heart, and equal pleasure in and out of the bedroom. The first time they made love was on their wedding night. William could barely control himself; he yearned for her body, ripping the dress right off her. He had waited so long for that moment, ever since that night in his hotel room in Venice.

They hardly ever quarreled or had heated arguments, immediately regretting having said ill words towards the other, and rekindled their romance instantly towards a more connecting relationship. They took long baths together, falling asleep in each other's arms in harmony, and made love almost every night, never denying the other that pleasure. A passionate, loving marriage, which soon became the enviable of everyone, including her two best friends.

It was a year ago to this day that William Cavill passed away. His head injury from the war had never fully healed like doctors expected, giving him pain towards the final few days of his life. The magnitude of the wound had gradually increased over time, and in the seventh year of their blissful marriage, William suddenly took ill without warning, and there was nothing Dagmara, his father, or any of the best doctors in the world could have done to save him. Jonathan Cavill flew in the best doctors to treat his son. He lathered their palms with money, but with all his wealth, he could not save his son from dying. No one could.

The last week of William's life was by far the hardest on his wife. Dagmara never left his side, not for a moment, staying with him in their bedroom day and night, having her mother tend to their son. She was not prepared. There was so much more she wanted to do with her husband that they would never get to share. Dagmara did not want to live a lifetime of regret for the things she did and had not done, so she granted William's final request, even though it killed her inside.

He wanted her to go on with her life, and live a life full of happiness, even if that happiness could no longer be with him. He wanted Dagmara not to let her spirit die, and be lost in grief, and stay locked in her room, till one day she turned around and missed her whole youth, and her future was gone. Even if that future was to be spent with another man, other than him.

So against her heart, feeling that it would be a betrayal, she said yes to him, she would comply to his last wish, and go on living, and in that moment, Dagmara Morrow truly loved William Cavill with all her heart, more than any other man.

She crawled in bed next to him, and stayed with him in his final hours, and as William passed away in his sleep, she knew he was finally at peace. William would now be reunited with his two best friends Stuart and Henry. They had waited a long time for him, to take his place alongside them, and the three musketeers would finally be together at last.

Dagmara's strength had deteriorated from lack of food and sleep, as she clung onto William Cavill's body, not wanting to ever let him go. Not wanting to leave her husband, the fairytale marriage they lived in, wanting to perpetuate the moment as she kissed his lips, knowing she would be kissing her husband for the very last time. And as her heart was breaking in two, it was Jonathan Cavill who had to pull her off his son's body and remove her from the bed, as sadness deafened inside their once radiant home, and darkness took fold in withering depth.

Dagmara was never the same again after William's death; a piece of her had died with him that night, never to be whole again. She had seen too much blood in her short lifetime, and death seemed to follow her, surrounding her everywhere.

A few months later, not being able to cope with the death of his son, with losing his only child, Jonathan Cavill took his own life one night with a revolver. All the booze in the world could not ease his pain, bereaved in unshakable depression, Jonathan Cavill felt he had nothing left to live for anymore, and left his entire fortune to Dagmara and his grandson.

The sudden death of her father in-law, who had become more like her own father shortly after she and William married, oppressed heavily on Dagmara's already fragile existence. The once vivacious young woman was now tormented by the death of two loved ones, and the suffering was unbearable. She took Jonathan Cavill's death hard, plummeting gravely upon being left alone, as he was her only link to William.

Hardly visiting her friends or family, Dagmara stayed in her large, empty house all by herself, with only her son for companionship. The devastation of losing William after only seven years of marriage ripped through her heart like a fiery dagger of death, and the agony of having to go on without him, was more than she could endure. The only thing that kept Dagmara alive, that kept her from taking her own life, from joining William and his father, was her son. He needed her, and equally, she needed him. He was her savior. The little boy that she held tightly in her arms brought her peace during the day, and gave her solace at night.

The weeks that followed were excruciatingly hard on Dagmara, and she distanced herself further from her family and friends. Losing interest in all things she loved most in the world, her vigorous flame started to flicker in the intermission twilight that followed in blackened sorrow, as one day moved into the next, till a whole year had suddenly passed.

Then one day she woke, as if the fog had been lifted, and she had been living in a darkened existence, a state of perpetual indifference for too long. William's words suddenly came to her in her sleep one night, telling her what to do. Telling her he would forgive her, and to remember the promise she had made to him. Dagmara decided there was one thing left undone that she had to do; she could no longer turn away from. She packed a suitcase for she and her son, hoping she had made the right decision, and left the servants to tend to the house.

Not knowing when and if she would return, Dagmara still had to face one last demon. She had prolonged the inevitable for as long as she could, longer than she should have. And when the grieving was over, and no more tears were left to cry, the cherishing memories she kept so close to her heart, had finally resurfaced.

Forced to relive the past, the painful remembrance, Dagmara Morrow *had to lie with the devil one last time*, and face the secret she had kept hidden from everyone. The secret that had kept her apart from everyone she loved, burying it deep within her heart, tearing at her soul. But she would have kept this secret until her death if William and his father had not died, not wanting to hurt either of them with knowing the truth.

Dagmara never told William about she and Colin, never telling him the intimate details of their relationship, of their one night of passion. The night she spent in the arms of a stranger, in delicious, rapturous, ecstasy. The agony of him knowing would have only caused him tremendous pain, and what good would have come of it; it would have only brought heartache.

But now she was forced to go back to that place she had closed herself off from, revisiting feelings she had sealed from her heart, and make things right, even if it cost her everything, everything she loved. She had no other choice. It was the only way.

"I will always love you William Cavill, and I hope you will forgive me for what I did, for what I was never brave enough to tell you. But I rather have you live a lie, than to know the truth that would have killed you, and your love for me. I did what I thought was best, for you, for us … for our son," Dagmara said to William in sadness, as she looked down at his grave.

Then Dagmara looked up into the sky, closed her eyes, and took a deep breath, knowing she now faced the toughest obstacle of her life. Then she opened her eyes feeling the coolness of the air swirl around her body. She stood up, brushed the dirt off her skirt, and took one, last, look at the gravestone, and then took her son's hand, and walked away. Walking away from a life that could have been, from a life she would have happily lived her entire existence in, if only William had not died.

The handsome young boy who was dressed impeccably held onto his mother's hand, looked up at her face, and saw her tears. He squeezed her hand tight, and she looked down feeling his added pressure, and saw a smile on his happy, innocent face.

"I love you mum."

"I love you too," she told him, and suddenly the tears turned into happy ones, and a smile crossed her saddened face.

And as they walked away together, hand in hand, Dagmara suddenly felt everything would be all right. Her strength and vivaciousness had returned. She was not one to lack the courage of her convictions, dealing with the enormous darkness of the past year; she would keep her promise to William, and live life to the fullest. She had stayed within the shadows long enough, and no matter what the outcome would bring, she had to go there and see him, face to face. To tell him the truth. To see if Colin Murphy was still alive.

And within each step she took, she moved one step closer to Colin, and one step farther away from William, distancing herself from her present life. Dagmara Morrow was never more scared, as if she had waited her entire life for this one, single, moment.

EPILOGUE PART 2

The view at the top of the hill was breathtaking. The dark green of the grass, the tranquility of the wide openness, as the orange and pink sunset illuminated the sky. Like a magnificent painting that was captured perfectly by a paint-brush, it reminded Dagmara of a place she once loved to lie within when she was a child.

Then suddenly she saw him. Colin Murphy stood in the middle of the field wearing only a pair of jeans and boots. His rippling abdomen glistened from the hard work, as his chest flexed in the coolness of the air. His sex appeal still made her heart skip a couple of beats. He had not changed at all since she last saw him. Her body still trembled with excite. Even now after all these years that flame had never burnt out.

Brady was with him, and off to the side coming from the house Dagmara saw another familiar face, Cillian. Then Dagmara saw a young woman carrying a small child in her arms. The woman walked over to Colin and his brother, and suddenly Dagmara's heart tightened, as she saw the woman move towards him.

Thinking she was too late, too many years had passed between, Dagmara started to turn around and walk away, when suddenly Colin looked up towards the top of the hill, and saw a woman standing there. Her long blonde curls moved within the light breeze. Her lips, red, ripe, and luscious. Her long black lashes flickered in the wind. She was dressed impeccably wearing a white blouse and skirt with a lace trim, as her slender figure accentuated the outfit perfectly, leaving nothing to the imagination.

She looked back down the hill as he looked up at her, and Dagmara was fro-zen in movement, unable to breathe. They stared at one another for several, long, impressionable minutes, as if they had seen a ghost from their past. Colin could not believe his eyes, wondering if he was dreaming. He dropped the cloth out of his hand, disregarded what Brady was saying, and started to walk towards the hill.

Closer and closer he moved towards her at a quickened pace, his heart beating fast, his pulse racing with excite, till finally he could see her face. His eyes opened wide at the surprising sight seeing it was Dagmara Morrow, thinking he would never again look upon her face. It was unbelievable that she was here, in Dublin, at his home, and she looked as pulchritudinous as ever. Her face, radiant. Her eyes, sparkled. She looked the same as the day he first laid eyes on her those long years ago. Dagmara had not changed at all, she looked as young as she did in France. Time had been generously kind.

Not knowing if Colin would even remember her, his feet started moving at a faster pace, moving up the hill in a run. He had not forgotten her at all. It was exactly the opposite. All the passing years inbetween seemed as if they had never existed, erased from memory, and time stood still once again for Dagmara and Colin, as if it was only a moment ago.

Dagmara's breathing deepened as Colin came near. Her heart pounded feverishly in daunted anticipation, not knowing if he would want to see her?

The closer he moved towards her, the clearer the image of Dagmara Morrow brightened. Her short hair was long again, now falling below her shoulders, as Colin had seen before. And suddenly he remembered the moment, when at one time he yearned to bury his face in her golden curls. She looked well tended, looking as if she had not aged at all, although her eyes would tell a different story. Her true innocence had long left, faded within time.

He moved closer to her, focusing his eyes on her face. The image was exactly the same as he had embedded in his mind all these past years. She looked beautiful. Then suddenly he noticed a young boy playing in the grass behind her. The boy had blonde hair and translucent skin just like his mother, and he was the most handsome child Colin Murphy had ever seen.

Dagmara moved towards him, and they stood face to face staring at one another. The smoldering silence seared through their hearts as they looked into each other's eyes, looking deep into one another's souls.

The sexy, arrogant Irishman was almost exactly the way Dagmara had remembered him. His hair was shorter, he had a little goatee, but his piercing stare that once captivated her presence had not lost its roaring power, and seeing him again, here, now, after all these years, had filled her heart with happiness.

He was alive. Colin Murphy was alive!

Dagmara did not know if he would want to see her ever again? If he would be happy to see her, if he would turn around and walk away? It had taken her over a year to come and see Colin after William's death, but she had to tell him the truth, about everything.

No words could describe how both of them were feeling at this very moment. Flooded with emotions of old and new, it had been too long, as Colin had to fight to keep his hands off her body. The desire deepened each second, wanting to take her in his arms and kiss her, feeling the softness of her touch upon his skin. Even now after all these years, she still lit his flame.

It was Dagmara who made the first move.

Gently she placed her fingers on the side of his face, gliding her hand down his cheek, caressing his skin. As he felt her touch, the softness of her hand, he could not resist the temptation any longer, and passionately kissed Dagmara on the lips. Vigorous fire exploded between their embrace, and the feeling was more new than familiar.

Dagmara let Colin kiss her, as he placed his tongue inside her mouth, and then she pulled back. Their fervor had been silently reawakened. Her lips intoxicated his senses, and Colin was instantly incited by the sensuous kiss. His kisses were still like novocaine that clouded her brain, stimulating with enticement through every part of her body. Dagmara had not realized how much she missed him, until now.

"You're alive," she said. "I thought you were dead."

"I did die when I walked out of hospital that day, and let you go."

"I did see you then. It wasn't a dream."

"No, it was not a dream," Colin replied.

"Then why did you leave?" Dagmara asked.

"You both belonged together. I could not stand in the way. I was ... an inconvenience. A slight detour," he answered, having his arrogance flow brightly through his words.

Dagmara missed that element that made Colin Murphy so irresistible. "No, you were never that. You knew that Colin," she told him.

Hearing her say his name brought forth an ardent feeling Colin had not felt inside his lonely heart since the day he walked out of the hospital, walking out of her life.

"What are you doing here?" he asked in the same arrogant manner.

"I had to come and see you. I didn't know if you would want to ever see me again, or if you would remember me?"

"I could never forget you, you know that Dagmara."

"Then why did you never come and visit?" she asked.

"Because I heard of your marriage to William."

Colin looked at her left hand, noticing the ring on her forth finger. The large diamond twinkling in the fading light, and then he looked over at the young boy.

"He's beautiful, just like his mum," Colin complimented.

Dagmara looked over at her son who was chasing after a yellow and brown butterfly, trying to grab it in his tiny hands, falling down and getting back up again with a playful smile on his face.

"Thank you," she replied, watching her son with pride.

"Where's your husband, William Cavill, right?" Colin asked, pretending as if he had forgotten his name. A name he could never forget.

"I guess you don't know, how could you," Dagmara started to say. "William passed away last year. His head injury from the war had never fully healed like doctors had hoped."

"I'm sorry, I did not know," Colin said sincerely, as Dagmara's eyes clouded with tears. He could see how much she loved and missed her husband.

"William was a good man … I loved him. He was a great father and husband. I want you to know that," Dagmara stressed. Then she looked straight into his eyes and asked Colin the question she was dying to ask ever since he left the hospital that day in France. "Why did you leave that day without even saying goodbye?"

Colin opened his mouth and was about to answer Dagmara, and then abruptly stopped, and decided to tell her the truth, the real reason why he had not said goodbye.

"When I came back into the room that day, I saw William at your bedside. The image of both of you sitting together as he held your hand and told you he loved you … I knew I would just get in the way. He was your fiancé. I was just a stranger. A man who fell in love with a beautiful, courageous young woman under strenuous, perilous circumstances. A woman that was promised to another man."

Dagmara could barely believe what Colin was saying to her. After all this time, she thought perhaps she did not mean that much to him, but that was not true.

"I knew he would take care of you, he loved you so much, I could see it in his eyes. And I tried to hate him because he loved you, because he was going to marry you, but I could not. No matter how much I tried, I could not hate him. And that's when I knew I had to leave. It was the only honorable thing I could do. It was the only way," Colin told Dagmara, as love and longing regret flowed through his words.

The interlude had not broken their connection; it had only made it stronger.

"I wished ever day that you were alive. That you, Cillian, and your brother Brady had survived the war, and were happy. Are you happy Colin?"

Colin noticed a change in Dagmara. Her maturity. She had grown up these past years, losing some of that childlike innocence, and he felt happy and sad for that loss.

"I wished every night before I fell asleep that you were safe, wherever you were in England, and that you and your family had made it through the war, unscathed," Colin answered.

His words moved her, knowing all this time he was still thinking about her. Then Dagmara looked down the hill at the dark haired woman standing beside Brady. Both of them looked up at her at the same time as Cillian walked over to them, and then she asked Colin the question she had to know the answer to, the question that plagued her thoughts ever since she arrived.

"Is that your wife?"

Colin looked at the woman and then at Dagmara, and suddenly a smile crossed his lips.

"No, that's Cassandra, Brady's wife. That's their baby girl she's holding," he replied.

A heart stopping feeling immersed within Dagmara's chest hearing those words, not knowing why this had affected her after all this time, Colin Murphy was free to marry whomever he wanted, he always was.

"You're not married?" she asked.

"No."

"No girlfriend?"

A smile crossed his entire face, as Colin knew what Dagmara was asking.

"No Dagmara, I never married, I couldn't … because I was still in love with another," he said, as his smile faded, and his tone became serious. "How could I love anyone else when my heart was forever connected to hers. Don't you see Dagmara, how could I possibly love anyone else … when I'm still in love with you!"

His statement overwhelmed her, enamoring her, never imagining Colin Murphy to speak such impassioned words. He still loved her, even after all this time. After all the long years inbetween, he still wanted her. He still desired her.

"I loved you from the first moment I laid eyes on you," he told her, and then Colin grabbed Dagmara around, pressing her body up against his bare chest, and kissed her rapturously on the lips, as a tear of release, of happiness, fell from her eye.

Then she whispered in his ear three words he had waited so long to hear, ever since that night. "I love you!" she told him, and it seemed he had waited his entire life to hear those words from her.

Colin looked at Dagmara like he was looking at her for the very first time. His eyes widened, his smile brightened, his heart fluttered with release. Words of just one syllable each had penetrated through eight years of loss and loneliness. Dagmara Morrow loved him, and softly he wiped away the tear from her cheek.

Colin looked over at the boy again. "What's his name?" he asked.

Dagmara hesitated for a long, fearful moment as she looked at her son, her heart pounding fast. It had finally come to this moment, the real reason for her unplanned, unexpected visit.

"His name …" she started to say, looking Colin straight in the eyes. "His name, is Colin," Dagmara answered.

Immediately Colin's eyes opened wide as he looked over at the boy and then at Dagmara.

"You named him after me?" he said surprised.

"I named him after his father."

Colin's eyes widened as he watched the boy play in the grass, as the shocking news registered in his mind.

"You mean … he's mine?"

"Yes, he's your son," Dagmara replied.

"I don't understand?" Colin said, somewhat in disbelief.

"I found out a few days after I got out of hospital. It was when I got back to England that I knew I was pregnant. And then we married so quickly … I had never been with anyone except you. And it all happened so fast. I didn't know what to do? How could I tell William I was pregnant with another man's child? I couldn't do that to him. He loved that boy so much … I couldn't tell him … It would have killed him."

Colin could barely get the words out. "I … mine?" he started to say; still dazed from learning he had a son. A son he never knew existed.

"It would have ruined William and his family's name, and mine. I didn't even know where you were, or what to do, so I married William, and I allowed him to believe the child was his," Dagmara confessed, finally telling Colin the truth. The long awaited truth that had plagued her thoughts, torturing her soul. The truth she had kept from him, from everyone, for so long. The secret she held for over eight years was now finally laid to rest.

"But you could do that to me," Colin stated in a harsh tone, angered that Dagmara could hurt him, but not William.

"No, it wasn't like that, you don't understand …" she tried to explain, and reached to touch his hand, and he backed away.

"I don't understand what!" Colin said, raising his voice, as tears formed in her eyes.

"A thousand times I wanted to tell you, but I couldn't. Too much had happened, too much time had been lost. But I want you to know, William was a great father to him. He loved him more than the world," Dagmara explained further, as tears streamed down her face.

"I have a son!" Colin repeated, as he stared at the boy.

"When William died, and after Jonathan Cavill's death, I told him where we were going, and a little about you. How we met during the war. How we had become friends. I had to come here and tell you in person, even if you hated me for it, for keeping this secret … from keeping your son from you," she told him, wiping away the tears. "I wouldn't blame you Colin if you never wanted to see me, or speak to me ever again."

Colin looked at his son and then at Dagmara. He could see the pain in her eyes, seeing how this was killing her inside. He could see how much she had suffered, through everything, even after the war. She had gone through so much, and he could not stand to see her in such agony, wanting to release her pain.

In a way, Colin understood why Dagmara had kept his son from him. Why she had said nothing to him until now. Even though he was hurting inside from the deception, from the years lost with his son, he could not blame Dagmara for what she had done. It took a lot of courage to come to his home and tell him in person, to tell him the truth after all these years. And he respected her even more now, knowing how hard it must have been keeping such a secret.

He stepped closer to her and moved his hands around her face. "The past is in the past, and should remain there. And I understand why you did what you did. You thought it was best for both you and your son, and perhaps it was. But hate you, how could I possibly ever hate you … when I'm still in love with you. Can't you see, I love you Dagmara. I love you so much!" he told her.

"You love me?"

"I've always loved you. There was no one else I could love."

And amorously he kissed her on the lips, as tears streamed down her face onto his. Overwhelmed with happiness that Colin did not hate her, she was equally moved knowing he loved her, he still loved her, even after she told him the truth. Colin Murphy was incredible. He was everything she could ever ask for in a man, and so much more. Not only was he seductive, an exquisite lover, he was also compassionate and forgiving, making Dagmara feel released from the suffering she had harbored for so long.

The kiss absorbed the pain, what words could not express, allowing them both to be freed from all the demons that haunted them from their past.

"I'm so sorry Colin," she apologized, wiping away the tears that had fallen onto his face.

"Sorry, for what?" he said kindly, not wanting Dagmara to blame herself.

"Because I should have told you, a long time ago."

"I have a son," he said with a smile. "We have a son, together, that is all that matters."

"What do we do now?" she asked.

Colin was about to answer Dagmara, as the boy tugged on her skirt, and Colin picked his son up in his arms and looked at his face, holding his child for the very first time. The elated feeling blossomed into a radiate smile that illuminated over Colin Murphy's entire face. He had a son, and as he smiled at the boy, he looked over at Dagmara and knew. He now had a family, the one he had always wanted. The one he had always wished for.

"Let's go home," Colin answered, and extended his hand to Dagmara, the mother of his child, his soon to be wife.

Just like that, all was remembered and forgotten. All was made right, and the long journey home, the long road to happiness, seemed a distant memory of fallen shadows of past and present. Dagmara's journey had finally come to an end. She loved William. He would always hold a special place in her heart, a piece of her heart just for him. But the torturous ache was over, she finally felt at peace. Dagmara Morrow had survived the long, horrid war. She had survived death, peril, and passion, and triumphed over the agony of love.

She placed her hand in his, as Colin clasped his hand tightly around hers, never to let her go, ever again. They smiled at each other, and started to walk towards his house, towards home, walking towards a new future, a new life, together. Colin had wished for this moment ever since he had walked out of the hospital that day in France, he had wanted Dagmara to be his, and now he had her, and a son.

Filled with joy, Colin Murphy now had everything he had ever wanted in life. Desire coursed through his loins, unleashing his lustful yearn he had for Dagmara Morrow, wanting to devour her entire body. To ravish her for lost time. Wanting to kiss every inch of her sultry, smooth skin, and make love to her till he could not breathe. Till his body was physically exhausted, and she could no longer withstand his vigor.

And as they walked down the hill together hand in hand towards Brady and Cillian, she could see smiles on their faces as they recognized whom it was holding Colin's hand. Dagmara felt she was not replacing William, she never could. But all was forgiven, bringing she and Colin even closer together in an unbreakable bond. Their one night of passion had given Colin a son, giving Dagmara a second chance at love. And somewhere destiny was shining. Fate had brought them together under the worst of circumstances, and now the same had brought them together again.

Two people from vastly different worlds, completely different backgrounds wound up being soul mates. Nothing could keep them apart, not ever again. Dagmara's smile brightened as she looked at Colin holding their son. She was happy now, they both were. And in the end, William Cavill in a way did give Dagmara Morrow the world, but Colin Murphy; he had made her his world. A world that now included three.

978-0-595-44336-9
0-595-44336-2